A Summer of The Forest Folk

by Maria Rodziewiczówna
and Tom Pinch

MONDRALA
PRESS

Mondrala Press is an imprint of
Ringel & Esch, S.A.R.L.-S
www.mondrala.com

Originally published in Polish in 1920 as *Lato Leśnych Ludzi*

Editing by InkScroll Editing
Cover Design by art_infinity

Publisher's Cataloging-in-Publication Data
provided by Five Rainbows Cataloging Services

Names: Rodziewiczówna, Maria, 1863-1944, author. | Pinch, Tom, translator.
Title: A summer of the forest folk: a classic tale of the healing power of nature / Maria Rodziewiczówna; Tom Pinch, translator.
Description: Ringel,Luxembourg: Mondrala Press, 2022.
Identifiers: ISBN978-99987-917-2-5 (paperback) | ISBN978-99987-917-3-2 (hardcover) | ISBN978-99987-917-5-6 (ebook:EPUB) | ISBN978-99987-917-6-3 (ebook :mobi) | ISBN978-99987-917-7-0 (PDF) | ISBN978-99987-917-4-9 (audiobook)
Subjects: LCSH:Women--Fiction. | Lesbians--Fiction. | Europe--Fiction. | Bildungsromans. | Polish fiction. | BISAC: FICTION/ Women. | FICTION/LGBTQ+ /Lesbian. | FICTION/Cultural Heritage. | FICTION/World Literature / Poland. Classification: LCCPN849.P72R632022(print) | LCCPN849.P72 (ebook) | DDC891.85--dc23.

CONTENTS

From the Translator

A SUMMER: READING BETWEEN THE LINES

I have been reading this book, on and off, for 50 years—sometimes cover to cover, sometimes just a few pages at a time before going to sleep or while taking an afternoon break.

Why would anyone do that?

Well, for the best of reasons: pure hedonistic pleasure. And the very many layers of it: the many layers of pleasure.

On the surface

Even on the most superficial reading, *A Summer of the Forest Folk* is a joy. On its surface, it is a simple, heart-warming story of the healing power of nature: three city men spending a summer in a remote forest cottage, far from the maddening crowds and pressures of modern city life. The place to which the three retreat (the Pinsk Marshes, in today's Byelarus) is the largest surviving stand of virgin forest in Europe. It is a mixture of forest, meadow, and marsh and is home to thousands of species of birds, fish, moose, elk, deer, wolf, bear, fox, lynx, snake, and the last remaining European bison. Early in the 20th century, three people had a cottage there and spent their summers hiking, fishing, growing vegetables in the garden, bird watching, picking mushrooms, and helping locals with simple farm tasks. If like me, you are a nature lover forced to live in a city, the escape the book provides is itself enough to enjoy it.

It also helps that the book is beautifully written. If, like me, you have spent a lot of your life dealing with texts, you may have, from time to time, become fed up with well-written Strunk and White prose and may well wish for an occasional gulp of something more unashamedly poetic. And, to my ear, this book provides that. There it is, on page one:

We shall talk about an ancient people here, as ancient as the eternal forest.

Yes, it does sound a little old-fashioned: the rhythm, the scansion. Maybe I am weird that way, but oh, for a break from the daily prose and the news it brings!

Yes, I am weird but apparently, not alone. These two aspects of the book – its topic and its style – have earned it a special place in Polish literature: 52 editions since 1920, never once out of print, not even under German occupation during World War Two (when paper was scarce). This book is known to absolutely everybody. And many phrases from it have worked their way into everyday language. It is a book grandparents read to their grandchildren – and, indeed, my grandfather read it to me. Because it is both heart-warming and well written.

Hidden meanings

But the book also has a fascinating history of interpretation. Some readers see it as a veiled statement of Polish political conservatism (even 'reaction') and others, more recently, as an LGBTQ *roman à clef.*

Like a French movie, the book does not say; it shows. And it expects you to guess, to read between the lines. And this makes it a richer read for those, like me, who go in for that sort of thing. *A Summer* presents the many delights of a Russian doll of meanings: a pean to nature, hiding within it a pean to traditional Polish gentry life on the Byelorussian frontier, hiding within it a fascinating story of a lesbian *ménage à trois.*

These multiple layers of interpretation have been a source of many pleasures (and discoveries) during my work on this translation, too. And I decided to write this essay to share them with you, hoping that my account of them may help you experience some of the same joys.

After all, pleasure in art is both its primary purpose – and it is catching. And the best pleasure is a pleasure shared.

Rodziewiczówna, the national icon

Who was Maria Rodziewiczówna?

Most Polish readers know her as an author of patriotic novels describing Polish resistance to Russian occupation (1795 - 1918).

Her life was shaped by that resistance. She was the daughter of a Polish gentry family who participated (as non-combatants) in the 1863 uprising. The uprising failed and ended in a national catastrophe: a colossal loss of life and destruction of property, followed by mass ethnic cleansing, exile, confiscation of property, and total elimination of any and all forms of local autonomy. Following the crushing of the uprising, even as much as speaking Polish in school became a punishable offense ("Speak Russian!").

Because they participated in the uprising, Maria's family had their property confiscated and were exiled to Siberia.

During the amnesty of 1871, they were allowed to leave Siberia but were not allowed to settle where they had once lived (near Grodno, in today's Lithuania) but only in a separate administrative area Russians assigned to Poles – a kind of "Polish Reservation" within the Russian Empire. The family ended up in very difficult economic circumstances in Warsaw, where her father took up a post as a building administrator, and her mother worked in a cigarette factory.

Their economic situation improved when they inherited a 3,000-acre property in Polesia (in today's Byelarus). The property was mostly marsh and sandy soil and burdened by debt. In 1881, following her father's death, 17-year-old Maria took over its management. At this point, presumably to make herself look more businesslike, and with her mother's permission, she cut her hair short and adopted men's clothing (and wrote in her journal: "I will never marry.")

Maria turned out to be a very talented farm administrator and a strict but fair manager of men. Over the next two decades, she improved the farm's productivity, paid off its debts, and built roads, schools, clinics, and churches for her employees and their families. She became involved in the scouting movement (a kind of crypto-patriotic organization) and the Theosophist movement. From the age of 18, she wrote and published novels.

Given her family background, it was natural that her novels tended to surround patriotic subjects: they dealt with the questions of foreign occupation, national survival, and national liberation. But, because they were published under Russian censorship, they could not address those topics directly. Instead, they had to approach them by a kind of symbolic code: since Polish writers could not write about Polish resistance against Russians, they wrote about Greeks resisting Romans or Poles fighting Tartars and Swedes (who conveniently happened to have been Russia's enemies at times, so were topics Russian censors allowed).

We see an echo of this situation in *A Summer*. In the penultimate chapter, the heroes discover the body of an 1863 insurgent and want to honor it by building a cross over the grave, but one of them says:

Too many Moscovite informers around. Moscovites will come and despoil the grave and probably destroy it, too. (...) Better we do something that only a few can recognize. So I will make a tombstone. But a secret one. Flat. Not seen from far away. And no one will know, only we.

A Summer was written relatively late in Maria's career and was not published until Poland regained its independence (1918), but she began writing it under Russian occupation, and, as you read the book, you can see that the early chapters are heavily encoded. In the chapter in which a farmer teaches a teenager how to mow with a scythe, he says:

Here is your scythe, young man. See how it is set. Here is the blade mounted on the haft and fastened with an iron ring and a wooden wedge, like the letter L. Though it may sometimes happen with us that one may mount it upright, and then the mowers are called scythe-men and mow enemy heads. The instrument thereby becomes ennobled, so one must honor it and keep it in respect, the way soldiers keep their swords because no one knows when and for what purpose they may be needed. Do you understand?

The reference is to Polish peasant battalions who fought Russians with scythes in 1795, and, yes, a Polish reader would understand, but a Russian censor might not – and let the text slide by.

The book is filled with this kind of coded speech, and, to many readers, decoding it is one of its great pleasures.

As it happened, the book was not published until Poland regained its independence (1918), and some of the more openly patriotic parts of the story (the exhumation of the 1863 insurgent, for example) were probably added at that point and intended for uncensored publication.

Rodziewiczówna the Catholic

Maria is commonly perceived as a political conservative not only because of her patriotism but also due to what people see as her Catholicism. You can see a lot of it in the novel: icons, prayers, blessings, etc.

But was Maria a committed Catholic?

It is hard to say. Under Russian occupation, Catholicism had become inextricably intertwined with Polish patriotism. Religious instruction was the only kind of instruction allowed in the national language, church organization was often used as cover for covert activities, and church festivals were the only occasion that allowed patriotic manifestations. And in this sense, it isn't clear whether the book's heroes light a candle before the icon of the Virgin Mary because she is the mother of Christ or because she is the titular Queen of Poland.

But it seems that Maria was religious. And thus, for example, *A Summer* features prayers like this one:

Quietly and slowly, he began, as if his thoughts detached from the bottom of his soul and floated upwards, looking to find expression: "Hail, to you, master of the wonders of beauty and wisdom! You are here with us in every shape, sound, and fragrance, and with you, we have spent this summer."

It is hard to imagine that these beautifully wrought prayers were a mere literary exercise. In the book, the character of Wolverine is a profoundly religious person, but his religiosity is not very Catholic. For one thing, in the first half of the 20th century, the church discouraged the practice of praying with one's own words (as untutored prayers could possibly be heretical). And the God whom

Wolverine worships seems to be, above all, the creator of nature and the natural order. If anything, Wolverine's religiosity is like that of Rudolf Otto's (*The Idea of the Holy*, 1917), in which he says: "A sacred tree is like any other tree except that something about it makes us perceive it as sacred." No hierarchy, no institutions, no popes, no priests: just a direct perception of the holy. It seems to me that Maria was personally religious in that sense; that as a member of the Polish gentry, she probably felt obligated to be outwardly observant, but in her personal religion, she was not especially Catholic.

And a Butch?!

So, there you have it: a religious, patriotic land-owner upholding the old social system and the old religion, safe enough for grandparents to read to their grandchildren.

And then an enterprising scholar (Krzysztof Tomasik, *Homobiografie,* 2014), prying about her personal life, broke a shocking story: "MARIA WAS A BUTCH! And the three Forest Folk (the heroes of the book: "Wolverine," "Crane," and "Panther") were really three lesbians living in a *ménage à trois*!"

A triple exclamation mark is in order because the surprise was so great. Three lesbians living in a *ménage à trois*! Goodness gracious!

But the evidence was undeniable: letters, documents, journals, memoirs, articles in the press, photos.

The best we have been able to piece the story together, Maria lived alone on her farm for some time. But, eventually, she was joined there by Helena Weychert, another butch/gentry girl in the agricultural profession (and with considerable farm managerial talent: she is said to have made significant contributions to the improvement of the farm).

I close my eyes and imagine the two butches riding around on horseback – each on her horse, thank you – and ordering their peasants about (crop in hand?). (Maria was once prosecuted for striking a recalcitrant (male) worker).

Then, for reasons we do not yet understand, the two women decided to move back to Warsaw. They bought an apartment in the city and a small farm on the outskirts. Perhaps they were there to enjoy the musical and theater season (November – April). And maybe Maria wanted to be close to libraries, bookshops, and publishers. But from then on, they spent their winters there and returned to the estate for the summer.

And then – we don't know when because the dates are sketchy – another woman appeared in Maria's life: Jadwiga Skirmuntt, her much younger distant cousin. I gather from reading her book of memoirs (entitled something like *A Memoir of Twenty-Five Years with Maria Rodziewiczówna*, in which she speaks glowingly of their deep emotional connection without ever mentioning sex) that she was the "femme" (as in "girls in dresses and frills.") She took care of the "domestic" side of the household – cleaning, cooking, pickling, preserving, drying, gardening, running the dispensary and the village shop. In *A Summer* she is Crane, who is "the doctor" (people come to her for cures), and fussy (bathes way too often), pouts, is often disapproving, and on whom the masculine Panther (Helena Weyhert) plays "tricks."

Krzysztof Tomasik, who has published the most on the subject, says that Helena ("Panther") and Jadwiga ("Crane") did not get along and that the *ménage à trois* was riven with jealousy. He says that Maria was obliged to spend her time with one or the other and rarely able to be together with both. There are echoes of this in *A Summer*, in which Panther keeps picking on Crane, and Crane is sometimes seen as holding a grudge or going off alone in a huff.

Now, anyone who has ever attempted to live in an open relationship or any sort of *ménage à trois*, knows how hard it is to overcome the most fundamental issue of jealousy. For every set of lovers that succeeds, as many – or more – fail. And in those that succeed, more often than not, one partner becomes dominant (as a primatologist might say, becomes the "alpha"), and the other two (the "betas") end up competing with each other for his/her affections. *A Summer* makes it plain that Maria was the dominant figure. Perhaps because of her age (she was older), or her status as the owner of the forest and the cottage, or perhaps simply because of her personality. The others call her "Chief." She makes all the decisions, and they are final.

And the competition between the other two isn't always nice. They try to do the best they can to appear agreeable (because Maria expects them to, and not to cooperate would appear unreasonably churlish), but they can be quite mean to each other. The novel pooh-poohs it. It says Panther put frogs in Crane's tea caddy because he once had the runs due to Crane's medication ("licorice powder"). But are we perhaps entitled to read more into this?

I wonder: is *A Summer* a work of imagination, perhaps composed for the benefit of Panther and Crane to show them how they *could* all get along with each other if they only tried? Or is it a record of a summer they did spend together, and which was perhaps not terribly successful, but which, Maria/Wolverine wanted to say – and show them – seen in a certain light, could well be seen as at least a good beginning to a better future? If you think of it that way, the chapter in which the two younger women (Crane and Panther) go fishing, alone, just the two of them, and capture a giant wels, and then survive a thunderstorm on the lake seems especially imbued with symbolic meaning.

Surprise?

Now, for a student of history like me, here is the weird thing: the Polish reading public was surprised to learn in 2014 that *A Summer* is a book about lesbians. Maria a butch? A Catholic patriot in a conservative nation under the most reactionary regime of the times – a lesbian?

But we really should not have been surprised. For, while Maria never openly stated that she was a lesbian, and never wrote openly about the subject, and concealed the gender of the heroines of *A Summer*, she also never made much of an effort to conceal her identity. Just looking at their photos: men's clothing, spiky hairstyles, flat shoes or riding boots, one could hardly accuse these women of being closeted in any sense. And we have the evidence of Romana Pachucka, a Polish feminist activist from the early twentieth century who wrote in her memoirs:

"I knew in those days three pairs of inseparable women: Paulina Kuczalska Reinschmit and Józefa Bojanowska, Maria Konopnicka and Maria Dulębianka, and Helena Weychert and Maria Rodziewiczówna. And in those pairs, invariably one of them projected a masculine image, dressed in man's clothing and flat shoes, moved swiftly and walked with a swagger, while the other," etc., etc.

Krzysztof Tomasik points to this passage as an example of "a lack of precise terminology for the relationship in the language of the day" (i.e., he objects to the term "inseparable women," wishing for something more explicit). And yes, he has a point, but is it possible that the passage also illustrates something else? Namely, that even in those otherwise very conservative times, at least in the upper echelons of the Polish society, it was okay to be different, as long as one did it "the right way," i.e., just didn't talk about it? "Yes," it seems people said, "Maria is... er... a little odd," and... shrugged. Mostly, it just wasn't their business?

Rereading this book now, with the "secret key" in hand, I had the feeling that I understood it a lot better than ever before. The psychology of the three Forest Folk and the attitudes of their neighbors makes a lot more sense if one knows that they are women, not men. That Wolverine and Panther might be worried, for example, when Crane (the girly girl) has gone off into the woods alone and isn't coming back; or that their neighbors might feel protective about them.

Reading between the lines can be so much fun.

And now...

A Summer of The Forest Folk

DRAMATIS PERSONAE

WOLVERINE	(a.k.a. CHIEF) scion of the local gentry, owner of the forest, author of the book (Maria Rodzieczówna /**Ma**-rya Ro-dzhe-vee-**choov**-na/)
PANTHER	his long term companion (Helena Weychert /He-**le**-na **Vay**-hert/)
CRANE	his other long term companion (Jadwiga Skirmuntt /Yad-**vee**-ga **Skeer**-moont/)
WHATISIT	his teenage nephew
ODROWĄŻ	local peasant, a former feudal retainer of Wolverine's family (Od-**rho**-vonsh/
SZCZEPANSKA	(a.k.a. MOTHER) daughter of the above /Shcheh-**pan**-ska/
SZCZEPANSKI	her husband /Shcheh-**pan**-ski/
JASIEK	(a.k.a. BEEKEEPER), their son /**Ya**-shek/

Action takes place in the Pinsk Marshes, formerly in the Polish Commonwealth (until 1795), now Byelarus; about the year 1900, under Russian occupation, which has very little time left to run.

GENEALOGY

We shall talk about an ancient people here, as ancient as the eternal forest. It has ancestors of all ages and all nations, for it is not a tribe of the body but of the soul, not of the inhabitants of a forest but of its lovers; of the true worshippers of the wood.

Of this family came the poet of Hellas, who sang the myths of Pan and his satyrs. And Baldur in Scandinavia. And that spiritual relative of theirs, who gave the Kupala Night[1] to the Slavs. Later, this family found a patron among the followers of the new religion – because he had their soul and their lineage: a lover and singer of the sun, a preacher to birds and fish, a friend of all God's little creatures, the seraphic Saint Francis. Thus, these folk can be seen to have sages

[1] Kupala Night was a traditional Slavic holiday celebrated on the shortest night of the year. It involved herb collecting, bonfires, and bathing in rivers.

and scholars and saints among their ancestors. And although they may at times seem to have been swallowed up by the general mass of humanity, yet they have retained a certain distinctive quality of their forest soul.

Yes, they have been snowed under by earthly upheavals, by the feverish pursuits of ordinary life, by complications and conditions, and by the very struggle for material existence. All of these removed them from nature: 1) civilization, 2) the so-called progress, 3) the destruction of nature through the expansion of industry, 4) the terrible burden of modern existence, 5) modern rights and obligations.

Seemingly, then, there is no place and no life for these forest folk.

But it only seems so because they have adapted the best they could to their conditions and make an effort to appear no different from others. They fulfill their daily duties. They work hard with and among others. They participate in civilization. They take part in progress. They use its inventions: know how to handle money, live in cities, dress like others, go to the theater.

Has the lineage and tradition of the forest people perished, then? Not in the world! Immortal is the spirit, and the lineage of the spirit is immortal; it's just that he who would know this tribe must stem from it. Then he will find his kind.

One need not look for this tribe in quiet villages or deep forests, among the people engaged in the business of nature (a.k.a. forestry or agriculture), which would be to say "in their proper sphere." One can often search there long and in vain but find it instead in a great factory town. One can find its member in a student's garret, where a boy, after finishing with his algebra, instead of going out to look for company in a stuffy bar, plays with and looks after his pet bullfinch; or in the basement shop of a shoemaker, who hardly knows the name of the bird that chirps for him while he's busy nailing leather.

One can recognize its members in a crowd by their peculiar behavior in certain unusual circumstances of city life. And thus, when the papers come out in the evening with the latest dispatches of a war, a scandalous trial, a sensational murder; and a certain person does not pick up the newspaper but instead studies with a smile how the sparrows settle for the night: she is of the forest folk.

And from this family comes she who, amid a solemn street procession, when everyone else is absorbed in music, uniforms, caparisons, the parading ranks of soldiers and civic societies, notices a chilled pooch in front of a closed shop door and opens it for him with a gentle word of kindness.

Among the classified advertisements, a member of this family will spot the address of a caged nightingale seller, ransom the prisoner, and release him from captivity with the arrival of spring, partaking in his joy of liberation.

The forest folk usually keep shy from others, hide their souls, and do not talk about their inner life, aware that no one cares about it.

In the monstrous mill of worldly life, where financial self-interest and the ruthless struggle for the luxuries of civilization reign; as they deal with others – with horror or utter astonishment in their eyes; they remain silent. They fulfill their social obligations and look out only not to allow themselves to be crushed and pulverized. They do not fear for their souls: those are safe from the world's pollution.

And so they vegetate, rare in the world and strangers to it. Occasionally, they find a friend. Then the doors of the soul fling open, and the newfound friends find solace in each other: dreams, needs, longings – all suddenly find their expression in words. As never before now, they suddenly give voice to their lust for freedom, for quiet, for communion with nature. They express their souls and strive to turn those longings into action: for life after their own hearts.

And precisely, that kind of life – a whole summer of it – will be our topic here. For those who had lived it, it will be a chronicle of happiness; for those who, in their worldly exile, only dream of it, a brotherly postcard and, perhaps, a call to action.

There were three of them.

The oldest, their chief and commander, was cunning, stubborn in his resolve, quick to decide, knowledgeable about nature's science, and experienced in living with it. He owned a vast stretch of land, some 3000 acres, and on it, agricultural land with a manor house – the nerve center of his agricultural enterprise. All around it lay various marshes and forests, cut by a network of slow-meandering streams and rivulets, set well off from public roads and wholly unappetizing to human greed.

There, in the depths of those unproductive marshlands, hidden like a secret lair, a forester's cabin came into existence one spring. For some time afterward, the shingle roof and sideboards shone white in the sun, and the deep ruts in the ground shone black, where the carts had brought the building materials. But within a year, all that newness was buried in the greenery of grass and moss. Wild rose and heather covered the walls, and the cabin melted into the surrounding landscape.

The forest folk called it their Refuge.

Life had robbed the chief of relatives; he had no family. But his house was full of God's creatures, who remained in the manor house under the care and protection of his companion – a friend whom he had trained and shaped after his own image. In their joking jargon, they called the chief 'Wolverine' and his friend 'Panther.'

Panther was the youngest, all made of steely muscle, swift, agile, and with his namesake's wildness and rapacity. He knew nature from living with it; he understood mountains, waters, meadows. He had a forest soul, through and through.

Later, a third one joined them, whom they called Crane. He had the purest soul of them all, the embodiment of kindness, gentleness, and inward sunny happiness. He rejoiced in the life of the forest as only youth can rejoice. He was a dreamer, a little absent-minded, quick to laugh, industrious, and of both iron health and constitution.

The three complemented each other and became regular summertime residents in that Refuge of theirs, the founders and builders of that life. There, they lived at one with the wilderness, like every other creature that arrived there in spring and flew away in autumn.

Their refuge, locked up for the winter, fell asleep at the end of summer. First, the roof was buried under golden leaves, then under snow, and then only animals drew their tracks about it. Tits and squirrels wintered under its eaves. Hares came to feed in the feeders, and snakes buried themselves to hibernate under the foundations. Finches came to feed on the frozen berries. And, from time to time, deer approached to nibble on the dried-up flowers planted there by Crane.

Meanwhile, far away, among the maddening crowd, the forest folk remembered their cabin and dreamed of tits and finches and the rest of their summer friends.

And awaited springtime.

EARLY SPRING

Wolverine and Crane wintered in the city. Panther remained near the forest, looking after Wolverine's manor house, some 15 miles away from their Refuge.

The three rarely exchanged news – like birds that do not sing in winter but only greet each other from time to time with the expressive "pain, pain, pain." Therefore, when, near the end of February, Wolverine saw an envelope addressed to him in a spindly scrawl, he said only:

"Spring must be early this year. Larks are surely singing if Panther writes."

They opened the letter and read it eagerly, looking over each other's shoulders, their eyes shining with joy:

Forest greetings to Chief and Friend!

I report that yesterday, our friend Stomper woke up. He had gone to sleep so fat that he barely fit into your boot, but yesterday, he emerged so thin that the boot shank fanned about him like a broad foyer. He promptly clambered into my lap, pricked me, and snorted: 'Food!' He then swallowed a mountain of cheese and a river of milk, swelled up hugely, and is now running about the house, terrorizing the mice. Thus, spring must be near.

But Jake does not agree.

Last October, on top of the ceramic stove, Jake made himself a nest out of several rags, my winter gloves, your cook's bonnet, and several branches of oleander. When the whole thing reached up to the ceiling, he crawled in it, closed it behind him, and went to sleep. He, too, woke up yesterday. The sleep had served him well. His fur is silver, shiny; his tail bushy like an ostrich feather, and his ear tufts are very rakish. He crawled out, stretched, drank some water, ate a few nuts, and went out to investigate. He did not investigate long: he returned angry, his tail wet, his paws dirty, and he spat out the buds he had picked, making it clear that they were bitter bitter bitter and that it was way too early and time to sleep some more. And that better times were surely still a long way away. He announced as much from the top of the stove and crawled into his house. And that's all we saw of him.

Bluetit, who had also wintered indoors (hunting moths and moth eggs), also insisted on being let out. Well and good: I opened the window, and out she went, like to a wedding, with a swing. She now peels worms off the maple tree by the window and chirps at me: 'It's time! It's time!'

And whom is one to believe?

Because the larks, you know, are back, too – and how! I went to say hello to them, far out into the field. In depressions, snow still lies and ice holds, but the glades are bare and blackened by molehills. The wind is like mint: it seems cold, yet it burns. And lark song is in full possession of our fields and will stay so till winter.

And now for the news about the travelers.

The first graylags came to rest overnight last Friday and raised a great hubbub. I went to hear what news they had brought from overseas. The night was clear and echoing with silence, still frosty. The edges of the ponds covered themselves with ice and stayed that way till noon.

Every night, crowds of traveling birds fall onto our black orchard. They fall, say hardly a word, and are off again at dawn. These will not spend the summer with us. These regiments have a destination farther north.

I have three pairs of partridges in the attic; I found them in traps set up by boys in the winter, and they ask me every morning how many more days of imprisonment are left of their sentence.

Sparrows are about it, too. Betrothals in full swing, like at a church fair. They all swear that spring is just around the corner.

But bees... are like Jake! I knocked on some of the hives and asked: 'Queen-mother, is it spring?' But they grunted sleepily: 'Pst, pst! Mother is asleep!'

Whom to believe, then? And how to remain patient?

It's not spring, yet, and yet, it's no more the Witch-Winter. It's not the summer's army, but it is its vanguard, announcing: "Time to get ready!"

So, the more impatient are doing just that. The flowers of the carmine hazel are still covered by husks against the cold, but she has already let out her catkins to the wind. Kingcups have been seen swelling at the bottom of icy waters, and anemones are slinking about under the leaves on the ground.

Everything is ready, and when you put your ear to the ground, you can hear that something is afoot, something a person cannot understand: is it the earth and its music? Or is it one's own heart? Ah, it's all one thing! They all cry: 'Life, life, life!'

I'll wait a tad longer, and when everything cries out like this, I will call you, saying: 'It is time!' Meanwhile, I make clogs, fiddle with the canoe, and fix all pots and baskets, and I wait, trembling with excitement.

Such was the letter. Wolverine looked it over once more.

"The earthworms haven't stirred," he said. "The witch will be back."

They both sighed. A longing twisted a knife in their hearts. Crane said:

“I felt the color, the smell, the taste, the music... How it hurts to wait! Let's sneak out beyond the city limits, listen and see. Let's drink the wind!”

“Let’s!” replied Wolverine. “For we still have yet long to wait. Until the solstice is another seven weeks!”

THE SOLSTICE

In March, Witch-Winter returned once more. She sent her troops – gray regiments of clouds and packs of northern winds – and hurled this army on the swollen trees, the creeping leaves, the multitudes of birds, all these creatures that had dared her with their wedding song.

From these evil clouds there now fell on all this starting life deadly droves of snow amidst the howling of the wind. The sun, pale like a ghost, remained behind this cluster of clouds, patient and confident in its rising strength and certain of its eventual triumph. Like a powerful, confident man, the sun allowed the enemy a few moments to vent, spend all her strength, and exhaust herself so that he might then shine his light and triumph.

"Poor Bluetit!" said Crane, looking at the clouds of snow.

'Ha! Bluetit probably knocked on the window during the first snowstorm and asked to be let back in," replied Wolverine. "It's worse for the critters in the forest: if the waters are up, Panther cannot take food to them. And if the Witch calls for frost support..."

"Trees are full of sap, and their branches are swollen, they ache when touched. We have to come to their aid!"

The two rushed beyond city limits, found a wood weighted with heavy snow, and began to shake off the white shrouds.

They recognized the trees and spoke to them as if to closest friends.

"Grow your beautiful corals, you mountain ash! Blow in the wind, you silver birch! Sway soft, soft, you fragile maple. This snow is too heavy even for you, dear spruce, you winter hero."

Tree branches flexed with relief, liberated. They laughed and warmed up, overjoyed and intoxicated by the March air.

Only twilight put an end to their work. And at night, it happened, just as Wolverine had feared. Frost-Killer squeezed his claws into murderous fists.

Woods groaned with the pain of burst tissue; broken limbs fell on the snow; the witch cackled with delight at the loss of young life.

"Why is all this?" Crane whispered.

"Why! It's the law!" Wolverine replied. "A law beyond our understanding. The law! But this is not death. Not real death. It is... a small death, a tiny and weak death. Without wind and thunder, she is like without fangs, naked as an earthworm. When a true catastrophe comes, no forest survives in her wake, no powerful animal survives, no speedy bird. All that's left is death."

For three days, the evil frost tormented the earth. For three nights, winds blew, wrestling and struggling with each other in clouds of snow dust, howling, hissing, growling, groaning, until one morning, on the new moon of the new month, a wave of air came suddenly from the south: the main army of spring.

The snow clouds fled before her like a wicked lot, and the victorious sun rose in the radiant blue. The air brought his strong, living power, the power of health, and it swarmed the earth, swirled, drowned, and played the hymn of rebirth.

Now, to the forest folk, a different message came from Panther, a short shout of a panting runner: "The forest is alive. He sings! He calls! Come!" They jumped up and began to pack feverishly, overwhelmed with panic, need, drive, lust in their souls like migratory birds.

Something in them called out, deafening all else:
"To life! To life! To Refuge! To Refuge! To Refuge!"

TO REFUGE!

There was hustle and bustle at daybreak in front of Wolverine's manor house. The morning was April all over: clear, sunny, damp with the rain that had passed through the previous night; passed, causing miracles. It peeled the sticky shells off leaves, washed away the rest of the autumn mold from grasses, opened the eyes of white anemones and violets, lured the gold of marigolds out of waters, washed willows and sallows, and covered them with suddenly conjured catkins.

In the silence of the night, the rain had woken them with its murmur, inviting them to a wedding; and when the sun rose, the earth turned toward him, fragrant, colorful, and seemingly singing with joy.

A long wagon now stood in front of the porch. It was being loaded with everything that was or could be needed during the summer. Crane packed food, spices, medicines, a handy first aid kit;

Panther, provisions for companion animals, nets, pots, baskets, clogs, craft tools; and Wolverine his boxes, manuals, and measuring rods, the bulk of nature research. All were so absorbed in their work that they drifted from home to the cart, like bees, loading, and loading. And the cart was piling up.

"And now only room enough for men!" said Wolverine, examining the cart. "If you have forgotten anything, you shall have to do without."

"Oh, yes, I am sure I forgot something!" Crane worried and groaned.

And now, the feeder of the forest folk entered through the gate: the bay-piebald Hathor[2], who had summered with them in the wood for years. She was skin and bones after the hard winter, her hair spiky and dull.

The animal knew what all this loading meant.

She went to Panther, sniffed his hands, got bread and salt, looked at the cart, nibbled on the hay, checked to see for the smell of potatoes and chaff, rubbed her neck on the wheel guard, and stood, looking at them with her gentle eyes, chewing slowly.

"Hathor! You want your Bambam?" asked Panther, bringing out of the house a tin cow rattle on a thong.

Hathor moved her ears negatively and reluctantly turned her horned head. No! Hathor didn't want her Bambam.

A few years ago, when she had first been fitted with this rattling horror, she became mad with fear and disgust and exhausted herself trying to get rid of the thing, plowing through thickets in the hope of tearing it off.

In this irritation, she had committed a criminal act: she had swung her horns at Panther, roaring grimly: "Murder, murder!" But that was a long time ago, at the very beginning of her forest service. Since then, Hathor came to understand that putting on Bambam meant the coming of the blissful life in the wilderness, in the abundance of pasture and water, and of unlimited freedom.

---

[2] Named after the cow-headed Egyptian goddess

There would be no cowherd and no stick, no dogs, no chain in the stuffy barn, no treacherous horns of envious companions. Hathor had lost her herd instinct over the years and, led out of the barn, she did not as much as grunt a single word of goodbye to her winter companions. Without enthusiasm, but also without protest, she allowed herself to be fitted with Bambam.

"Panther! Harnesses up Patch Pelt! I'm going to fetch our householders. You take the birdcage, Crane!" commanded Wolverine, entering the house. Crane now placed on the cart a large basket covered with a colorfully embroidered napkin. Panther and Hathor breathed the scent with delight. They smelled fresh rye bread.

"The chief is such a driver today that breakfast somehow went missing," said Panther. "I can't resist it when it smells like this." He reached for a knife in his belt, lifted the napkin, made a sign of the cross over the loaf, and sliced off a hunk. He broke it, and they all shared it. Hathor's wet mouth slipped in among them for company.

"Ah, right! Chief ordered harness!" Panther remembered, turning to the stable. Soon, a piebald mare came out into the sunny yard, treading cautiously. She pulled Panther down to the well, drank her fill, and then went up to the wagon of her own accord. She tasted the hay, searched the muzzle bag for chaff, snorted, yawned, stretched, and, with resignation, gave her head to the collar.

"Do not complain about the load!" said Panther. "We know you're with a foal. When we come to mud and sand, we will jump off and go on foot. Now, come on in the thill!" He pulled the straps on, harnessed her, and stood ready for the journey, sharing his bread with the beasts.

"Crane! Tell the chief that all is ready! The way is long; we'll barely make it for supper!"

Meanwhile, in the manor, Wolverine struggled with the householders. Stomper (a hedgehog) and Jake (a squirrel) were the height of contradictions of customs and preferences. They knew little of each other but enough to hate each other, if only because neither would let the other one sleep.

During the night, Stomper frightened Jake with his incessant tramping. The squirrel stuck out his head from his nest and cursed:

"You filthy crawler, centipede-eater, slipper-sleeper, may you choke on a frog! Your stomping prevents us from sleeping!"

And during the daytime, while rummaging around, Jake would peer over the armrest of the couch and, trying to stash away a few nuts, drop them on the sleeping Stomper, who wiggled and hooted furiously.

"You brawler! You mischief-maker! You jester, clown, scarecrow, birds' laughingstock! May tree resin stick your tail to your nose! May your mouth never close on your teeth!"

This quarreling lasted all winter. If the two had anything in common, it was their hatred for Mrs. Barker. She actually lived in a stable but sometimes came into the manor house, sniffing everywhere, upsetting everything, noisy and annoying beyond all expression.

She was true poison! Although Jake was safe at the top of the stove, the very appearance of Mrs. Barker gave him palpitations, and he held his hands dramatically to his puffed-up chest. Stomper, under his couch, suffered from liver attacks and asthma.

Today, taking advantage of the turmoil of the trip, Mrs. Barker slipped into the house, causing terrible panic.

She chased Jake onto the wardrobe, barking threats and impertinence at him until she ran out of breath. She then sniffed Stomper in Panther's old boot and, unable to get to him, dragged that boot all around the room. At this, Wolverine arrived, grabbed her by the neck, and unceremoniously threw her out of the house; but by then, all the householders were in total rebellion.

Stomper was so angry that he jumped up and down in the boot and snorted:

"That's it! That's it! I don't want you! I don't want to go to the forest! Don't touch me! Go away, away, you wicked, false friends! That servant of yours wanted to eat me! In fact, she may have eaten me for all I know! I can't even tell; I am so upset!"

"No way I am coming down, either!" Jake squawked from the height of his perch, his little hand pressed to his heart. "I'm not stupid!

I am not leaving here! No way. Nobody in my entire clan has ever heard so many insults as I did today from that evil creature. You've got to make up your mind: it's either her or me! And, no, whatever it is that you are holding in your hand is not going to change my mind! Even sunflower seeds! I have my pride! You have abandoned me to that beast. What? Am I to take that sort of abuse?!"

"Very well," said Wolverine, "suit yourself!" and, putting a handful of nuts back in his pocket, picked up the boot with Stomper.

"Stomper, that beast is not coming to the forest with us. You will play to your heart's content there. Remember how many greasy worms there are? And how soft the moss to sleep in? And in the hut, how much milk and cheese and fish livers you can have any time you want? Get out of that boot! Are you not ashamed to be carried around in that, like some sort of troglodyte?"

"But I happen to want to sleep in this boot!" snorted Stomper and froze.

"Well, Jake, are you staying behind? Because I'm in a hurry. Goodbye then, the window is open."

"What do you have in that pocket? Show me," Jake jumped down on Wolverine's head and slipped into his pocket. There was a crack of the walnut shell and a soft purr of satisfaction. Peace had been made.

"Ready?" Crane stuck his head through the door. "Grab your fiddle, and off we go!"

"Off we go!" commanded Wolverine, sticking the boot with Stomper among other packs and jumping onto the wagon.

Crane held onto his crates, Panther jumped onto the thill, the mare snorted eagerly, Hathor swayed, and the caravan started.

They went through the gate, onto the dirt road, bumpy and muddy, and looked at the bluish line of forest far away. The breath of the open spaces enveloped them now, relaxed their lungs, brought color to their faces, and lit their longing pupils with the fire of joy.

"The anthem! The anthem, chief!" Panther reminded them.

And Wolverine sang to the blues of forests and fields:

It's time to go, it's time to go,
You commander of our armies!
Here's the oaken wreath for your helm,
The rosemary club for your hand,
Your golden arrowhead!

"You will lead us, you will lead us
Onto our golden trail!
Where hearts and songs have time to bloom,
Where dormant forests quiet wait,
And the eagle's silent flight!

"You'll take the world, you'll take the world
In your triumphant march!
Where out of ashes new flowers bloom
Where dawn breaks out from the jail of night
The battle of our lives!

THE SETTLEMENT

They passed fields, human settlements, crossroads, and golden marigold meadows and headed on and on towards the wood.

The trail became more and more indistinct, and the forest turned gradually from a distant smudge into a dark, massive wall. Until, like the advance party, old pines suddenly burst onto their path just as they came over the edge of a hill; behind them stood a solid wall of trees, lined with juniper and heather. They were greeted by a gentle and solemn hum, like a prayer, carrying with it the incense smell of resin; they were about to enter the sacred temple of the forest. They took their hats off and looked up, their lips moving in silent greeting. No one spoke. They listened intently.

The mare led the way. Without thinking, she picked out cracks in the forest wall, a barely visible path. She did not hesitate at turns or in the narrow passages among wetlands. She found foot bridges thrown across treacherous dykes. She wheeled and wove, so sure of her memory that she picked at snacks along the way: now a bunch of rush, now a twig of birch, and she chewed on them for fun.

The ground descended slowly. They rode over ancient levies made of oak logs centuries ago, where maybe once Swedish or Cossack armies had passed. They moved along the edges of great peat bogs, cleared a trail through marshes, and got stuck from time to time in the thickets of reed and rush. The sun was in their eyes, at their backs, to their left, to their right, and, finally, the only trail to be seen was the one they made, as clear as a path trodden by an elk.

Then water flashed among the thicket, a stream spilled into a wide ford, disappearing in sallow beds. They had reached the boundary of their summer kingdom.

"Here is our Rainbow Bridge!" said Crane. All three gave a shout – the usual chord with which they called each other when separated during their expeditions.

The mare entered the ford eagerly, bowed her head, stroked the water with her lips looking for the deepest reach, then stood and began to drink. Hathor followed suit, and the men drew water into their hands.

"Let us drink of Lethe's[3] stream. Forget the other world!" said Wolverine.

"It's as delicious as birch sap. Like wine!" said Panther.

"And it's full of fry. Look, there, against the sand at the bottom, can you see?" Crane pointed out. "Oh, and a green-headed drake is there, can you see, under those trees?"

The beasts of burden, their thirst slaked, raised their heads and opened their muzzles. The mare neighed, and Hathor tugged at her rope. Both sensed their summer pastures. Even Jake, sitting on Wolverine's shoulder, measured the distance to the first clump of birch and, as soon as they cleared the ford, gave a leap and was gone in the treetops.

---

[3] Lethe, the river of forgetfulness, is one of the five rivers of the Greek underworld. The shades of the dead were required to drink the waters of the Lethe in order to forget their earthly life.

The men jumped off. Hathor was released. Wolverine took a cage with the partridges and the basket with the hare – animals that had wintered with Panther on the farm. Let go, the hare was in no hurry to run. He stood on his hinds, scented, raised his flaps, glanced at the men, and slowly hopped off into the heather. The partridges, like yellow balls, rolled in single file behind him.

"Do not curse us, you godly martyrs! We are innocent of your misfortunes," whispered Wolverine.

When he returned to the wagon, he was alone. His comrades, carried away by the sudden frenzy of freedom, had rushed ahead on foot. Jake accompanied them along the treetops, and the mare pulled on her own in the direction she knew so well.

Wolverine caught up with her and walked alongside, steering her from time to time so that the cart would not catch on trees, but he, too, was busy with his thoughts.

He read the story of his country's winter.

Here, he knew every tree, every foot of earth, and he welcomed it all like his dearest friends. The forest had kept no secrets from him: it told, showed, bragged, and complained.

Here was the old pine tree with the killer sparrowhawk's nest; and there, another, bent and limp, which had once been broken in her youth. Here was a birch with a monstrous burl and an enormous rowan, which they called The Stunner and that had so many corals in autumn; and a hornbeam, split in half by lightning, that had survived the blow but shone with the black streak of the old wound; and there, a birch felled by frozen sleet; and a squat willow with an old squirrel hole where wild bees had already moved in. And there was the huge anthill, already crawling with life: the great empire of black forest workers, strewn with white lumps of resin and traces of winter raids by black grouse. And here was an alder ditch full of holes, fissures, chasms, roots, torn half out of the ground by a storm, a hideout for snakes and vipers.

The forest whispered softly, a kind of quiet panting of the revival of spring, and the man, staring and listening, lost himself in this great, mighty whole and felt how its great forces entered him, how he absorbed their power, how they now coursed inside him.

Beyond the ford, the ground rose. Their refuge was like an elevated island amid the bogs, surrounded on all sides by peat and swamp; peat and swamp crisscrossed by small rivers and overgrown with impenetrable thicket.

On this miraculously fertile island, a forest stood in a full riot, birch trees darted towards the sun, swaying their green gauze-like slender dancers; lovely hornbeams bloomed, stocky like virile farmhands; alders, ashes, oaks, lindens, rowan trees, maples all pressed together and upwards towards the sky; and lower down, hazel, viburnum, bird cherry, buckthorn; at their feet, raspberries and blackberries covered the ground. The clearings in the forest were white with anemones, and tall grass fluttered like the ready background for a tapestry yet to be woven by the coming summer.

The lingering cries of his companions woke Wolverine from his reverie; he glanced at the sun, then lightly nudged the feeding mare.

"Home, home, to the cabin, Patch Pelt! We also deserve dinner. Ah, here comes the scout!"

"Krr, krr," a voice said among the branches. Jake fell onto his shoulder, rubbed his tail on his cheek, and dove into his pocket for nuts.

They went on – to the left, then to the right – under the braids of birch trees, through wreaths and arches of bird cherry, until a large oaken cross with a carved figure under its own little roof appeared. Then the forest wall parted, a wide clearing opened up, and in its center stood the cottage of the forest folk. Its walls were gilded with streaks of resin and covered by the lace of wild roses and woodbine. The hut was low, spacious, on a high fundament, but still closed for winter, secured with locked shutters.

In front of it lay a garden surrounded by a fence – "Crane's patio," as they called it, planted with various forest flowers, and shaded from the heat of the sun by a linden tree.

Panther and Crane were waiting for him at the gate and soon began their report.

"A blackbird has a nest in the vine, next to the wall. A bush-robin moved into the box on the Linden tree. Lilies of the valley are peeking out. I found a viper on the porch. We're hungry!"

Wolverine was silent. He untied the mare and hung the harness on a peg under the roof. Only then did he take out the key and open the hut. The cold winter air blew over them out of the interior.

They entered the main room; the sun followed, gilding the holy icon of the Virgin Mary on the wall directly in front of them.

They bared their heads, and Wolverine greeted the Queen of Poland[4] with prayer and bow:

Salve Regina Mater misericordiae, vitae dulcedo et spes nostra!

And three voices joined together:

Salve!

Then Wolverine lit the lamp in front of the icon. Crane placed a loaf of bread on the table. Panther took down the bars and opened the shutters. Spring blew its color and warmth into the room.

"Ah, the house didn't fail to house winter residents!" they laughed.

In one corner, forest mice had built a sheaf-sized nest on the bench, and an anthill had materialized under it at the opposite end; the intruders had to be turned out. Crane began to cook a meal. Smoke blew out of the chimney; the cottage came to life.

Jake sat at the open window and watched the work. He had upturned his plume over his head and, feigning hunger, gnawed on a pine cone, spitting bits out on the folk crawling under the benches. But because they were too busy to pay any attention, he turned to bother Crane.

And he, having set the pots in the kitchen, started to unpack the cart and carried sacks and bags, pots and boxes to the pantry. Jake liked it. He sniffed and tasted everything and, finally, discovered a box of sunflower seeds and began to nibble without ceremony

"Don't ruin it!" Crane took it away.

---

[4] In a uniquely Catholic rite, Virgin May was crowned Queen of Poland in 1656

Jake was indignant.

"Mine! Mine! Mine!" he croaked.

"Yours, but not now. You're too fat, you glutton!"

"Mine! Give it here!" protested Jake.

"I will not, you greedy glutton!" Crane became impatient.

Then there was a brouhaha and ballyhoo, and suddenly, Jake flew out of the pantry. Disheveled, his plume erect, he climbed to the top of the linden tree and screeched and screamed from there.

"What happened? Where's the harm?" asked Wolverine.

"Harm! Exactly!" Crane replied. "He bit through three bags, bit open a box, bit my ear, and now he's screaming for help! Now, you all finish up because the gruel is ready!"

"And my stomach, too!" Panther said, rising up. "We swept the swarm away. The rest can wait. Eat!"

"First the beasts!" Wolverine reminded him.

"True!" said Panther and bustled about.

He dove into the pantry, then into the hall, and took out two buckets – one of potatoes, the other of oats – and set them in front of the gate. Then he took the trumpet off the wall in the room and sounded the bugle call.

The sound slapped the silence, flew into the forest, shattered the air. The signal was well known because it was answered immediately by a neigh and the distant sound of Hathor's clapper. Leaning against the forest fence, Panther waited. The mare was the first to show up; she snorted with delight and buried her head in the oats. Hathor stoically approached; Panther crouched by her side with the milking stool.

"Here's asking kindly for the milk, Hathor! And don't hold back because we're exhausted and ready to eat!" he spoke to her gently.

"Lunch on the table!" cried Crane from the room.

On the white maple table, under the paintings, lay a loaf of bread, a beautifully painted, steaming clay bowl, and three wooden spoons. Crane had even decorated the table with a wreath of marigolds. They took their places on the benches and dipped in deep, like honestly hungry folk. Jake assisted, trying each slice of bread, then wiped his mouth on Wolverine's sleeve with disgust, jumped on the window sill, and started his midday nap.

Humans eat disgusting things, he thought with a grimace, closing his eyes.

When the spoons scraped the bottom of the bowl, Wolverine said:

“I'm going to take the boat, check up on the fish, and set the traps. Panther will inspect and ready the stable. And Crane will clean the rest of the cottage and check the vegetable garden. Tomorrow, we will hoe and plant!”

"First of all, I'd like to change my hide," said Panther, inspecting his clothes.

“Well then, you two go change, and I'll smoke a pipe. And we need the clogs, too.”

The bedroom was behind the hall, wide and bright. It was where Wolverine and Crane slept at night. Panther slept in his alcove just beyond.

Soon, they were completely changed. They wore their forest uniform: gray linen outfits and light linden clogs, a leather belt with a knife in a sheath attached to the loose jacket, and a felt hat on the head.

“Now, the forest will recognize us as its own!” Panther laughed with delight and, taking an ax, went to work in the stables. Crane started to wash the pots. And now, it was time for Wolverine to get going.

He straightened his limbs with delight, changed his clothes, and unloaded his personal box, full of zoological books, collections and scientific instruments, and thousands of other small items he used for his studies and guarded as a treasure.

Then he hung the old sheepskin sleeve high under the ceiling – Jake's nest – and put the boot with Stomper in its corner. He finally loaded himself with fish baskets, took an oar and an ax, and went to find the boat. It had its place beyond the spring, under the old alder, by the stream. Wolverine bailed out the rainwater, loaded the baskets, unhooked the bast strap, and pushed off.

The expanse before him was endless because the bogs were still flooded with spring melt water; one could paddle in every direction, among the beds of the barely green and young shoots of the rushes. On the water lay spring duckweed, the favorite spring snack of Hathor and Patch Pelt, and he soon found them up to their bellies in the water, feeding.

They raised their heads and talked in the forest tongue.

"Good! Wholesome!" snorted Patch Pelt.

"A bit watery," muttered Hathor.

He patted each of them as he passed and said:

"Just you remember not to go to the deep end, beyond the spring, where you nearly drowned last summer. Both you and we nearly died! Remember, you gluttons!"

Swarms of marsh birds raved over the shallow water. Lapwings, curlews, and snipes screamed like at a wedding; golden marsh sallows smelled of honey; birch and alder smelled of balsam; the oar scooped up golden marigolds and clumps of water mint, and the sun, working its miracles, laughed to see its work.

Wolverine paddled up to the water fence, checked the depth, tied the canoe to a stake, and slipped into the water.

He inspected the whole length of the fence, mended gaps with twigs, and, at the inlet, where the current ran, he placed the basket. He worked slowly, methodically, observing all the rules of the fisherman's craft, guessing how the fish might go based on various minute observations, engrossed in his work, and all the time ospreys wheeled over his head.

The forest folk knew the rules of communing with nature. They avoided sudden movements, noise, frightening, and scaring. They kept a shotgun in the cottage for emergencies, but that hardly ever came, at most as a measure against some predator. Beasts and birds had fast accustomed to the sound of Hathor's knocker and their mealtime bugle, and the whole forest now knew well that no harm would come from the three.

A small gray boat with a gray man inside it, churning water with a slow stirring of the oar, was now a picture completely familiar to the birds: familiar, daily, and common; so common that the lapwings no longer bothered with their usual tricks designed to lead a potential hunter away from their nests. Flocks of teal fed carelessly along the path of the canoe.

Wolverine set up a second basket and a third, paddled about various fishing waters and bays, inspected the usual hiding places of fish, renewed last year's acquaintance with his companions of forest life, and completely forgot about the time.

He was just rummaging in some corner of the lake by the sandy hills to the west when, suddenly, the air burst with a polyphonic, predatory cry.

There was in it the blaring of ancient military horns and something like the call and answer of the scouts.

"There! Awake! Watchman, awake! There! Watchman, awake! It's twilight! It's twilight! It's time! Watchman, awake!"

It was the cranes sending their evening song from their inaccessible bogs.

Wolverine glanced at the sun and, obeying its signs, turned the boat back towards the cottage.

The treetops were red and gold, and a silver mist rose from the water. Birds rushed with the last tidbits of food and the last blades of grass to their nests. The time had come for rest and evening prayers.

I will be late! thought Wolverine. But he did not rush because rushing would frighten the birds.

The crane trumpets came three more times, more prolonged and more insistent each time.

"Evening light! Evening light! Awake, watchman, awake!"

And then, the bog suddenly burst in the croak and chortle of frogs; green-headed drakes began to splash at the edges of the water and call hoarse, luring calls; the mists thickened; the surface of the water wrinkled with the feeding fry; up in the sky, white clouds bloomed pink like roses; a song thrush on top of alder trees began its call to prayer. Dusk was nigh!

When Wolverine landed at the clearing, there was the usual bustle of the ending day. Crane, with Jake on his head, was bringing buckets of water from the spring. Panther was leading Hathor into the stable, and the mare stood in front of the gate, demanding her evening oats.

"Hello, chief! We couldn't wait!"

"Wait for what?"

"Wait for you! Because we have a lot of news. An owl has wintered in the attic and still lives there. The attic is full of mouse fur. A furrier, one would think!"

"Probably also a lot of feathers. We shall have to ask her to leave."

"And the old water serpent is still in the shed. It has grown a good two hands."

"Great tits have settled in the bird boxes – and in one, a wryneck."

"The wild pear tree is all white, like a bride."

"And there will be plenty of hazel this summer – the hazel bush is covered with catkins!"

"In the heathers by the vegetable patch, a black grouse sits on six eggs."

"Stomper has set out to hunt."

"Bees buzz in the hive."

Crane stopped to rest with his buckets; Panther came out of the barn with a mug of milk; the mare came to join them for company. And so they stood in the middle of the clearing. Patch Pelt repeated one thing over and over: "Oats! Oats! Oats!"

"Stuff her mouth, will you, Panther!" Wolverine laughed.

"Oh! But no one can! That's not a belly; it's a gaping abyss! Come, you bottomless barrel!"

"My goodness, the water's boiling!" Crane heard the fizzle of the stove and rushed into the hut.

Wolverine took sleepy Jake into his hands and slipped him into his sleeve-nest under the ceiling. The doors of the stable creaked as they closed behind the mare. For a moment, one could hear the chopping of logs and the clanging of pots in the kitchen. But the sounds of work slowly faded; the twilight was diminishing in the sky. But they felt no urge to go inside and eat.

Around them, the trees and bushes, beds and rushes, water and earth and heaven began the last act of the day, the evening prayer of all creatures.

At the entrance to their cottage, the forest folk sat down on an oak log, looked, listened, and fell silent.

And then, quietly, Wolverine said:

"Praise be to you, Lord, who made all these miracles."

The sickle of the moon rose above the trees and silvered the face of the saint on the cross, who seemed as if hugged by the mist rising from below and appeared to float miraculously above the ground.

The air, cooled by dew, brought the scent of honey and balsam, and the nightingale lute-player began to sing on the birch tree by the spring. The frog orchestra struck their double bases; a bat circled noiselessly overhead, chasing moths. Calmed by the great silence, night descended on earth.

And thus ended the first day of their forest life.

THE DAY OF THE SWIFT PANTHER

Panther slept in a tiny little alcove beyond the main room. That first night he woke frequently, impatiently awaiting daybreak.

At first, he could only see the ruby lamp burning in front of the icon, but soon, the window began to glow with the light of approaching dawn. He lay sleepless, listening to hear who would be the first to get afoot.

He heard the gibbering of black grouse, the pathetic pow-pow of nightjars, the far-away bleating of bucks, the giggles of owls, and the tearful love song of nightingales: the song of the night.

At last, he distinguished a different song.

"There it begins!" he whispered.

As if on a signal, the nightingale piped down. The ground of frogs held up, but from its secret hiding place, a single whirring voice asked: "Now's the time? Now's the time?"

And then, suddenly, the confused, blaring brass of cranes resounded from the marshes.

"Hey, day! Come by! Come by! Hey, day, your master is here! Hey, day, awake! Hey, dawn, awake!"

The entire chorus, several thousand strong, burst into song all at once. "Day-break! Day-break! The master's here! The master's here! Life-life! Life-life!"

Thus, the forest welcomed the rising day.

Panther jumped up and, still in his nightshirt and barefoot, leaped out of the window.

The clearing in front of the house was paved with the opal of dew; the air was moist, fragrant, warm, the birds flicked their feathers, stretched their wings, and flew to water.

Panther stretched out his shoulders, wiped his face with a damp branch of birch, and ran to the stream to bathe.

When he left the water, he rolled on the grass, ran across the meadow, and returned to the hut as red as a crayfish.

Jake stuck his snout out of his nest but only yawned and buried himself again.

"Not gonna wet my precious fur in this dew! That's good for the hairless," he purred dismissively.

Panther put on his clothes, took the milk pale and, whistling, went to his work.

He let the mare out and woke Hathor.

A steel-gray grass snake had been warming himself by her side and reluctantly slithered away as the cow stood up.

"Hiss-Hiss, you want milk?" Panther spoke to him. And it seemed he did want some because he hung about. Hathor, having paid her tribute, followed after the mare. Panther poured a few drops of milk into a shard of a pot.

"There, Hiss-Hiss! And then off you go hunt for frogs!" he said to the snake. He set the milk in the hallway for Crane and peeked through the crack in the door into the bed-chamber, but all was dark and quiet.

"Oh, these sleepyheads! All they ever learn in that town of theirs is bad habits. It's an embarrassment before the entire forest. But it suits me!"

He sat down on the parapet, put on his clogs, put a piece of bread in his pocket, stuck an ax in his belt, drew a small bundle from under the thatch roof of the barn, and set off for the canoe.

But as he walked, he conceived of a prank. He caught a small frog, went back to the main room, and stuffed the frog into the tea box.

Crane will have a fit when the beast jumps into his face, he thought.

Now, it was the chief's turn. Panther set off with the boat for the fish baskets and loaded each with some strange object from his secret bundle: in one, he put a horse's skull; in another, an old galosh; in the third, a rabbit skin; and then he slipped back to the landing.

Now there was movement in the hut – the other two were talking; the chimney was properly smoking; there was a smell of coffee.

Panther hesitated for a moment. The chief had ordered him to hoe the garden, but he'd just fly into the forest for a little, check a few secret sites, burn a little energy, and be back with news and loot. And away he rushed. He waded through the thickest brambles, slipped under fallen trunks, rolled over the carpets of anemones, mocked the birds, whistled, and sang. He scared a deer family from their lair and chased them for a while.

"Ha! I'll jump on your back, grab you by the horns, and ride, ride, ride!" he whispered at last, out of breath, watching as they leaped through the marshes. He lay down under a birch tree and felt hungry, thirsty, and delightfully sleepy.

He had bread; there was no shortage of water, but as a true forest gourmet, he broke a birch twig, bent a piece of bark into the shape of a cup, and dipped the bread into the sap.

"It's barely dripping. All sap's gone into the buds!"

He yawned at last, stretched out, and dozed off.

Curious tits swarmed briefly around him, inspected him, and returned to their work. A finch couple building a nest in the birch tree pretended for a few moments that they were only passing through but soon calmed down and went back to their elaborate construction work; nearby, a snipe landed, bleating. The sun rolled up a little higher and woke up the sleeping man. He looked at the sky, at the shadow of the trees, and he sprang up. "It's ten o'clock! They must be at work! I can't show up without some prize!"

But what? He started looking. He first came upon the foundations of a chaffinch house, but that was nothing special; after a little more digging, he found two eggs on a snipe clump: another ordinary thing. At last, he noticed a yellow bouquet of mistletoe on a distant birch tree on the marsh.

"Ha, I'll get that! Chief wanted to hang mistletoe in the cottage. Off I go!"

There was not enough water in the swamp for the canoe, but only a few steps away from the edge of the forest, the bog went deep. The grasses and reed made only a thin crust that wobbled and sank underfoot. He had to crawl.

Panther cut some reed, tied it in bunches, fastened them under his armpits and around his chest, took a long stick, lay down, and began his adventurous crawl.

He crawled, pushed with his legs and elbows, fell into the slime, cut himself against the reeds, tore his shirt, spat out water and mud, and, after all these heroic hardships, reached his goal.

He was drenched in sweat, dripping with water, black with slime, and nearly naked, but he won his prize. He immediately climbed the birch tree, sat astride a branch, let the sun dry him, let the wind cool him, and looked around.

"I'm a fool! A little to the right is a hump of land and a crest of reed. I will go back to the other side like on a highway! Ah, one can see the crane nesting grounds from here! Oh, they are circling everywhere! We must get to them this summer. That will be an expedition!"

He hacked off the mistletoe and started to retreat. The newfound "highway" was comfortable enough that he sank in the marsh up to his neck only twice, left the remnants of his shirt on the coxcomb of reed, and reached the solid ground clothed only in black mud.

Then, realizing that it was already close to noon, he rushed back to the cottage.

Along the way, he heard the bugle, met Patch Pelt on her way to lunch, jumped on her back, and thus reached the gate.

"Jesus and Mary! A forest spirit, not a man!" Crane shouted at this sight.

"Mistletoe for the Chief. Our first bouquet! By my life, how hungry I am! I will eat your ear, Crane, if there is no food on the table!"

"I'll bring you a bucket of water to wash up in, you dirty boy!" said Wolverine, laughing.

Panther jumped off the mare, turned a few flips on the grass, and, a little on his feet, but mostly on his hands and head, went to bathe.

"Chief! Throw me a new suit, will you? I want to dress properly for lunch! A white tie, a tuxedo, and, of course, a gardenia in the buttonhole! Oh, oh! I will take Hathor to lunch, arm in arm!"

He bathed, splashed, scrubbed, changed his clothes, and wondered if Wolverine had yet been by the traps. Asking would give his game away, but he could guess nothing from the faces of the other two as they sat at their lunch bowl.

Everyone talked about their morning loot: Crane had found a rare flower – a lady's slipper. Wolverine had spotted a sparrowhawk nest. They hoed a few rows for potatoes and planned to plant vegetables the next day.

After the meal, they rested for an hour, and then the three went to work. They had worked the vegetable patch for a few years now, so the ground was soft and plump, a stretch of beautiful black earth near the stream, surrounded by a fence against Hathor's gluttony.

Panther hoed furiously to make up for his morning hooky. The sun was warm, and sweat stood out on their shirts. And then it was finally evening.

"Won't you check your traps, chief?" asked Panther at last.

"Oh, I was just about to ask you to do it in my place today. I got severely winded with all this hoeing."

"But for me... that is... I don't quite know where you set them," pleaded Panther.

"Where I set them? Why, the usual places."

"Er... won't it wait till tomorrow?"

"No, it's time! Go have fun! You like beavering on the water!"

There was no way to refuse. Sour, Panther went to the boat. He found all his surprises in the traps and threw them away in irritation. The trick had failed, and until today, Panther still does not know whether sly Wolverine had been at the traps that morning or not. In any case, in keeping with his name, he evaded the trap set on him, and this ruined the rest of Panther's day.

He returned, humorless, to port, threw a bunch of pikes threaded on a withy in a bucket, and spent the rest of the evening painstakingly washing his soiled rags.

THE DAY OF THE VIGILANT CRANE

In the bed-chamber where the two of them slept, the shutters were closed at night. Bird chatter woke Crane up. Half dozing, he lay with his eyes closed, enjoying the music, and waited for the ruby signal.

Then the rising sun hit the shutters and shone through the knots like red torches. And Crane got up.

He walked to the spring to fetch water and read the clearing along the way. There were traces on the silver dew: mare's round hooves, Hathor's long ones, and Panther's light feet. A snake's trail twisted like a ribbon from the barn.

Hiss-Hiss would drink his milk and go hunting. But he had a habit of making a detour by the spring, and Crane would often meet him there. Raising himself high above the water, Hiss-Hiss studied his reflection as if in a mirror, swaying coquettishly.

"What varied life forms inhabits the vice of vanity!" philosophized Crane, amused. "Look at him, admiring himself! Eve would be jealous!"

He returned with the water, lit the fire, swept the room, and went to his bath. Then he shaved and dressed and, as usual, found the entire company in the room at breakfast.

Then the day's work was discussed.

"I have to mow rushes for the litter," said Panther. "We'll have a foal any day now. If you ask Patch Pelt, she thinks it will be a girl."

"And her name may turn out to be Magpie."

"I'll go beyond the Praying Birch; I have to build a salt lick for deer," said Wolverine.

"Perhaps you might look for crayfish, Crane?"

"In the afternoon, maybe! I haven't yet finished with the garden and have a whole bucket of milk to do something with."

"Then give me salt in a bag, and I'll be off!"

They put on their clogs. Panther sharpened the scythe, and both took off.

Crane washed the dishes and went to his beloved plants. In a small garden next to the cottage, he experimented with the domestication of forest flowers. He brought from the forest orchids, mints, red gladioluses, meadow rues, valerians, wintergreens, and meadowgreens, and planted them all with loving care.

He stretched out in the yard and was examining his plantation when he heard a rustle by the fence.

He scooted aside for fear of a snake but was surprised to see Stomper instead.

"Why is Sir Stomp not asleep at this hour?"

The hedgehog raised up his snout as high as he could, and the man lay low; and thus, they were in perfect position for a conversation: nose to nose.

"Maybe Sir Stomp is hungry?"

But no, judging by his girth, Sir Stomp had had his fill.

"So, how about some cottage cheese? Yes?"

The damp honker touched his hand. Stomp had business, but the man had to guess it.

Crane stroked him gently over his folded spikes.

"Come home with me, Sir Stomp. We've got fresh fish livers. Hm?"

He rose and looked around. Stomper moved slowly, with a limp. Then Crane took him up in his arms and saw it.

Stomper's hind leg was swollen, and when he touched it, the beast hummed and twitched. Crane sat on the threshold and carefully examined the disability. The foot was entangled by roundworm, which had buried itself into the flesh and caused it to swell.

A surgery took place. It was apparently very painful because Stomper puffed and tugged his leg and, at one point, even bit Crane's hand, but he did not stand his spikes and did not twist away, and finally, when he felt relieved, he licked the man's hand with his tiny tongue.

Then he got his promised fish livers and, incredibly, swelled even more – so much that he barely managed to cram himself into his boot and, huffing goodbye, fell asleep until evening. Jake watched the whole operation from the window sill, where he basked in the sunlight.

What a perverted sense of aesthetics! he thought. *To spend such a wonderful time of day sleeping in a cave. I understand that this is done in winter, but now? Fool!*

Crane noticed how high the sun was and set about cooking lunch.

Hearing the creak of the pantry door, Jake turned up to assist. Crane was touched by his attachment but also worried a little: due to his life of plenty and no cares, Jake had become a complete Sybarite. He rose late. For the first few days, he allowed himself to be persuaded by Wolverine or Panther to go for a walk in the forest. But he soon learned that there were no nuts on the hazel or seeds on the cones, and he was too much of a gourmet to chew on buds: he left that to the undomesticated rabble.

He knew, however, that locked in the pantry under Crane's care, there was a large tin of nuts and another one with sunflower seeds.

He, therefore, often hung by Crane's side, and the latter took the snobbery for attachment and fed him as much as he could bear.

When Crane sat down on the threshold to peel potatoes, Jake settled next to him with his nuts.

The sun now stood high above the clearing, and the first butterflies were floating in the hot air. The birds had piped down, as they usually did towards noon, and now there was such a silence that both Crane and Jake raised their heads instantly when they heard an unusual rustling in the oak tree.

On a branch, near the trunk, sat a wild squirrel, distrustful, ready to flee at any moment, and watching the beautiful fat bachelor at the cottage door. Jake ruffled his mustache, jumped on the fence, and turned a couple of cartwheels.

"Krr-krr-krr!" they said to each other.

The wild squirrel retreated somewhat, luring the bachelor to follow her; soon, they started chasing each other around the trunk. There were chuckles and taunts, and finally, they ran off into the forest along the treetops for their spring wedding.

When the forest folk sat down to dinner, Wolverine noticed the absence.

"Where's Jake?"

"He was seduced by a ginger temptress," replied Crane.

"High time! All the nests around have their first litter already, and these two are starting only now!" said Panther.

"Goodness. He's such a city kid! An owl will devour him at night."

"Never fear! Jake's not so stupid to spend the night in some wet tree hollow! He'll be back to his sleeve by evening."

"And he'll be hungry, little creature."

"That'll be good for him. You feed him mercilessly! His skin is about to burst!"

Immediately after lunch, Panther harnessed the mare to the cart and went to collect the reed litter. Wolverine paddled out to the fish traps. And Crane was left alone again.

He quickly cleaned up the pots, worked a little more in his herbarium, and then, remembering the crayfish, began gathering the tools needed for his hunt.

"Actually, it would be easier to bait them with scraps of fish, but that works best out on the water, from the boat, where it's deep. But Wolverine took the boat away, so I think I will try to rustle a few from their hiding holes at the shore," Crane consulted with Panther, who had just arrived with the reed.

"Wait for me! I'll bring the rest of the reed, and we'll go together. I know the best places."

"Yeah, sure. I bet you have some trick up your sleeve. I already had a mouse in the box of toothpaste today. Oh, and a sewn-up shirt sleeve. Enough for a day!"

"By God, that was not me!"

"Not you? Who then? Maybe Wolverine?"

"No! The Tennant![5] You probably didn't offer him honey in a walnut shell to greet him!"

"Ah, yes. Must be the Tennant! I bet he hung Wolverine's stuffed owl under the eaves, too, so that birds would not let us sleep at night!"

"Oh, he could do a thing like this easily. He's one scary trickster!"

"And the Tennant left the peeled snake skin in my bed linens?"

"Could not the snake have peeled his skin in your bed? After all, you also change your clothes there."

Laughing, Panther rode the mare away.

Crane took the net on a ring, a bag for crayfish, and went out.

There were no roads in their country, but everyone had a map of it in their head, never wandered, and always took the most direct course. As time went on, they trod their own paths, like those of animals, and never lost their way.

Crane was soon out of the clearing and into the thicket of reed. He found last year's footbridge thrown over a narrow dyke, climbed

---

[5] Poltergeist

over a hump overgrown with alder, forded a few streams, skirted the peat bog, and headed straight like an arrow for the great oak on the lake shore. The water lay smooth, spilled wide, and ran inland with a multitude of little coves. On the opposite bank were white sandhills, like an island, and behind them again the black forest wall.

Under the oak, Crane threw off his clothes, down to underwear and clogs. He slung his bag over his shoulder and stepped into the water. He waded waist-deep and stuck to the shore. The bottom was slushy, and the shore was full of holes. Every few steps, Crane set the net at the water's surface and stomped about the holes with his foot. When he raised the net, he found mud, beetles, and, on his third attempt, a dark carapace and two large pincers raised up belligerently.

"There you are," he said triumphantly, taking his prey carefully by the tail and tossing it into the bag.

He was soon seized with hunting fervor. He no longer bothered about the depth of the lake, his surroundings, or the sun, but only plunged the net, stomped, lifted, and filled his bag. And then, suddenly, he lost ground under his feet and lurched with his whole body – head and all – into some bottomless underwater cave under a huge alder tree.

The water suddenly boiled about him; some great fish slithered between his legs. Crane swallowed a goodly gulp of water but soon regained self-control and emerged into the air. He must have swum a dozen meters before he touched bottom again. He then swam out to catch his hat and the net floating on the surface, and he crawled ashore.

"Well, this time, it definitely was the Tennant!"

He felt the bag; it was empty. All his crayfish had swum free.

The evening was close; mist began to rise on the water, and chill pierced through his linen, but Crane continued his hunt, working his way back towards the great oak. But the runaway crayfish must have alerted their tribe because he only found adolescents now, and he soon became discouraged and gave up.

Teeth chattering, he ran back to the cabin. Along the way, he slipped over one of the ditches and fell deep into the mud, and then he heard from far away the trumpet of alarm and the hooting of his comrades.

They were coming his way, anxious.

"Did you lose your way?" asked Wolverine.

"No. But I wasn't paying attention and fell into the deep under the alder tree."

"And the wels was not there?"

"He was! This close! I could have taken him with my hands, but I was thinking about saving myself and not about catching him."

Panther groped in the bag.

"What's up? Just a handful of tweezers."

"Yeah, the big ones got away when I took my bath. Brr! I'm freezing! And is Jake back to his sleeve for the night?

"We did not look! We were looking for you!"

"And there is no supper?"

"Oh, yes, there is! I cooked dumplings in milk, but we waited for you before eating and finally set out to look for you."

It was nice and warm in the hut, but Crane felt cold and went to put on a sweater. When he emerged again to join them to supper, he said with some disappointment in his voice:

"You know, Jake is back in his sleeve."

"But you were worried about him spending the night in the forest!"

"Yes, well. Still, it's a sign of total Sybaritism."

"Now you're starting to see things in their proper light!" Wolverine laughed.

Crane started eating; the warmth of the cottage inclined him to daydreaming, and great sleepiness came over him.

"Be careful not to get the soup in your ear by mistake," Panther teased him.

"I still have to wash the dishes!" Crane mumbled, leaning against the wall. But they left him to doze and finished the house chores themselves.

He did not remember how he got to bed, but he remembered everything the moment he felt two crayfish under his pillow – a gift from Panther.

THE DAY OF THE CUNNING WOLVERINE

Ruby lanterns in the shutters and Crane's bustling in the kitchen normally woke Wolverine. He then went to bathe in the stream and was usually late to breakfast because he always got sidetracked on the way back. Of all the creatures of the forest, birds were dearest to his heart, and he watched and studied them with enthusiasm. There were tree boxes all around the hut, and Wolverine knew the history and affairs of each school of birds intimately. None of the forest folk could ever boast of having discovered some new nest because whenever he barely started, the chief would guess: "In the hazel, almost on the ground? I know! It's a shrike!" Or: "On that pine, behind that hornbeam. Yes, I saw that; it's a crested tit nesting in an old squirrel hollow."

He had special favorites.

Every day, he visited a certain robin sitting on eggs in a rotten birch stump near the spring. On the first day, she flew away; when she returned, she found a handful of ant eggs in the nest. On the second day, when she saw the face of a giant looming over her, she froze, motionless. The black beads of her eyes expressed limitless horror. The giant threw a few ant eggs again and walked away. She immediately grabbed the delicacy, and from then on, whenever she heard the cracking of twigs under the giant's foot, she awaited him eagerly, no longer afraid.

After breakfast, Wolverine refilled the lamp in front of the Queen's icon, chopped wood, pulled on his clogs, and went out into the forest.

He took with him a bag, an ax, and a rope with a hook at one end and was gone without a trace. He usually walked very slowly, his hearing focused. From time to time, he would stop, snuggle up to a tree trunk, or stretch out flat on the ground under a bush and observe, motionless.

The forest was just now barely growing its first tiny leaves; it was the best time for bird watching, and it would be short: one had to make the most of it.

Every day, Wolverine also visited the bees. For several years now, they had occupied a hollow in an old willow tree. He knew them well. They were true forest bees: black, tiny, and they stung mercilessly.

The forest folk found them in their first year in the cottage. But so far, they had no honey from them.

The hollow was leaky and rotten; the tree itself was doing poorly. Green woodpeckers got at the beehive from time to time, sometimes a mouse; in springtime, after winter, there was scarcely a handful of the nation left, and before they could grow the colony, winter would arrive.

And this year was the worst. They barely managed to go out to forage on flowers, the work was slow, and they were not bringing pollen back to the hive.

"There is no queen-mother!" Wolverine said to himself after careful inspection.

He set off farther into the forest, lost in thought.

The forest violets were now in full bloom, and the reed catkins were swarming with wild bees. There had to be, Wolverine reasoned, another wild beehive nearby because bees could not fly this far from human settlements, from orchards and fields, through all these swamps and marshes. There had to be one, but where? Over the years, Wolverine had searched for it, from one end of their refuge to the other, but he had found nothing.

Now, he had to find it. He had to rescue these motherless orphans. He lay down in a clearing, all lilac with blooming violets.

All around him, workers scrupulously picked the sweet nectar and flew away. The forest man followed each with his eyes and, at first, did not understand what he saw: the insects seemed to fly to and fro without any logic. But eventually, he realized something: they were not all the same. Some were small and dark, and others were slightly larger and yellow.

After an hour of patient observation, he realized that the former always returned to the familiar willow, but the others rose above the trees and flew east. And as they flew, they carried at their feet as if baskets of golden pollen, and they hummed merrily as they worked.

Wolverine arose with triumph.

"There they are, and my queen-mother!" he said to himself and struck out east, following the bees.

He inspected every old tree along the way; he stopped in the clearings, observed the insects, and then followed them again until he arrived at an insurmountable barrier: a bog trench.

"Ha! I see! They have their hive on the other side! So, that's why they are yellow like resin. That I didn't think of it! There they are, I'm sure, in that pine!"

Beyond the stretch of marsh, as if an island in the sea, was a small elevation, overgrown with old pines.

He inspected them: their golden trunks, gnarly branches, and blackish crowns. The biggest one, the lead dancer, bore an enormous wreath of a stork's nest on her head.

"It seems one could reach them with his hand, but the bog says 'away, or you are drowned!' It's bottomless: not a bush, not a tree on her, but she's narrow! Not more than fifty paces! I have to get there!"

He lay down and began to hatch a plan. He tried the ground, stepped back, and started to chop reeds and tie them into sheaves.

His work was interrupted by the lunch signal. When they sat down to eat, everyone recounted their new discoveries.

"You know, Chief? I saw a hoopoe looking into one of our boxes!" Panther boasted of his discovery.

"You inspected the boxes?"

"An overwhelming desire took me to imitate Jake! I've peeked into seventeen."

"That's a nice day's work!"

"Ha! It would have been more, but in the end, a cunning branch turned on me. I crashed to the ground and strained my arm."

"And?"

"And nothing! I called the doctor; he reset the arm in no time but forbade me playing Jake for the next few days."

"Even without my forbidding, you would not be able to: you pulled your tendon."

"And what did you find in the boxes?"

"For the most part, great tits. Most already sit on young; in one box, I counted twelve open mouths! Twelve! Some job to feed such a crowd. Also, a few flycatchers, the smaller sort, all sitting on tiny blue eggs. And the blue tits sit on their eggs with such resolve you could take them with your hand. In one, I was angrily hissed upon by a wryneck: she hissed like a snake. And in another, two starlings set on me. But my worst reception was in the ash tree. Guess who's there?"

"Hm? A woodpecker?"

"Bumblebees! The small, light gray sort. They went straight for my eyes, so I got frightened, dashed for safety, and – crashed!"

"And in which box did you find that litter of naked baby mice, which you so kindly put in the coffee mill for me?" asked Crane conversationally.

"I? Mice? What? When?"

"Ah, of course! That was also the Tennant! Why didn't you call him for help with your dislocated arm?"

"Ghosts make lousy doctors!"

"And I have bad news. Our bees have lost their queen!"

The other two were sad to hear this and began to discuss possible measures.

"I'll go to Odrowąż for grubs," Panther offered.

"The foot planks on the way to Odrowąż are still underwater, and the path is so winding! Easy to lose your way and fall into the swamp."

"Or should I go back to the manor house? We don't have much bread either. I don't understand how it disappeared so quickly," said Crane.

"Ha! Must be the Tennant! Either hid it or fed it to Hathor," laughed Wolverine.

The two looked meaningfully at Panther, who, with an innocent expression, kept busy threading a bast string into his clogs.

"Can't go home next few days," he said calmly as if he hadn't heard the last of the conversation. "Patch Pelt has breathed rather meaningfully in my ear to send for a midwife. Would the doctor be so kind?" he turned to Crane with a courtly bow.

"Well, I found another hive." Wolverine resolved the issue.

"Well, then, why all this theater of asking our advice?"

"The theater is to fill the time while I have my pipe. And give you time to wash the dishes. When you're done, we're off for an afternoon of hard work. The beehive is on Pine Hill, beyond The Drowning."

"So, we will have to tie fasces[6] and lay them across the bog. What a chance to get thoroughly filthy in the mud! Sounds wonderful. Let's to it!" Panther rushed to clean the table and wash the dishes.

---

[6] Fasces: A bundle of rods which in ancient Rome signified the executive power of the consuls. Reference to classical learning, not political sympathies.

Soon, all three set out, leaving the hut in the care of Providence. Even Jake, scandalized by this general abandonment, followed, jumping onto Crane and snuggling into his pocket for an afternoon nap.

They followed Wolverine through the thicket and talked about the coming project.

"Every year, on Saint Anne's Day[7], I look towards Pine Hill and rack my brain on how to get there," said Panther.

"Why especially on Saint Anne's Day?" asked Crane.

"Because 'Saint Ann sows mushrooms.' Haven't you heard? And at Pine Hill, mushrooms have grown since the beginning of time, and no one has ever collected them! It must be a gold mine! But it's so hard to get there even in winter. That cursed Drowning!"

"Damned to others, blessed to us," said Wolverine wittily. "Would we have this world to us alone if there were a road to our hut? We'd run away after a week because visitors would poison our lives."

"Sure! Peasants to sell potatoes, and women to Crane for medicine, and Jews for fish, and... guests! Good grief! When you hear me weeping in my sleep at night, you know what nightmare I am dreaming."

"As soon as the water clears the footbridges to Odrowąż, he'll be here directly to tell us about his arthritic pains!" said Crane.

"Oh, he's all right. He belongs here. He's one of us," smiled Wolverine. "He taught me all I know about survival here."

They now arrived at the edge of The Drowning and immediately set to work.

They tied their 'fasces' and laid them over the boggy ground like a bridge. The swamp wobbled underfoot; they had to keep clear of pools of water and look for ground with some growth at least, even the smallest clump of whitish, spongy moss. First one, then another slipped and fell in the marsh, and his companions had to pull him out with the help of the rope. Drenched, black with slime, they exerted themselves with furious determination, fighting for every foot of

---

[7] 26 July

advance, so stubborn in their resolve that they did not even speak. And all this to obtain a brood of grubs for the orphan hive.

When cranes began to trumpet their evening concert, Wolverine, half wading and half crawling, crossed the quagmire and lay down breathlessly on the shore of Pine Hill. His companions, choosing a more secure path, were not far behind and also without strength.

"It'll be dark soon. Time to head back to the cabin!" said Crane.

"You two go ahead; I'll stay the night here. Tomorrow morning, bring me some rope, a pot with embers, a hat with a net – it's all hanging on the wall in the bedroom. And maybe a piece of bread for breakfast."

"Oh! You'll be hungry and cold in your wet clothes!" objected Crane thoughtfully.

"I have matches and tobacco in my cap, and they have made it across dry. Also, an ax and a knife, and there is no shortage of brushwood. I'll have a comfortable night. At dawn, I'll find the hive and prepare everything. This is not a civilized beehive with a roof to pull back; there will be some trouble getting at it. I will rest before the hard work. Go, go, before it gets dark!"

"Till tomorrow then! We'll be back at daybreak."

Wolverine was left alone. He rested for a moment and then began to look around and examine his surroundings. He was astonished by the deathly silence of this isolated spot. He had expected it to be a paradise of birds, but it seemed deserted. Neither singing, nor chirping, nor the usual bustle of the late afternoon.

The pines stood motionless like mutes; all around seemed completely deserted while life positively teemed just on the other side of The Drowning.

"Some enchanted corner!" he whispered to himself. He walked along the shore, looking around. Farther on, the old pines mixed with spruce, and the ground was overgrown with ferns and blackberries.

When he stopped for a moment, trying to find a path among the undergrowth, something like a dog barked in a pine tree behind him. Instinctively, Wolverine retreated behind the trunk and looked up.

On a thick branch, side by side sat two huge, gray immobile figures. Two pairs of bright yellow eyes stared at him, blinking; the faces of these old criminals were finished off by black, powerful, bent beaks and crowned with tufted horns.

Without least movement or sound, the man and the pair of great robber knights stared at each other. Now, Wolverine understood the silence and emptiness of this wilderness. Here was the fortress of a robber baron with a plume on his head.

The cause of the silence was clear: the killer knight had destroyed all life around him. He reigned and ruled, a mighty one above all law.

"There you are, you Teutonic monster!" growled Wolverine. "You heraldic dogcatcher! You executioner of forest creatures, you wicked tyrant, you terror of the weak, meek, and peaceful! Now has come your time of reckoning! Now it's over for you! I have often heard you at night, your bloodthirsty war cry, and the screaming of your victims. I have been looking for you. And now the great keeper of the birds has brought me here so that you might pay with your throat for your criminal life. This is your last night on Earth!"

He turned and walked away. Taking advantage of the last moments of daylight, he located the beehive. He was pointed to it by the workers coming back from fieldwork, and he was glad to see that the hollow was not too high and the opening was quite wide.

"Now, I will rest and listen to the silence," he said, stretching out on the moss.

But he could not rest. The sun had gone down, and cool vapors rose from the marshes. He felt a chill, so he undressed, rubbed his body with moss, and pulled his damp clothes on again. Now, warmed up a bit, he lit his pipe to kill his hunger and built a small fire on the shore.

The lords of the island were offended.

Their gloomy "Uhu, uhu!" was menacing. A black shadow popped out of the thicket; soft wings practically brushed him in flight as the scarecrow wheeled over the fire then glided over The Drowning into the forest in search of prey. After a while, the second one followed.

"Uhu, uhu!" *Unguibus et rostro!* "Claws and beaks" is their heraldic motto and their war cry: "Uhu, uhu!"[8]

Stretched by the fire, Wolverine listened. The spring wedding music thundered from the forest: the weeping of nightingales, the mumbling of the black grouse, the barking of the deer. Then the robber's war cry, a sudden moment of silence, and again the joyful hymn of young life.

Then the air was split by a scream of pain, horror, and death – and there was silence again.

"He took a hare!" Wolverine whispered.

The moon had climbed into the sky. In its ghostly light, the mists were a procession of swaying figures in long, trailing shrouds. Frog orchestra played for them; an occasional breath of wind rearranged the figures in groups and circles.

Some distance away, water splashed, something rattled, clattered, disturbed the procession of mists. "A moose is fording the bog!" Wolverine whispered. "The Drowning is no bar for him!"

Like a ghost, without the least rustle of feathers, the murderer flew over him again and into the trees beyond.

He's back with the loot! He has little ones in his nest!

But at last, Wolverine grew drowsy from exhaustion. He still watched as the smoke of his fire wafted towards the mists and mingled with them; he heard the warning croaking of a mother mallard; and then he also wafted away, joining the smoke and the mists.

And he was now as light as them. Day came, and he floated over the meltwater, looked into nests, stroked birds with his hand, swam in the river, wrapped his arm around the moose's neck, watched, standing one step away, how a recluse bittern sank his beak into the slime and buzzed loudly, and with his fist knocked away the eagle owl from a piebald deer foal.

---

[8] Medieval knights adopted heraldic emblems, mottos, and war cries. The author continues the symbolism eagle owl = Teutonic knight.

And with this magical dream ended the busy day of Chief Wolverine.

In the morning, the blaring of the crane trumpets woke him. He jumped up. The light in the east was barely amber, and there was still drowsiness in nature. Pine needles had dew beads at their tips; a few sentry bees came out on the doorstep of the hive and rubbed their wings. No birds sang. Creeping, sidestepping twigs underfoot, Wolverine moved towards the thickets.

On their branch, the eagle owls sat motionless, puffed up, with folded tufts, and slept, full of murder. Slippery blood glistened on their beaks and claws.

Wolverine retreated, stoked up the fire, and again fooled hunger with tobacco.

Meanwhile, the world was waking, coloring, and singing with such eagerness and enthusiasm that the woodsman, infected with it, began to hum in an undertone:

Every morning, singing soul,
Praise the Virgin!...

"We're here, Chief!" a call sounded from beyond The Drowning. Wolverine jumped up.

"Well, hello! Did you bring some rope?"

"Lots of it."

"Then tie them together. Attach one end to that birch on the bank near you, and throw the other end, the one with a hook, over here. Take a good swing, Crane, because Panther is crippled!"

"Good idea! We'll have a handrail without the attached bridge! Or, wait, maybe we shall walk the rope?" Panther called.

"Quit your useless banter, Panther! You rush back to the hut and bring my shotgun and four cartridges!"

"What's that? You found a lynx?"

"A far worse criminal than the lynx! Go! Run!"

The hook plunged into the water near the shore. Wolverine fished it out, tied it to a tree, and soon Crane arrived, laden with goods.

"Bread!" asked Wolverine and got a bagful.

"Death to... whom?" asked Crane.

"I'll show you."

Meanwhile, he ate his bread dipped in milk; and his face grew ruddy.

"Did you find the hive?"

"Yes, it's in that crooked pine. Have you brought the tool bag?"

"I have."

"You're my lad!"

"So many years in your school... I have learned. And here's the news! Last night, a boy came from the manor to say that a guest had come to see you."

"Who? What, the devil?"

"The boy said it was some 'young master.'"

"Lucky thing it's not some 'old auntie.' Any 'young master' can wait. There is plenty of place to sleep and plenty of grub to eat. He'll be all right. Well, I'm full."

"Then show me what you found."

"Let's wait for Panther's return. Let's not frighten the beast away."

So, they waited, chatting softly about their life. Then Panther's scout appeared: Jake ran along the rope, greeted Chief, and dashed into the pines. Behind him came Panther, laboriously splashing through the mud and jumping from clump to clump.

They were just about to start inland but barely managed to line up when Wolverine saw Jake and pointed to him with his hand. The squirrel was flying back, breathless, along the ground and looking behind him with horror. He caught up with Crane and pressed himself into his sweatshirt, deep under his arm. His tiny body was trembling all over, and he gave two pitiful squeaks.

"What happened to him?"

"He met... Death. Let's go, but soft, like hunters!" Wolverine took the shotgun, loaded it, and set off, ready to fire.

They crept up without a rustle. Then he raised the barrel, and the others followed it with their eyes.

"A monkish tribe of robbers. Robbers!" he whispered.

"Junker Eduard and Kunigonda!"[9] Crane completed the line.

"Give it to them, Chief!" Panther growled.

A shot went off; a second later, another. Eduard fell off his branch like a thunderclap, and Kunigonda barely had time to unfurl her wings. She now hung by them on a spruce thicket, already dead.

"That was some shooting!" Panther said.

"Ha," said Wolverine sadly. "Many years ago, when I was young and stupid and thought it was a fine sport to kill, some people sometimes said that I was a good shot."

Wolverine set the rifle against a tree.

"But this morning was not sport, only the meting out of punishment. 'Might makes right' has met his reward: he was brought to court and paid his fines. The forest is my witness that I am only a righteous avenger! And now, let's go find their nest!"

"On the ground?"

"Odrowąż told me that they nest in different places: sometimes on stumps, or in tree tops, or in hollows. Anyway, we will recognize it by the mortuary. Look what feathers and bones are here! Oh, look! A green drake cap, some lapwing tufts, black grouse's steering feathers. And that – that's a fresh hare. I heard his death cry last night.

"Our little lover-boy! Colorful and beautiful, young and happy with spring sap and love, felled by this insatiable thief, murderer, glutton, plunderer. Ripped to shreds and devoured. This is a mass grave of the whole forest. Nobody had a right to life here, only the thief."

"Chief! There it is, on the spruce: a pile of dead branches! But today, I will not climb it!" exclaimed Panther from the thicket.

Wolverine pushed in between the crowded branches and wiggled his way upward.

---

[9] The eagle owl = Teutonic knight simile continues. Junkers were a social class in the Prussian state: estate owners obligated to military service. Prussia was a successor state to the Teutonic State.

"Aha! They took over an old eagle's nest and laid their damned brood here. There are three young ones. Still white, barely hatched, and already snapping their jaws and pecking my hand! Shall we take them alive and raise them as slaves?"

And then there was a mournful cry of Panther from under the spruce tree: "O, criminals! Look, this is what's left of Sir Stomper!"

"What? Impossible!" cried Crane. "Is the forest not full of them? Show me, and I'll recognize him. When I dressed his leg, I had to cut one claw off."

There was silence. Wolverine asked:

"Well?"

"Alas! Our Stomper is no more!" replied Crane, and Panther cried out in vengeful delight, "Chief! Do not raise this hellhound brood! Twist their necks off!"

Wolverine threw down the nest with its brood.

"There. Perish, beasts!" he growled.

The forest folk had taken their revenge.

They returned to their pine tree and set up camp.

"By next spring, this cove will be a bird's paradise. Wood-cocks will toot their horns, woodpeckers will hammer in their smithies, kinglets will hang their baskets, and pigeons will settle in the spruce. The old natives will return, peaceful, cheerful, and gentle. And repopulate the desert!

"Hang these criminals up by their feet!"

"No. I'll take them home and stuff them beautifully. They will replace the old, moth-eaten owl and scare the crows away. And now – to the hive!"

"If you don't need me for anything, I'm going back," said Crane. "I swell like a monster from bee-stings, and Jake has scratched me and is still shaking with fear."

"Smart cookie, Mr. Jake! Stomper, the nocturnal tramp, trusted in his spikes, and that was his undoing. Yes, Jake, there is nothing like an old sheepskin sleeve. There, Eduard had no chance to find you and take you. Aren't you a lucky thief."

So, Crane returned to the hut, and it was only there that Jake finally dared to come out into the world. But from that point on, he never went away any distance, not even to chase his redheaded suitor.

NEW ARRIVALS

The morning after the execution of the executioners, Crane was woken by a loud knocking on the bedroom door.

"Not yet, not yet!" Crane mumbled and continued dozing.

"We've had an increase in the family! A baby girl! Mother and child doing great!" announced Panther through the door.

"Spotted?"

"Like autumn chestnuts with which children play."

"Shall I get up?" Crane awoke.

"Too late! You missed a chance to earn your fee!"

"So, why did you wake me?"

"You sleepyheads! Is it not a pity to sleep on such a spring night? I'm off for a walk."

"Stomper did that, too, and it ended badly for him."

At daybreak, everyone first went to look in on the new member of the household, bringing various treats to Patch Pelt. The foal, still shaky on its legs, looked out curiously at God's creation from under her mother's belly.

"Regular geological survey map," laughed Crane, looking at her spots.

"You'll grow to be a great beauty yet." Wolverine stroked her.

Panther tied a red string around her neck – a charm against evil spirits.

And then, laughing, he said:

"Crane! I happened to see the Tennant last night. He climbed onto the shelf and put something in that pot. A gift for you, I suppose."

"Better you see for yourself. I am fed up with these gifts."

But Wolverine grew curious and looked in the pot.

"O, kind Tennant! Good Tennant!" he said, pulling out something gray, round, and about the size of a lemon.

"What's that?" asked Crane distrustfully.

"Stomper Junior! A teenager, spikes are barely through his skin. Where did you find him, Panther?"

"At night, on the path to the spring. His mother came first, and she puffed at me big time; and behind her, four such little grubs."

"When we got him, Stomper Senior was even smaller than this, almost naked. Let's make him a bed in a box with moss and dry leaves. He'll be drinking milk by tomorrow."

"I will raise him!" Crane rejoiced.

"Our household is increasing. Our biggest livestock inventory so far!" said Wolverine, sitting down to breakfast. He then immediately began to work on his eagle owls. He took up the whole table and immersed himself in this difficult work so much that he neither smoked, nor spoke, nor raised his eyes, nor heard what the others were saying.

He wasn't even aware that they existed until Crane stood over him.

"Hey there! What about this boy, waiting at the manor?"

"Don't block my sunlight!" muttered Wolverine, cleaning the bird's skin with a lancet.

"Diogenes[10] said!" Crane laughed. "But we don't have any bread left at all, and potatoes are running out."

Silence. The last few cuts, and the skin was off. Wolverine admired his work with triumph.

"Even Master Lastowski[11] would be pleased by this," he said. "Now, all I need to do is rub with arsenic and stuff it."

"Do you have the beads for the eyes?"

Wolverine thought for a moment.

"I do, but did I bring the box with me?"

He went back into the bedroom and rummaged around for a bit.

"Alas! The box is in my desk in the manor!" he said.

"And thank goodness. So, maybe now you'll agree that we need to go to the manor?"

Wolverine lit his pipe and, with a sigh, made his decision.

"Yeah. I'll go. Write me a list of what food we need. I'll take a cart from the manor and have the groom bring me back as far as the Rainbow Bridge. Meanwhile, let us hope to God that this guest got tired of waiting and left. Oh, how cruel is life! To have to change out of these clothes and leave this place! If it wasn't for that box with the glass eyes, I wouldn't be going."

He finished his preparations, changed his clothes, gave Panther some instructions, and left.

"If this guest is still waiting and wants to keep Chief there for a few days... then, God bless him, I wish him fun!" Panther laughed.

"I forgot to write in the note to bring newspapers!" hissed Crane.

"Oh! Never fear! He wouldn't bring them even if you did! Who wants to read the newspapers here? And when? Do we really need more information about the revolution in Mexico? The turmoil in the Balkans? The exchange rate or the earthquake in Calabria? Far

---

[10] Diogenes was an Greek ascetic philosopher. Famous for telling Alexander the Great: "You are obstructing my sunlight!"

[11] A well-known Warsaw furrier of the day

more interesting is the question of whether our bees will manage to raise a queen mother from the brood of grubs we gave them. And does the hoopoe take the box? And have the footbridges to Odrowąż cleared water yet? And most of all: will I find a bittern's nest? Or a penduline tit's, or a black stork's? Because we need these to complete our collection, you know. Why don't we take the boat and paddle out to that alder tree? Maybe we'll find the wels."

They took double nets on long poles, went out and paddled up quietly. Panther rowed, Crane steered, barely brushing the water. Through various narrow passages, they emerged onto the lake. It lay silent, smooth as glass, almost without a trace of the river's current that flowed through it. The lake narrowed towards the far end and disappeared among the black overhanging reeds and alders.

It was an April afternoon, and the lake was busy. Panther pointed out the birds to Crane in a low whisper:

"Look over there! A pair of grebes. And there, that's an auk! Ah, it has already disappeared behind the trees."

"And ducks among the bullrushes. And – look! Terns!"

"Over there, do you see? Swans!"

"They're only passing through. And look how the fish are jumping!"

"The water has dropped a lot. Look, you can already see the foundation stakes of the old mill. When was it built? Must be centuries ago! All right, we're in the channel. Steer for the alders."

"Which one should we try?"

"Why don't we start with that one over there, where the old canoe lies? That's where I took my bath the other day."

"Let's turn our boat sideways and hold it fast. We'll put the nets down together – but gently, or we'll fall in!"

Crane gritted his teeth because they chattered with hunter's excitement. They approached the shore slowly, stealthily, communicating with eyes rather than words. Panther pointed to a protruding alder branch, took off his belt, tied it in a noose, and hooked a knot.

Then they attacked with lightning speed. They dipped the poles with nets into the water and covered the entrance to the underwater hole. Then, holding onto his belt with his teeth, Panther hit the water with his oar, muddling it all the way to the bottom.

"There he is!" Crane shouted, feeling a sudden heave against the net.

"Grab it! Pull it! Into the boat with it! Careful! You'll capsize us! Hit him on the head! Stun him! Now, fast! Ashore with him! Ashore! The shore!" Panther cried and carried out his own orders.

There he was. Entangled in the double nets, a black, slippery, giant-headed monster thrashed at the bottom of their canoe. The boat danced and took on water, nearly capsizing several times.

Panther let the belt slip from his teeth and hastily tied the giant in the net. Crane grabbed the oar and paddled the wobbly boat towards the bank, chasing hordes of frogs into the bush. Now he grasped the tree branches hanging over the water and held the boat tight in place. Both were drenched and out of breath, and ecstatic about their catch.

"Whoah! That's a patriarch! It will weigh twenty kilos!" said Panther, dragging the net with the giant ashore.

"I reproach myself that we went out on this hunt without Wolverine," said Crane.

"Oh, he had a few of them in his life! Besides, though he does go fishing, he's really a bird-man! Now, we have some hard work ahead of us; we won't be able to take him back alive, or he will capsize us when he comes to. So, you, doctor, will have to perform euthanasia. And check to see if he perhaps has a police boot in his belly."

"A what?"

"Odrowąż claims that this monster is a cannibal and especially likes to eat policemen."[12]

"Hm... It might be better to return him to the lake when he is in such a respectable business."

---

[12] 'Policemen' would have been functionaries of the Russian Empire (and eating them was therefore "a respectable business")

"Wait a minute, now! I also need to eat something during Lent!"[13]

"Very well then, I'll look for the shoe! But this head, my my, such a head! We should try to preserve it!"

"It'll be easiest to give it to the ants to clean. I know an anthill as huge as a haystack. I'll bury the head there tonight."

An hour later, they were already paddling back. The lake had changed: a westerly wind had picked up, and rain clouds were rushing in from the west. The air grew muggy. A storm was brewing.

"Paddle harder, or we won't make it before the rain!" Crane studied the sky anxiously.

"It's wonderful to be on the lake in a thunderstorm!" laughed Panther.

"Look how the clouds are rushing now. Like a herd of galloping horses! Ah, listen to the distant cracking of the whip! That's thunder. Soon, everything will be dancing!"

The clouds began to boil overhead. There was a sudden zigzag of lightning, a sudden whirlwind turned the canoe, and then the clouds burst open. The lake and the sky became a single mass of water, black clouds, foam, waves, blinding flashes, and thunderclaps as if the world were cracking open!

Crane began to bail water because the canoe fast filled with rain, but Panther stopped rowing and sat erect at the canoe's nose, enjoying the downpour, the flashes, the thunder as if they were the world's greatest pleasures.

His nostrils flaring, his lips laughing, his eyes sparkling, he responded to every lightning bolt with a wild exclamation. His heart was flooded with elemental joy.

"To shore! We're drowning!" Crane shouted.

"Nonsense! We will not drown!" Panther laughed insanely. "It will be over soon! Boom! Boom! Oh, what happiness, to be such a power! To play like that!"

---

[13] When Catholics abstain from meat

But he agreed to turn the canoe towards the bank and tie it to some reed. And helped to bail the water.

"Oh, it's over! What a pity!" he said, looking at the sky. "Now, we'll have to work fast with the oars to stay warm! Wow, how wonderful that was!"

They turned back to the middle of the current.

The water was smooth again, the sky blue; the birds began to sing, and the air acquired a delicious, sweet scent.

When they arrived home, there was no sign of the storm that had just passed, except one: a birch tree near the spring had been torn asunder by a thunderbolt, clear from the top to its root.

Patch Pelt neighed to welcome them from the stable, and Jake briefly popped his snout out of his sleeve.

"Crane, let's eat!" Panther called.

"Wait up! I'm kindling the fire right now. You want a change of dry clothes?"

"Not worth it! Only after we carve the wels! Then I will change."

"How do we do that?"

"First of all, we will rub it with ash to get rid of the mucus. Then we will wash that gunk clean off with water, then we quarter it like a hog and salt it and leave it for a few days. Then, in a couple of days, I will build a smokehouse out of that old barrel there. And I will bury the head in the anthill."

"So much work! I'll come to help you soon."

"No need! Just make us some supper. After this storm, I feel like I'm drunk on champagne! I couldn't possibly sit still!"

He lifted the monster on his back and threw it in the grass in the clearing before the hut and started the arduous work with panache, singing, and whistling. He worked so hard that his shirt began to steam on his back. But when he finished, cleaned up, and sat down for supper, he ceased to speak and laugh, ate fast, and disappeared in his alcove. At first, Crane thought that he went to change, but, when surprised by the silence, he looked in on Panther, he saw him fast asleep, still in his wet clothes and clogs. There was no use nudging him or calling him, so Crane only slipped his clogs off and left him like that. He also felt tired and sleepy.

The following day, they both slept in, missed the crane clarions and the morning choir of birds, and were only awakened by the lowing of Hathor, the neighing of the mare, and the squealing of Jake.

"O, no! The storm has brought mosquitoes!" said Panther with a troubled expression, sitting down to breakfast.

"There will soon be swarms of this filth. We'll have to cover the windows with nets and gather pinecones for smokescreen! I think I'll sew a shirt for Baby Patch, or the mosquitoes will eat her alive. Even Wolverine can't come up with a solution to this plague."

"He spent all winter mixing some ingredients and said he had a few creams to test. Do you think he'll be back today?"

"I doubt it – if the guest is there. But let's try going out to the Rainbow Bridge tonight. Maybe we can play a trick on him? Scare him witless?"

"Scare Wolverine?" Crane laughed. "How would you scare him?"

"Eh, you're right. We could probably find a way to scare him, but the beast won't let on, so it's no fun. All right then, I will build the smokehouse today. Chief also ordered me to dig some tar wood for torches and check the fish baskets. But first of all, I have to see if the hoopoe has moved in."

He went off and disappeared into the forest. He forgot about all the work and probably got lost in his usual adventures because he returned all scratched up, with a torn shirt and only one clog but with plenty of news.

"Orioles have arrived. The black grouse is sitting on eight eggs, and the garganey has laid her nest right by the bog; she seems to think we will have a dry summer. There is a redpoll sitting on the birch tree, indifferent to me like a loaf of bread. I killed a viper sneaking into the nest of a garden warbler. I also found a nest of earth bumblebees and stole some honey. A bit tart, but nice."

"And the tar wood? The smokehouse? The fish baskets?"

"A trifling, my dear! A trifling! I'll get it all done after lunch!"

He dutifully worked all afternoon. He chopped, sawed, and carried and, before evening, was ready to go meet the Chief.

They left Jake at the cottage. The wood, bathed with rain, smelled like magic.

They stopped at times and took in the beauty of the spring bloom with their eyes, ears, and lungs, stunned by the majesty of these sensual masterpieces. Finally, they arrived at the boundary stream. The colors of the sunset lit it like molten gold, end to end.

"This is not a Rainbow Bridge, but a Golden Bridge today."

"And it glows like raw silk. It's the fry playing at the surface!"

They stretched out on the grass and listened.

"I can't hear the wagon. But let's wait and watch. Geese usually fly this way; this is their usual route."

But, perpetually restless, Panther soon stirred.

"I'm going to fall asleep right away unless I move," he muttered and began to cut beautiful bast shoots and shell them for clogs.

"They're coming!" Crane whispered. They pricked their ears and held their breath.

"They're coming. Oh, they scared a deer. Do you see? She went into the hazel. They're coming. You can feel the rumbling in the ground. And they're talking. Let us call them our way."

They bellowed. First a long call, then a short one. A clear echo ran along the water's surface, bounced off the forest, and returned. They listened.

"Why is Wolverine not responding?"

"Is he talking to someone? Who?"

In the distance, two horse heads appeared. The water splashed.

"What's that? Someone's there, with Wolverine."

"Has to be the groom."

"No... the groom is the third. Let's disappear!"

"What, again?! If Wolverine is talking to someone, it's a guest. Maybe Odrowąż?"

They watched as the wagon neared.

Next to Wolverine sat a teenage boy in a gymnasium cap and black blouse.

"Some kid... Like we need a baby!" Panther muttered.

"Oh, I know!" Crane whispered. "It's probably that boy, Stefan, Mrs. Anna's boy."

"Chief's nephew! That wastrel!"

Crane barely had time to nod because the wagon was upon them, and Wolverine was already speaking:

"Well, hello there! I'm bringing you a recruit!"

The wagon stopped. The groom began to unload various bundles. They said hello.

The forest people studied the new recruit suspiciously.

A city ladybug! said Panther to himself.

A softie, thought Crane.

But one must bear his outrageous fortune bravely, so they each offered the boy a handshake.

"Uncle said I could work here with you," he said, his voice uncertain.

"Well, no," Wolverine corrected him. "I promised you a place here if you can manage it. Now, put your trunk on your back, and off we go!"

The groom turned the team around and left. Panther threw the largest bag over his shoulder. Crane and Wolverine loaded themselves with the rest.

The recruit slung his trunk over his shoulder and followed them, stumbling on the roots. It was getting dark; there was no pavement, no road, no path; branches slapped his face, low shoots were tripping him up, the weight of the trunk weighed him down.

And the others walked lightly, quietly, quickly, and disappeared like ghosts in the thicket ahead.

After a while, the boy sweated and gasped, his heart pounding; he felt overcome with fear and shame. He gritted his teeth and tried to make an effort but felt he couldn't cope. Finally, a branch ripped off his cap; he began to search for it, and when he found it, he found himself alone in the thicket.

Alone and directionless.

“Uncle!” he cried fearfully.

But instead of uncle, Panther appeared.

“What's up? Why have you stopped?”

“I haven’t. Only some branch took my cap off, and I lost sight of you.”

“Ha! The cap has peeled off because you did not bow to the forest. And the forest is a great and mighty lord. One must have respect before him.”

“And the others?”

“They left. We will not all babysit you, you know! Well, your bundle is heavy. Pass it here! I will help.”

“Thank you, sir. I can handle it.”

“Ha! Here, “sir” means ‘forest’ and ‘lady’ means ‘water.’ I am a forest folker – Panther. Don't pretend it; your hands are shaking with effort. Here, thread the trunk's strap through that branch. That's right. Now, sling this end over your shoulder like this. Ready? Off we go! And follow in my footsteps: left, right, left, right!”

"Won’t we get lost in this darkness, without a path?" asked the boy after a moment.

“What do you mean, without a path? This is a path. Look, marked by trees like post boxes.”

“And what are all those lights glistening near the ground? It must be wolf's eyes glowing in the dark!”

“Where? Oh, this? It’s the fireflies.”

“What's that?”

“Well, we call them Saint John’s bugs. If you catch a few dozen in a glass jar, you can read by their light like by candlelight. Why are you jumping like this?”

“Because there was something under my feet! Probably a viper!”

“A viper? Vipers sleep at night. A frog jumped from under your foot, probably. Go straight, and don’t pull!”

A moment of silence. Suddenly, the boy flinched and stopped midstep; the trunk slipped from the pole and fell to the ground.

"What's that?" he whispered.

"For goodness sake! Now what?"

"What was that cry there?"

"An owl! There, she sits up there. Can you see? Hurry up, will you? Pick up your bundle! At this rate, we won't make it for supper, and my animals need me!"

They walked in silence again. The boy kept glancing in all directions, anxious and puzzled. The isolation, the darkness, and all these unfamiliar cries made him him uncomfortable.

"Sir! I mean, please, Panther... Are you not scared here? All alone?"

"Oh, but this place is positively crowded! Listen: that's a billy goat barking. And that – that's a black grouse. You can hear the frogs, yes? And that – that's the harriers calling on the wing. There is more life here than in the city."

"But no people!"

"Ha! And that's why it's safest. What can be more dangerous to man than another man?"

"But it's so dark!"

"Never fear – they'll light up the heaven gas lights soon. Besides, only fools are afraid of the dark. What is so terrible in the forest? What bad thing can happen to you here? We're in our world!"

"Still far away?"

"Not far. Don't you smell smoke?"

"No. What do you mean, smoke?"

"Smoke means that supper is cooking."

"Are they already at home?"

"Long since! They don't crawl like us!"

"It's so hard to walk fast in the dark!"

"Well, well. Then do not try it, or you may fall! Oh, you can see the light in the cottage."

"Thank God!" the boy whispered.

Then they heard Wolverine's voice:

"Hey, you there!"

"Hey, we here!" Panther shouted back.

"Hurry up, will you? We were wondering whether we should go looking for you."

"No kidding."

Wolverine met them at the gate.

Panther threw his sack and the boy's trunk to the ground.

"Goodness gracious! What's in your trunk that it is so heavy? There, Chief, you take the recruit. I'm off to look after the animals."

The boy, finding himself in the brightly lit room, breathed a sigh of relief and began to look around for coffee.

"First, you greet our Queen!" Wolverine showed him the icon.

The boy crossed himself.

"Maybe I should do something?"

"You will do everything we do. But for the time being, take a rest here, on a bench."

"How wonderful it is here!"

"Do not rush with praise until you have seen it all! You will sleep in the entryway. Tomorrow, you'll change your clothes and shoes and be assigned your tasks."

"I wonder what task!" cried Panther, entering the room with a bucket of milk. "And I would also be curious to know what we will call this newcomer. Though I've already thought of a name for him."

"What is it?" the boy asked.

"Why, 'Whatisit,' of course! As we walked, every step of the way, he cried out: 'what is it, what is it, what is it?'"

Crane set a bowl of soup on the table. They all sat down.

The boy was given a wooden spoon and a slice of black bread, and, seeing what they were doing, he began to shovel from the common bowl.

"What is it?" he asked after a while.

Everyone laughed.

"Precisely! Panther baptized you well! You will be Whatisit until you earn a different name. You ask what it is? It's a fish soup."

"A wels soup! You know, Chief? We caught the big one! This has been a week of great hunting: eagle owls and wels catfish!"

“And new arrivals: new foal, new Stomper, and now new Whatisit.”

“And baby blackbirds have hatched in Hathor’s stable!”

Whatisit wanted to ask what blackbirds were but was too embarrassed. He decided to find out for himself in the morning.

After supper, Crane called him to help wash the dishes, but he only managed to get himself dirty and break the bowl. Then Panther summoned him and led him up a ladder to the attic, where they loaded a huge sack of hay.

"You'll sleep on this, Private Whatisit. Now, you go down carefully, so you don’t go the way of the bowl. Ha! Wouldn’t you know it, there he is sprawled on the ground!”

The boy had hooked his heel on a rung and fell into the hall, but luckily onto his new mattress. He jumped up, embarrassed, but Crane and Wolverine were feeding Stomper Junior and didn’t even turn around, and Panther, jumping down gracefully and lightly from the attic, said:

“Good thing you aren't made of clay, or you wouldn't last long. There, make yourself a bed here on the bench and rest after all these adventures.”

The boy stood helpless for a moment. How could he sleep without a bed, without a pillow, without a nightstand and a foot rag? His trunk had been left outside, and the very thought of looking for it alone at night sent a shudder down his spine.

And no one seemed to take the slightest interest in him. Crane and Wolverine went into their chamber; Panther blew out the candle and, exhausted, lay down in his alcove and fell asleep immediately. In the total darkness of the hut, only the red light before the icon was visible. The boy sat down on the mattress, near tears. The entrance door was not even locked! In the forest, something murmured, stirred, and called. And something was walking around in the room! How was he supposed to sleep?

Then the unhappy Whatisit began to curse his mother, his uncle, his fate, and the whole world. Then, exhausted from all the grief and bitterness, he closed his eyes because they burned him with all the spring sun and spring wind, and then he remembered nothing because he fell asleep.

The blackbird chicks also fell asleep under her mother's wings, as did the foal at the feet of Patch Pelt. She slept standing up but woke at the slightest rustle and poked her child with her muzzle as if to say, "Do not be afraid! Sleep! I'm watching over you!"

Only Stomper Junior, true to his tribe's tradition, ran with mincing footsteps all over the house and hunted insects that had dared to come in during the day.

WHATISIT

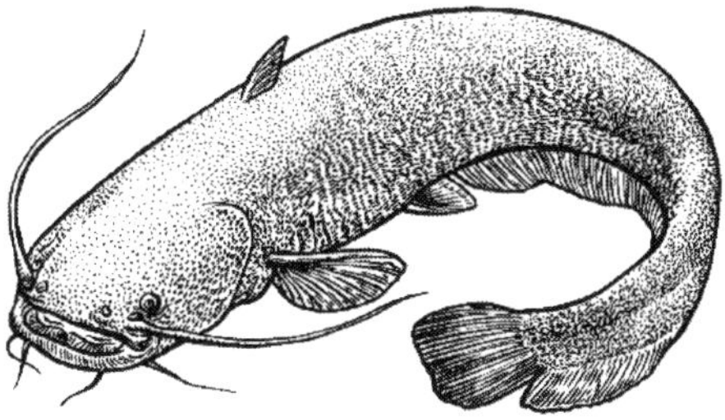

Wolverine was stuffing his eagle owls. He made up for his lack of skill with stubbornness and enthusiasm. Because he got in everyone's way in the main room, he had set up his studio in the bedroom and, after three days, accomplished his deed.

"They worked out well!" he said triumphantly to Crane.

"Perhaps now you will have time for other things," muttered Crane humorlessly.

"What's so urgent?"

"Mostly, the boy."

"He went into the forest to look for nests. He said he wanted to make a collection of birds' eggs."

"He won't find any eggs! He's scared of everything. I bet he's hiding in a nearby thicket, waiting for the lunch bugle. You really should take him in your hand. After all, you brought him here. To our mortification."

"What was I supposed to do? I couldn't leave him at the manor because he'd run away from there in a thrice, and my sister begged me to keep him for a few months. She said he was exhausted with his schoolwork, had had typhoid, fallen in love with his forty-year-old teacher, and wanted to duel over her!"

"I would like to know how we can possibly help. And why we should babysit him!"

"Probably so that we do not get too comfortable here. I've been watching him. For the first two days, he was amused by the novelty of the situation and is now experiencing the inevitable period of longing and boredom. And, of course, all those memories of his star-crossed love. We best let this stew, ferment, and pass on its own."

After saying this, Wolverine, who was rarely moved by anything not related to the life of the forest, smoked a pipe, loaded himself with his bird instruments, and set off for the wood.

First, he checked on the bees.

He stood near the beehive and watched.

At first, it seemed to him that the "nation" was moving about as before, but after he observed it for a while, his face began to brighten and at last formed a quiet, joyful smile. The way the insects buzzed and wiggled when they entered the hive carried a message. And he heard it clearly and repeated after them in a whisper:

"The Queen-mother has arrived!"

And only then did he notice a human voice in a nearby sallow bed, frustrated and complaining. He recognized Whatisit's voice.

"Please, Panther, what kind of a life is this?! It's good for the elderly and the hermits. Why! For misfits and misanthropes! But I love, and I want to be alive! And no one will understand me! I do not want to be here. This place drives me crazy! I miss her so much!"

"Oh, misery!" said Panther's voice. "Then why don't you abscond? I'll take you to the edge of forests, and off you go to your sweetheart. Seriously, we need you here like we need a stove fitter in July."

"But my mother hasn't given me any money!"

"Then why don't you earn some?"

"Where? How?"

"Hmm... How about this? Catch some fish, salt them, dry them, put them in a bag, and sell them in the market. Or, try to find a nest of a rare bird, like a penduline tit or a short-tailed wren or a siskin. Chief says one can sell them to collectors for good money. I would not wait another week if I were you; I'd start right away. What a man desires, he has to go out and get. Besides, you may not need money; you could just stow away under a bench in a carriage. Poor Jews do that to save a penny; surely you can do the same for love?"

At this, Whatisit fell silent; he did not like any of these ideas.

"If I could only borrow the money for the road..." he muttered.

"Hmm!" Panther cleared his throat. "And how will you repay the loan?"

"Mother will have to give me the money."

"For a trip to your sweetheart? Why, if she had wanted to help you in your *amour*, she could have done this back in Warsaw instead of sending you here, yes? It seems unlikely to me that anyone will lend you money on this security.

"Life's tough, Private Whatisit! Instead of seeking such fraudulent loans, better do honest and righteous work. Lurk at night by the roadside and rob passersby. Or stand at the church door and cry, 'Merciful people, spare a penny to save a wounded heart!'"

"Please, Panther, you are mocking me!"

"What nonsense! That's what I would do if I were in your desperate straits."

At this, Wolverine, sensing the need for an intervention, lifted the curtain of the sallow branches and emerged in the back of the speakers. Frightened, Whatisit jumped up. Panther flashed his teeth in a broad smile and continued to peel the bark off the bast and twist it into a string.

Wolverine also got down to work, and the boy, ashamed, stood sheepishly, uncertain what to do with himself.

"It's all God's truth," said Wolverine, as if he had been part of the conversation from the very beginning.

"You are bored here because you are deaf and blind to the world around you. Our eyes and ears usually open late in life. That is, if they open at all! Perhaps because many people don't have them to begin with, and many others feel no need for the insights they deliver. Plus, at the age of eighteen, there is also another powerful obstacle to prevent us from seeing things: the disease of love. I know it because I, too, endured the curse in my time. However, were you to abscond from here and flee for Warsaw, as Panther suggests, you would not find your beloved there because she's gone to Ciechocinek[14] with her children."

"She has children?" Panther burst out laughing.

"Four. Including a fifteen-year-old daughter."

"Whatisit?!" cried Panther in mock horror.

"I'm not surprised. At his age, I was in love with a widow who had a grandson. But that's not the point; I am asking whether you want me to give you money, against your mother's will and probably behind her back, so that you may go to Ciechocinek to see your teacher."

"Please, Uncle, I would like to return to Warsaw because I feel useless here. And I am bored."

"I cannot send you back to Warsaw because you are here at your mother's request. What would you do there anyway? You know that your mother went to Odessa with her aunt. So, think about this for a day. If you tell me tomorrow that you have decided to go away, then we'll return to the manor because I have no money here. There, I will give you the money, and you will write me a receipt stating that, at your firm request, you are leaving me and going to Ciechocinek. I must have such a document to show to your mother, you understand."

"No, Uncle. There is no need for me to think about it. I don't want to do that."

"What do you want, then?"

"I would like... I would like to... I don't know! I would like to do something! Be something!"

"You don't want to be Private Whatisit?" laughed Panther. "Well, then make a few clogs. Or weave basket traps for fish. Or a snare for birds. There are a thousand things that you can do, all easy and

[14] Ciechocinek /che-kho-**chee**-nek/ a summer resort

simple. I believe that you are bored because you live in a populous country but do not know the language or the customs of the inhabitants. Indeed! You don't even recognize one face from another. If you want, I can give you seven assignments, and if you complete them, I promise to fulfill your seven wishes."

"Please, Uncle, are you angry with me?" the boy whispered shyly.

"Not at all. I understand, and I would like you to be able to overcome your frustration. But I don't want to embarrass you. Everything here lives freely and strives upwards towards the sun. Before Panther comes up with those seven assignments for you, why don't you come with me, and I'll introduce you to the locals." He looked at the sun and added, "We have an hour and a half until lunchtime."

Whatisit looked at his watch.

"You're spot on! That's quite a trick!"

"I can do better tricks," said Panther. "Chief must look at the sun to know the time. All I have to do is listen to my stomach! And I know exactly what kind of show you will see. Chief will set Eduard, or Kunegunda, on a perch; you two will hide, and then he will start calling various birds. I can show you something similar tomorrow by the Rainbow Bridge."

The two set off.

Wolverine asked:

"Have you found many nests?"

"I've had no luck. I walk and walk, I climb trees and... come up empty."

"I'll teach you. Look! Three hundred species of birds lay their eggs in these parts! In trees, in bushes, on the ground, on the bog, and on piles of flotsam on the water. Of these three hundred, some seventy are easy to find by the dozen. The rest require a little effort, and perhaps thirty require great art. Or luck. I have a collection of two hundred species but now find only a handful of new ones each year, and there are a few I have been looking for for years without success. Haven't you collected anything in your life?"

“Ah, yes – insects, stamps, coins. But this year, I became a little discouraged.”

“You write poetry, don’t you?”

“How do you know? Did Mom tell you?”

“No. But if you pay attention, you get to know a lot about the life cycle of creatures. Here, in the spring, all denizens wear beautiful colors and sing. And eighteen-year-old humans experience their May. Write, boy! Sing! Dream!”

“But I would like to find these nests that you have not been able to find.”

Wolverine smiled.

“Very well, then. But first, I will show you how to look for the two hundred that I already have.”

He slowed his pace and pointed, without pausing, to a bush of bird cherry.

"You see there? To your left, a meter above the ground? That bunch of flowers and that dark spot above it? There is a garden warbler sitting on five eggs. He has a dark cap, and the female is ruddy. During midday hours, the husband relieves her from the boredom of brooding. Then she flies free to relax and is right there right now, on that birch tree, cleaning her feathers and stretching her wings.”

Whatisit's eyes widened, then he stopped. Frightened, the “husband” flew out of the bird cherry and joined his wife on the birch tree. The two looked in horror at the giant, who now spread open the branches of their bush.

“Can I take one egg?” Whatisit asked.

“Yes. If it's light-colored. That means the embryo is not yet developed. Otherwise, the egg will crush when you try to blow it empty.”

“I have a start of my collection!” smiled Whatisit, showing his trophy. Wolverine reached into one of his pockets and handed him a glass tube stopped up with cotton wool. There was a little ruddy-spotted egg at the bottom of it.

“And what is that?”

"This is an egg of a crested tit. I found it yesterday in an old squirrel nest."

Whatisit now looked carefully at each bush of bird cherry.

"Pay attention to junipers, too. They're gold mines of nests. And look there! There is an exquisite finch basket on that birch. There, you see? Glued to that branch, as if a knot of wood."

"I'll climb there!"

"Go at it!"

The boy jumped to it. He struggled rather clumsily, and finally, a branch broke under his weight, and he fell.

"Wait!"

Out of his bag, Wolverine took a rope with a hook at one end and threw it over the branch.

"There – this will help you. Tie this end around your waist. There is a knot in the middle of the rope for better grip. Now, pull yourself up."

Whatisit clambered up.

"What a lovely little basket! Lined with red silk threads. Two eggs, like light-gray pebbles with dark spots."

"Take one! These pair have only just begun to lay. They may not notice if one goes missing."

"But how can I carry it down?"

"Why, in your mouth, Whatisit, just like the cuckoo carries hers."

Whatisit carefully placed his catch into the tube.

"You have good eye-sight!" he marveled.

"The eyes of the forest folk, like Panther says! But it's not the eye; it's the familiarity. I know everyone in my neighborhood."

Now, Whatisit began to stumble because he looked up at every birch and bird cherry as they walked.

Suddenly, a tiny yellow-and-gray bird flew from under his feet.

"Uncle, there is something here!" he cried, falling to the ground.

"That was a wood warbler. Or maybe a willow warbler. I can't say; I didn't see exactly because I was listening to the male. He's crying now, can you hear? "*Pea-pea-pea*"! Be careful, or you will trample the nest. The nest has a hole on one side, near the ground, maybe under that dry fern. Do you see it?"

"No, there's nothing here."

"It's well hidden. Keep looking and listen to the male; the louder he cries, the closer you are. It's a bit like playing 'hot and cold.'"

"Ah! There it is! A hole in the ground! Lots of eggs, like tiny beads!"

"Take one, and off we go because – just listen how they lament!"

"Uncle... This was my find, yes?"

"Yes, but do not tell Panther, or he will call you 'Warbler' when the time comes to name you."

"And you will name me?"

"Yes. When your forest eyes and ears open and you feel the forest soul within you."

Whatisit stared at the gray clearing covered with dry grass.

"How do they manage to raise their young like this? Underfoot, without any protection?"

"They do! In a few weeks, a whole bunch of them will fly out to enjoy the summer. Then in autumn, they will all fly overseas, not a care in their hearts! There is great power in these little things. They obey the Law and believe that they received life in order to live it, and therefore live it they will! Life on Earth is mostly made up of the weak and the small, and they are obedient to their task. Can you hear him? He's happy again already! The monster has passed, the female has returned to their nest, and he is there, on the upper branches of that alder tree, feeding and singing his melody: '*Chirp, Chirp, Charp! Chirp, Chirp, Charp*!' I hear him every day, from early spring to late autumn, and I always smile when I hear him because his song is so funny."

"I can hear it now, and I will try to remember it."

Wolverine stopped.

"You see that enormous juniper? For three years now, I have found a green finch nest there. I'm guessing it is the same pair, enlarging their nest every summer. You can see the clump of moss from here. See if they have survived the winter and are back."

Whatisit went up, pushed apart the stiff, spiky branches, and raised himself onto his toes.

"Three eggs! Blue, with red spots!"

"Well, then. They have been lucky to survive and return! Happy summer to them!"

"Do you know every tree here?"

"Almost. Here, all are old acquaintances. Some are closer than others. There are outstanding individuals in this corner: some are old with age, others remarkable for their beauty, others yet catch the eye with their graceful movements. There aren't two alike – one only has to look to see it. We live in a crowded neighborhood here, with thousands of inhabitants. A perfect place to observe them, get to know them, and learn to tell them apart. Sometimes, even individual character quirks can be observed by total strangers like us. Crane and Panther call various friends by name and tell whole stories about them during our Sunday socials."

"What do you mean? How is that?"

"Ah, yes, you'll see! It's Sunday the day after tomorrow."

They walked on in silence. Eventually, Whatisit asked:

"And what nests haven't you found yet?"

"Let's see. Bluethroat. Penduline. The Eurasian short-tailed wren. Grasshopper warbler. And, of course, siskin. People in these parts say that the siskin puts a pebble in his nest, and this makes it invisible."

"But I don't know anything about these birds. I don't even know what they look like. Do you have an atlas you could lend me?"

"Five! In different languages. With colored plates."

"Then let's go home! I'm going to set to work immediately."

"You head back alone, then. I'll just dive in those bushes there for a little while."

Whatisit looked about him helplessly.

"I won't find my way."

"Oh, just try it! You go this way and keep heading east. Along the way, you will pass a clearing with a large spruce tree. You must pass it on your left. Then you will go past three birch trees; one of them has a broken top. And then you will see a path through the heather. Follow that until you come to a large pine tree with a whole lot of pine cones piled up by a woodpecker at its foot. There, you will turn right and soon come across the trail to the Rainbow Bridge.

"And if you get lost, do not panic, but sit down and listen: Crane will soon give the lunch bugle from the cottage. Then you will hear the clatter of Hathor's rattle, and she will lead you home."

Whatisit shook his head doubtfully, sighed, and headed east.

Wolverine waited for him to disappear into the thicket and then, smiling, followed him from a distance.

After a short while, the boy began to meander, veering now to the right, then to the left. Finally, after a great deal of searching, he found his way to the clearing with the spruce. Then he heard the lunch bugle and, soon after that, Hathor's Bambam.

When the horned head emerged from the brushwood, Whatisit sighed and followed her, ignoring all other signs. But Hathor did not follow any trail: she ripped straight on, through bush and mud and stream and mud and bush.

Fortunately, she was full and therefore not in a great hurry, or else Whatisit would not have been able to keep up – cows have long legs and walk fast. Still, he got winded, muddy, and wet, scratched his face and hands, and when, all sweaty, he emerged onto the path at last, he saw Panther standing in front of him, laughing.

"From all that racket, I assumed that a bear must have risen from the dead and was chasing Hathor. But no! It's Private Whatisit rushing for his grub. You wade like a moose, my friend, straight through the swamp!"

"Please, Panther! Do you know? I found a warbler nest by myself! I have the egg!"

"And your uncle's housekeeper finds eggs in the chicken coup every day! Big deal! A warbler! I found a *heistun*."

"What is it?"

"A black forest stork. Chief will be happy to know. It was not far from where we collected bast this morning."

"We'll blow our eggs together!"

"Together? That won't be easy. But I'll show you how it's done. Only I have to see to the animals first."

They both hurried to the cottage. There, leaning against the fence, Wolverine awaited them.

"You didn't get lost?" he asked.

"Yes, I did! But I was saved by Hathor!"

"At least he's not a liar – there is hope for him yet," said Panther.

Right away, Whatisit asked for the atlases and became so absorbed in them that he forgot about his hunger.

"And all of that lives here! Nesting! Singing!" he exclaimed in amazement as they sat down to eat.

"And not only that: also mammals and reptiles and insects and plants. There are as many inhabitants here as stars in the sky."

"It's more crowded than in the capital."

"Here, you are spoiled for choice with whom to make friends. We will give you letters of recommendation! I will write to fish and reptiles, Crane to her sticks, and Chief will write to the race of birds!" said Panther.

"Just the other day, I was invited to a lizard wedding at the Widow's Hill. It was a very classy affair: the groom had a green tux, the bride a pale gray dress, and they left immediately for their honeymoon under the heather bush. The tits, of course, talked the entire time, the frog orchestra played, and the thrush sang *Veni Creator*. There were various speeches from both families, but I can't remember what they said. I only remember that the dowry contained a rotten trunk full of fireflies and an anthill next to it."

"I like birds more."

"That's Chief's department. But, I warn you, if a reptile bites you, you will not be able to ignore it. And Chief can't possibly show you the serpent king with a silver jewel on his forehead. Only I know where he lives."

"And you will probably introduce him to the Tennant, too," smiled Crane.

"Well, well, pass the eggs; let's prepare them," said Wolverine.

And so Whatisit was hooked. He was drawn to the beautiful illustrations and curious descriptions, to the idea of collecting and of a treasure hunt. He barely managed to sit through their midday meal, waiting for the afternoon adventure to begin. And then, full of enthusiasm, he found himself on the path, laden with a large bag, following Wolverine, who was carrying a forked pole on his shoulder and a stuffed eagle owl under his arm.

They went out into a stretch of sandy clearings, overgrown sparsely with birches and pine, and, at last, stopped at a great juniper bush. Wolverine glanced at the sun.

"It's a bit early; we'll have to sit for a while, but it's a good test for you. In ornithology, one must have the patience of a Hindu ascetic. Birds are more active in the morning and in the evening, but in the afternoon, they like to laze around. Do you have good eyesight?

"Not bad, I think."

"Well, then, let's take our position!"

He mounted the stuffed eagle owl on top of the stick and stuck the stick firmly into the ground, right next to the juniper. Then, out of his bag, he took something like a tent canvas made out of a greenish see-through fabric and placed it on sticks, giving it a shape like an extension of the bush. He then placed a few pine branches on top. They both slipped inside and closed the opening behind them.

"Now, sit comfortably and stay still! Hunters stalking black grouse sit in tree huts, in frost, sometimes six hours at a stretch. That's hard: it's a pain to sit still without moving. We don't need that much time. This stick is called *stark* in the old hunting language, and our hiding place is called *shaterek*. Now, find a good opening in the cloth to see through, and keep your eyes peeled open!"

"What are we waiting for?"

"In this way, you can hunt goshawks, crows, magpies, and Eurasian jays. They hate the eagle owl and scream at him and attack him. I once had a live eagle owl for this purpose, and, over the course of a summer, I shot maybe three dozen birds."

"It's a pity you didn't bring your shotgun."

"Oh, I am reluctant to meddle in the affairs of this country now. I do not feel comfortable interfering. There is a kind of order here that exceeds my understanding. Everything in this world is connected. Everything complements every other thing. Everything fulfills some task assigned to it and serves some great law, often incomprehensible to us, which maintains a wise balance. On observation, I find that whoever stands out by courage, strength, or predation, or who merely multiplies beyond what the law allows, is promptly brought to measure by the Power That Be, whoever it is. And it's ever more rarely, and only when my emotions sway me, that I act to defend the small and the weak. There! Look! Listen! As usual, the first to notice the eagle owl are the tits. Hear their racket!"

He lowered his voice and explained:

"Tits come here in five species, the common ones. The yellowish one with a black tie, that's the great tit. It's the largest and most common of them all. That other one, on the birch tree, that's a blue tit, blue like a jewel. The coal tit and the crested tit have not yet heard the news. But there is a chaffinch, a male with a brick-red chest, and – of course! – that daring midget – the short-tailed wren. This one would throw himself at an eagle. Do you see?"

"Yes, I do! It's wonderful!"

"And now, look, ha! All sorts of other small fry are already here. A European robin, the one with the orange chest. And a garden warbler, a tiny whitethroat – people say 'lesser whitethroat' – and a yellow 'icterine' warbler, and the spotted flycatcher – 'spotty' on account of his underside. Look, what a horde of them! And now, even the phlegmatic longspurs have shown up. And all shouting, cursing, swearing, and egging each other on. A regular riot!"

"And that spotted one? It stretches its neck and shakes its head!"

"Ah... that's a wryneck. He's a tricky dodger! Well, now we have to save our eagle owl. Jays and magpies are already screeching, and, look, that's a goshawk circling overhead. Our show is over! Soon, they will start attacking, feathers will start flying, and our trick will not work a second time."

Wolverine parted the canvas and stretched his limbs. The crying crowd dispersed, flew to more distant trees, shouted and cursed, wondered, and finally scattered through the forest, spreading the shocking news:

"The Pine Hill Killer was seen in broad daylight on the Widow's Hill! Oh, fate! Oh, perdition! He's back! He's baaack!"

"Hush, hush, hush," soothed the tits. "The mighty spirit of the forest has appeared, saw him, found him, caught him, imprisoned him! Hush! He'll lock him up!"

"Oh, never fear! If he does not imprison him, you just watch! I'll gouge his eyes out tomorrow!" cried a tiny goldcrest fiercely.

Wolverine and Whatisit walked home, where Whatisit repeated his lessons.

"I already know some of them, the colorful ones: chaffinch, robin, bluetail, great tit! I have them still in front of my eyes. Now, I will read the atlas with a better idea of what I am reading!"

"And so, the desert here fills up for you with creatures!" At that moment, Wolverine cocked his ears to a reedy whistling and turned in that direction.

They came upon Crane, who, while walking lost in thought and listening, whistled on a willow pipe.

"Blackbirds will answer you! You imitate them perfectly."

"If you listen carefully, you can hear a *kujawiak*[15] rhythm in the blackbird song."

"Where are you going with that bag on your back?"

"Why, it's Friday! They're supposed to deliver our bread to the Rainbow Bridge."

Wolverine stashed away his load and wrapped the eagle owl in the cloth.

"Then let's go to the concert with you!"

---

[15] A regional folk dance

They followed Crane down the path.

"Now listen! Don't look, don't think, just listen!" he whispered to Whatisit. A late, sunny, clear May evening was approaching: the time for the greatest arias.

Whatisit closed his eyes and listened. At first, he heard only the general racket, but then he began to distinguish individual soloists among the accompanists and orchestra.

Against the background of the monotonous hum of the forest and the steady ground base of the frogs, he now heard a song, a duo of silvery whistling, coming from a nearby treetop. Crane's pipe repeated the first voice, the tenor.

"It is a song competition between a thrush and a blackbird!" Wolverine whispered. "Blackbird sings the first part!"

Short, dancing accents answered the duo.

"Those are finches and buntings, harmonizing."

"Hey, ha! Boys and girls, come together now, fast!"

"Bravo, bravo, bravo!" a passing cuckoo cut in.

And then the nightingale's song drowned out everyone.

Wolverine lifted his hat.

"Well, hello, Master Bekvark[16]!" he smiled.

The lute player outsang the whole crowd of singers. His voice towered over the choir and the orchestra: artful, full of weepings, passionate confessions, love whispers, eternal oaths, and raptures, the love song of spring.

Suddenly, everything stopped. Crane slipped his flute into his pocket. Wolverine pointed to a gray shadow slinking among the branches.

"The killer!" he said.

"The owl! The owl! The owl!" cried the tits and followed her.

Words formed in Whatisit's head; rhymes flooded in. He felt he would write a beautiful sonnet.

And now, they were standing at the Rainbow Bridge.

---

[16] Renaissance Hungarian composer and virtuoso lute player at the Polish court

"Stay here! We'll be back in a moment," said Wolverine as he entered the ford with Crane. At first, Whatisit listened to the splashing and their conversation, and then he turned to the concert again.

There were no soloists here by the water, only the general racket: noise, shouting, whistling, applause, laughter, calls, interrupted from time to time by the grim growl of a bumblebee.

And then the clarions came, the cranes sounding their evening song.

Loaded with a week's supply of bread, Wolverine and Crane came over the ford.

"What's that frightening tooting?" Whatisit asked.

"It's the cranes in their summer nesting grounds. That's how they greet and bid goodbye to the sun every day. Well, time to go back to our cabin."

When they arrived in the clearing, they found Panther collecting their drying laundry off the grass and tree branches. Hathor and Patch Pelt, with her miniature daughter, were walking behind him, asking for their evening feed. Jake did double flips in the willow tree. The light of the fire flashed from the hut.

"Have you checked the fish traps, Panther?" asked Wolverine.

"Oh, yes, but I have not cleaned the fish yet – I left it for Whatisit."

"Why, of course!" The boy offered himself eagerly, grabbed the wet sack, placed it on the special bench reserved for the job, and set about the work.

"You madman! Light some incense and put an extra shirt on your back, or the mosquitoes will eat you alive!" Panther called to him.

Indeed, the mosquitos from the marshes were a curse of their refuge, but Whatisit decided to endure the suffering like an Iroquois warrior under torture and even whistled as he worked.

Shortly, Wolverine came to his aid, and the smoke of his pipe chased away the swarm of mosquitoes.

"I can see our recruit wants to join the forest tribe," said Panther, standing over him.

"I do!" Whatisit said, wiping his face with his sleeve and smearing fish blood all over.

"And you seem to think it an act of heroism to fall prey to mosquitoes? But it's the opposite: to protect yourself, that's the true forest trick. Look at us: they bother us less than you. Chief defends himself with his pipe, Crane defends himself with some vinegar of his invention, and I have a special herb for it. Patch Pelt Junior would be dead by now if I didn't rub her with it three times a day."

They took the cleaned fish to the cottage. Whatisit asked, "And when will I become a member of the tribe? It seems to me that there are many things I know already. I'm not getting lost anymore and I recognize various birds."

"And have you met the Green Ghost? And weren't you afraid of him? And have you spent a night in the wilderness? Have you walked across a bog that sinks under your feet? Can you swim? When a cramp grips you on the water, do you know what to do? Can you save yourself if a viper bites you far away from Refuge? Hey, hey, Private, it's still some time before you can have a forest name!"

"I will learn all these things!" Whatisit said stubbornly.

As they sat down to supper, Crane said:

"I hereby make it known that the footbridges have cleared. I had my first patient today: a woman with fever and ulcers. She was overjoyed that we were back, and so... my peaceful days are over!

"We could sabotage the footbridges, you know."

"Ah, these peasants are like beavers: they will repair them in no time! Too bad, but I have to live with it; I had committed myself!" Crane sighed.

"Day after tomorrow is Sunday, Whatisit!" said Panther. "You haven't come on our social calls yet because you were busy moping about in the bushes. But now, you should know that on Sunday, after prayers, we go to the forest together, and each boasts about some peculiarity he has spotted over the week. You, too, have to come up with something.

"I think you best spend the day looking for the Green Ghost. He likes to sit in ditches or spruce thickets during the daytime. He's tiny, only his head is huge, and he sports one large horn on the forehead. It shines like touchwood at night."

Here, Panther grabbed Stomper Junior rummaging under the table, placed him on his lap, handed him a bowl of roe and fish livers, and, while stroking his folded spikes, he continued:

"And you still do not know our House Tennant. There is a house-elf in every household, and he plays tricks or helps, according to the mood of the moment. Ours gets along with me, I am pleased to say, but he has no mercy for the doctor. And the beginning of that animosity was that the doctor once poured green licorice[17] on the floor. The elf, terribly hungry for sweets, ate it, and he has hated Crane ever since. Isn't that right?"

"He must have complained to you!" laughed Crane. "You probably had to come to his aid in that adventure."

"Whatisit!" said Wolverine. "You listen to what Panther has to say. Later, old Odrowąż will tell you more of the wonders of the forest. But remember this: to be a forest man, you must lose all fear and all anger and stir in yourself a loving kindness for everything and everyone who lives with you under the sun. And now sleep. Tomorrow, we will rise at dawn and go to the old clear-cutting. We will dig old dead trunks for firewood."

Whatisit left the hut one more time. He had become so used to the night that he wandered as far as the clearing – avoiding, however, the proximity of the thicket – and he stood there for a while, listening.

A night in the forest never has the majestic silence of the night in the fields. In the depths of the forest, something always slinks, rustles, lurks, sneaks, flashes, crunches. Creatures feed and hunt and murder in the dark.

Two birds began to circle over the clearing with a flight of bats. There was a pathetic *"pow, pow,"* and a wing brushed against the boy's temple. Somewhere nearby, a dry branch cracked beneath an invisible foot. He quickly returned to the hut.

---

[17] An emetic

Each of these creatures will go into this darkness, and none will lose his way! he thought and sighed. He still felt fear! But once inside, he felt safe, weary, and sleepy.

He undressed quickly and fell asleep, already used to his stiff bedding.

He was awakened by the steady tapping on the wall close to his head. He jumped up and suddenly saw a terrible sight.

In the depths of the hall, by the wall, a luminous, great, glowing face stared at him. Its shining eyes blinked, and its wide lips moved as if they were saying something or giggling soundlessly. Floating in the air, it seemed to waft towards him. At first petrified with fear, the boy now gave a wild scream and rushed towards the bed-chamber door, groping in vain for the door knob in the dark.

The door opened, and Wolverine's voice asked calmly:

"What's happening to you, my boy?"

"Uncle! Something terrible has just appeared!"

The moon's bright glow enveloped the hall, and the mysterious face was gone.

"It was clearly visible in the dark!" Whatisit whispered, clutching Wolverine's sleeve as he closed the door. "Can you see?"

"I sure can!" Wolverine replied, going towards where the apparition had been and laughing as he struck a match. "Here is why I am missing several glass tubes!" He called out:

"Panther!"

But silence answered him. He went into the room, lit the lamp, and brought Whatisit to the ghostly face.

On the wall, glass tubes hung, intricately attached with threads and studs and filled with fireflies, forming the shape of eyes, a nose, and a big mouth. It all glowed, moved, and swirled. Whatisit looked embarrassed, but Wolverine comforted him.

"I'm not surprised you screamed! What a trickster! Well, we have to let these poor things out. And since it's almost dawn, let's go meet the forest before *ledvukhna.*"

"It's a bird?"

"The woodlark. *Ledvukhna* is what our honorable canon[18] Kluk calls him."

He disassembled the device and put it into the alcove.

"Panther has played his trick and has spirited away! Be prepared that it will not be his last trick, and learn to control your fear!"

They went out onto the porch and, sitting on the platform, put their clogs on. The world was barely pearly, and the depths of the forest were dewy and silent. They walked along invisible paths and spoke in whispers, not daring to disturb the silence. The dew, the power of the air, and the words of Wolverine slowly seeped into the boy's soul.

---

[18] A priestly rank

SUNDAY

Without even lighting the fire in the kitchen, Crane set a jug of fresh milk and a loaf of bread on the table. Panther brought a handful of flowers and laid them before the icon. And Wolverine brought out from the bed-chamber Sunday clothes for everyone.

"Sunday!" laughed Whatisit and ran to bathe in the stream, leaving his first pair of hand-made clogs at the threshold for all to see.

He was proud of them as if they were a masterpiece and felt a little worried when, upon returning, he saw Panther inspecting them.

"Do you have a spare pair? We will be in the forest all day today: bag lunch! And we will not return to the cottage before dark, but these poor things won't last two hours. Look, the sole has not been threaded twice; the ear flaps look very flimsy, and the heel is not fully covered. You'll be limping barefoot before noon."

And he scornfully threw the masterpiece away.

"They're not that bad!" said Wolverine encouragingly after studying them. Crane inspected the clogs and gave the boy another pair.

"You'll end up barefoot, a viper will bite you, and I'll get stuck looking after you!" he said.

The masterpiece flew over the fence.

They washed up, changed their clothes, had their breakfast, and went to the cross. Wolverine read the prayers, and they sang *Who Shall Take You in Her Care.*

Whatisit took the ceremony to heart and was scandalized that, throughout the proceedings, Panther kept nudging him and pointing with his eyes to a bird box suspended high on a birch tree.

As soon as they finished, Panther shouted:

"Chief! The hoopoe took the box!"

"You saw it?"

"And how! As we sang *He Shall Free You from the Hunter's Snare*, the hoopoe thrust his head out and raised his crest! I was trying to point it out to Whatisit, but he didn't get it that he had a friend there!"

"What is hoopoe's Latin name?" Whatisit asked.

"Whatisitus vulgaris."

"Best not to quote Latin, Whatisit, or Panther might christen you that, and it just might stick!" laughed Wolverine, looking at the birch tree in delight.

"Which generation of residents of this box is it, then? Let's see." He counted. "First, there were three generations of tits: the great tits, the blue tits, and the marsh tits; then, we had black flycatchers, then wrynecks, then starlings and woodpeckers, and now, the hoopoe – seventh."

"The eighth will be hornets and the ninth red mice," said Panther. "Then we. Ten generations in the forest!"

"Off we go!" commanded Wolverine. "Shoulder bags, axes; any special equipment for your projects. Stop up the hut door with a stake. Leave feed for our comrades by the fence. Off we go!"

They bustled about and took off. The day was divine, clear, and a little hot.

"We'll get sprinkled with rain this afternoon," said Crane, looking at the sky.

The leader, Wolverine, intoned their forest anthem. A joyful song filled the forest and their souls with warm enthusiasm.

You will lead us, you will lead us
On your sunny trail,
Where hearts do sing, and songs do bloom,
Where sleeping forests await the wind,
Where birds await their flight!

"Whoever has a special find, let him lead the way!" said Wolverine.

Crane volunteered:

"I have two flowers and a mushroom."

They walked without a trail now, bypassing bush and bog in a fantastic zigzag.

"This would be a great place to leave you alone!" said Panther to Whatisit.

"Very well! Let me try it!" Whatisit replied audaciously.

Finally, in a wooded marsh overgrown with birches and lined with weed, Crane stood and pointed. There was, in a blur of color and subtle grace, a slender flower of fantastic form all alone.

"A lady's slipper! A flower no bigger than a field lily," quoted Crane and fell to his knees to collect it for his herbarium.

"Spare him for now!" said Wolverine. "It bloomed here so wonderfully among all these weeds, all alone, like a beautiful soul among a coarse crowd. Dig it out properly tomorrow, and move it directly to the garden with a large lump of soil."

"Ah, that's a better plan. I will do it tomorrow."

They admired the sight for a goodly moment, and then Panther, searching the tree branches with his eyes, said to Whatisit, "See that birch by the glade, with a bulge by the branch? There, to the left?"

"I do!" the boy replied after a moment of searching.

"And do you see those black quills sticking out of that bulge in all directions?"

"I do."

"Do you know what it is?"

"Lichen."

"Well, yes, outside. But inside?"

"Inside? Some kind of growth on a tree."

"Seven little birds. And the quills are their tails sticking out."

"No way! I'll go and check."

"Go carefully, though, because the ground is boggy here. That's a house of yet another kind of tit: the long-tailed tit. The whole bird is as small as a nut, and only his tail is magnificent. How can so many fit into such a tiny hut? Because they always crowd so; sometimes, there are seven or more. But the tails don't fit, so they make holes and stick them out."

"Uncle! Do you have such a nest in your collection?"

"I do! Anyway, you should not take this one because it is occupied."

As Whatisit touched the trunk of the birch to climb it, the lichen cottage began to stir. White balls of fluff began to pour out of the intricately covered opening at one side. Soon, the parents turned up, and there was a racket.

Whatisit managed to get one chick in hand; he studied it, kissed it, and let him fly.

"What a wonder!" he said, returning. "They're as beautiful as flowers. I feel a little silly now for having disturbed them."

"It's all right. Sometimes, these little gluttons torment their parents for too long. See how well they fly already. They don't need nursing anymore!"

They moved on, deeper and deeper into the swamp. In time, they found themselves in a field of irises in bloom.

"Ah, the Field of Gold! We're going to the Black Eye," said Panther. "Crane will show us a water wonder. Only pay attention on the footbridges!"

Soon, they climbed onto some logs, slippery and round, and Whatisit slipped into the black morass with one foot. Wolverine pulled him out, but the boy became so frightened by the experience that he let himself be led on as if he were blind.

"My God! Is it still far?" he whispered despairingly at last.

"We're there! Look up and see!"

They stood over a smooth pane of black, still water, covered with a carpet of blooming water lilies. Alders framed the pond, and its loneliness, isolation, and danger seemed as if emphasized by the snow-white of the lilies.

"This is not a pond but a window to the bottomless unknown. We measured it with ropes once, but however many we tied together, the stone at the end seemed never to find a true bottom. And yet, these water lilies must find it to raise these flowers to the sun. There are no such depths to any swamp that the soul could not break out into the light. Only a person rarely has the will, the faith, and the wisdom of water lilies," said Wolverine thoughtfully.

"Well, well. But where is your miracle, Crane?" asked Panther.

And Crane raised his hand.

"Do you see that flower?"

"Ah, yes. One is bright pink. How come? Why?"

"There, at the bottom of the swamp, there must live the creative thought of the master of the universe."

"This flower has to be picked," Panther decided, looking about for a way.

But the flower grew too far to reach with a rod or to throw a rope, so Panther began to undress.

"Leave it alone," objected Wolverine. "Don't you remember the rash we got when we tried to measure the depth here?"

"Big deal! It was over in three days! I must get that flower for Crane. I have to. Don't ask me why!"

He laughed and, naked, leaped into the black depths.

"His conscience touched him! He wants to make up for all the pranks of the house-elf," smiled Wolverine.

Panther swam effortlessly like a fish. It was clear he was enjoying himself.

He paused for a moment at one bunch of plants, and they saw a little bird fly out from among the leaves. Then Panther reached the pink flower, plucked it, tied its stem around his neck, and swam back ashore.

"Uncle! Teach me to swim!" Whatisit asked.

"Very well. We start tomorrow."

Panther sprang ashore, spat something from his mouth into his hand, and handed it over to Wolverine.

It was an egg.

"This is not in your collection yet. The nest lay on a leaf, like on a plate – five eggs! And, here, the house-elf brought a gift for Crane. He swam just ahead of me, guided me, and helped me pull out the stem. I suppose he forgot all about that licorice powder."

"Well, good boy. He'll get honey and milk!" Crane laughed. He crouched down, opened his can, and carefully stowed away the prize.

Meanwhile, Panther had rubbed himself down with grass and put his clothes back on.

They turned back. Again, Whatisit slipped on one of the footbridges, and they made their way to solid ground.

"And here you have my third miracle!" said Crane, standing in a clearing.

"Osina-in-the-collar."

"Is that a mushroom?" Whatisit wondered.

"Yes, a kind of oyster mushroom, but of phenomenal size. The tree is half dry. We'll saw it off tomorrow and take it home. It's big enough to sit on!"

"The best tinder is made from this mushroom," Panther said.

Here, he looked at the sun and stretched out on the ground.

"Lunchtime! I won't take a step farther unless we eat."

Everyone lay down. The clearing was dry and covered with wildflowers. Bees buzzed. They felt drowsy.

"A storm is coming," Crane whispered, settling himself comfortably. And everyone fell asleep.

Wolverine was woken by a rustle. He opened his eyes and stared motionlessly. At the edge of the clearing, somewhat in the shade, stood a pair of moose – mother and child.

Clumsy, as if the last survivors of a failed experiment of nature, spirits of the forest, gods of primeval earth: heavy, oversized heads; hooves gigantic like skis; oddly overlong limbs.

The mother moose rubbed her neck against the tree; the foal, hidden a bit behind her mother, nibbled on a twig. Finally, the female, reassured by the immobility of the men, snorted and walked past sleeping Whatisit, pressing his hat into the ground with her heavy hoof; the little one sniffed it curiously.

At that moment, the boy woke and jumped up. The animals made a mighty leap, there was a crack of broken bushes, and they were gone.

Now everyone was up, and Whatisit lamented while hearing Wolverine's story.

"I should not have moved!"

"Well, she may have stepped on you, and you would look like your hat now."

"Mercy! Eat!" Panther rummaged about the food bag.

They spread out the contents. There was bread, cheese, dried fish, and, in Panther's pot, a few dark, sharply pointed eggs.

"A true gourmet! Lapwing eggs!" laughed Wolverine.

"This is revenge. Yesterday, in the marshes, this cursed bird beat me in the face with its wings! It screamed and cursed, even though I was not in the least interested in her nest! I was looking for a bluethroat that had flashed at me from the reed. But this thing did not let me look in peace and scared away all who lived there. Well, I figured, since I took the punishment, I might as well do the crime.

"Here, Whatisit, try this delicacy! Oh, I see! You don't dare? Well then, you won't get any."

And Panther swallowed the last egg himself.

"And you didn't find the bluethroat?"

"How's that? Would I let a stupid lapwing defeat me? It would be shameful for Panther to have nothing to show on a Sunday! Let's go! We can make two kilometers before we're done chewing these fish."

Panther led the way.

Wolverine named various features for Whatisit's instruction, pointing out their characteristic features.

"Look, this is 'Beggar Woman.' This birch tree, bent down by some catastrophe, with its skeletal branches and head to the ground. Doesn't it look like a beggar at the church gate?

"And this enormous mountain ash, covered with snow-white flowers, isn't she a 'Beauty'? How many thrushes, fieldfares, and bullfinches visit her in autumn and sing concerts while feasting!

"And in that stand, that tangled pine with some parasitic growth, does she not look like a 'Witch'?

"And that's 'Janosik.'[19] That spruce, tall like a mast, in that black thicket.

"The forest, like any community of men, has ordinary crowds and outstanding individuals. Some stand out for their beauty, others for their strength, personality, or thoughtful old age. Look at these three oaks! Three Wise Men. They alone survived a storm that laid all the other trees around them low. There was once a dense stand of their peers here, and their trunks can still be found rotting among the blackberry. What glorious fellows they were, a regiment of giants!

"These three sometimes retell the legends of that past. You just need to understand their sough. So many fell to lay a causeway for cannons going against the Swedes; so many gave life for Napoleon; so many, through human greed, went down the river to Gdansk, and then some others fell to pay the penalties imposed after the

---

[19] Janoskik /Ya-**no**-shik/ a legendary bandit, the Polish Robin Hood

Insurrection[20]. The last fell only recently; their rotten bodies are still sticking out here and there, tangled with bushes. The Hangman Muraviev[21] ordered vast clearcuttings as he hunted for the last of the partisans hiding here.

"The three old men have seen it all. They know the whole chronicle of the forest. Let's bow to them to honor them!"

They uncovered their heads and walked for a while in silence until impish Panther said:

"I am afraid that that old man, that fellow who's a bit bald, has a tenant in his hollow."

"What?" said Wolverine, surprised.

"I'm not sure who. It might be a lynx. Though we have never seen one in these parts. Or maybe it's a marten or a polecat? The hole seems to be freshly scratched. I will keep an eye on it."

"And I!" Whatisit whispered pleadingly.

Panther only nodded because he was carefully looking around to orient himself. At last, he plunged into a stand of reed that covered the marsh's edge. It was green at the top and brown-dry at the bottom, higher than their heads, so that soon, only the reed tufts swaying overhead marked their passage. Shamefully hard stumps hurt their feet, and they were barely able to push through the thicket. Wolverine shook his head. Even he wondered how a man without the smell of a weasel and the eyes of a cat would find a nest of a small bird in this jungle.

The hike was long. Panther had to change direction more than once, but finally, he crouched down to the ground and, parting the dry stems, showed them a carelessly constructed nest of reed stalks with five blue-spotted eggs. Crane, wiping sweat from his forehead and not half as enthusiastic about ornithology as Wolverine, asked:

"Explain to me how one finds such a needle in this haystack!"

---

[20] The 1863 Insurrection against Russian rule was followed by mass confiscations and tax penalties

[21] A Russian commander during the 1863 uprising famous for his reprisals against the civilian population

"Piece of cake! First, you find a clump of reed on the mud with a bulrush mace in the middle – that one. Then, you make sure to keep that birch in front of you – and that's it! Now, all you have to do is stretch your arms to measure distance and then look for this!"

And he plucked a black grouse feather tied with a red thread to the top of a bulrush mace.

"Panther, you rascal!" cried Crane. "You've been in my medical box again! That's surgical thread!"

"I don't know anything about it," replied Panther, undaunted. "I was once looking for a sewing thread to fix a hole in my jacket, and I took what I found. Here, I have the rest in my pocket!"

And he conscientiously handed back the dirty, tangled knot of precious threads.

"First incarnation of a troglodyte![22]" Crane growled, throwing away the ruined thread. Wolverine carefully collected the nest and eggs for his collection and explained to Whatisit:

"It is a lovely and rare bird, a relative of the nightingale, though not a soloist at all. He has a beautiful blue shield on his chest. Hurray, Panther, for finding this trophy!"

"Is it over already? Chief and Whatisit have nothing to show?"

"First, let's dig ourselves out of here and let me secure these eggs. I did see something lovely, though perhaps it is gone by now. But I'll take you anyway."

"*It* went away? What could that be?"

But Wolverine remained silent, and when they stood on solid ground, he pointed to a solitary spruce visible from far away, and they headed in its direction.

As they crossed a heather-covered glade, they suddenly saw something red rushing along the ground.

"Jake!" Crane rejoiced.

There was a joyful *"Krr, krr!"* and – *hop!* – Jake was on his shoulder, wet, winded, and thin-looking.

---

[22] E.g. "little better than a caveman" (on the theory that souls gradually improve with each subsequent reincarnation)

"Look how the scoundrel found us!" Panther teased him. "The cottage is closed; no nuts nor milk!"

But Crane had clearly been waiting for his pet because soon, there was energetic cracking of a nutshell and a happy purr from his pocket, warning off all and sundry from his feast.

The spruce to which they finally came after a long march was not Janosik. His name was Seer. Its dense and spreading branches formed a kind of stepladder, and, at the very top, there was a platform made with a few boards. With a pair of good binoculars, one could see the entire country of the forest folk from there.

Wolverine and Panther climbed first and, after a while, from the top came:

"There it is! It did not go away!"

Whatisit climbed impatiently behind them. Panther gave him the binoculars and pointed out the direction.

"See that clearing in the thicket? With birch trees all around it, like a garland?"

"I do! And something's standing there, nibbling at the grass. A deer! And something else moves around it – all covered in funny spots!"

"It must have been born yesterday. I spotted it last night. You can watch them from here without frightening them. Anyway, that clearing is surrounded by bog on all sides; it's difficult to get there."

"And you can see our hut and the nets on the stream and the Boundless Swamp and the Black Eye. Now I know it, too. And the lake. You can draw a map of the country from here. I'll do it tomorrow!" Whatisit said.

"And you can also see that cloud coming our way. And thank goodness; the heat is stifling. Now, all down, on the ground, and lie low in a clearing because there will soon be thunder music here!"

They hid their bags and clothes, the nest, and the can with the water lily, and even their axes and hats under the spruce tree. They stripped down to their underwear, and with their heads uncovered, they lay down in the heather, looking at the sky, waiting for a bath.

The wind rattled the forest and wrestled it. Somewhere in the distance, a tree fell with a crash. A blinding flash tore a glowing sign on the black cloud.

And then the world boiled. Rain poured down on them; the air shuddered with thunders. The wind blew torn leaves and branches; it seemed it might carry whole trees.

Whatisit, blinded, stunned, looked at his companions. Panther was gnawing on dried fish. Wolverine covered the bowl of his pipe with his hand to keep it from going out. Crane took off his shirt, wrapped Jake in it, and was rubbing his torso with a handful of moss as if in a Turkish bath. No one even blinked an eye at the incessant dazzling lightning, as if they were deaf to the roar of thunder.

Whatisit decided to show carelessness too and began to whistle, but Panther nudged him rather rudely.

"Hey! Be silent, you worm!" he shouted amid the roar of thunder. "Lie there and listen carefully. This is a divine sermon!"

"No whistling then? But eating fish is okay?"

"It's okay because I'm hungry. But even a dumb blackbird knows that it is rude to whistle in a storm! Oh, there, you've got your punishment!"

Suddenly, hail poured out of the clouds; very fine at first, then gradually getting thicker. Whatisit covered his head with his hands and, following the example of his companions, holed up as much as possible under the moss and heather. The ice balls snapped painfully; the clearing whitened with them.

Panther finally crawled under a juniper, and Crane, red as crayfish, did also, not forgetting to take along Jake wrapped in his shirt. But that was the end of the storm.

The cloud moved east; the sun came out.

"And now, run home!" commanded Wolverine.

They gathered their belongings and ran. Panther broke into the lead and disappeared into the thicket. Crane was pulling on his jacket as he ran. Whatisit, his teeth chattering, tangled in his scuffed clogs. Wolverine covered the precious nest with his shirt. The exertion soon warmed them up, and when they reached the hut, their wet clothes were steaming.

"No need for quinine today," said Crane, entering the hut.

Panther kindled the fireplace, and soon, the four of them – not forest folk anymore, but three wild, naked men – were changing into dry clothes.

"And now sleep!" said Whatisit.

"Really? And leave the work to the house-elf?" Panther was indignant. "Collect those wet rags and hang them up neatly in the attic to dry! Then throw some firewood down from there. Then wipe the floor dry, peel potatoes for supper, and milk Hathor! You can see that our two friends are lost to the world, buried in their eggs and herbs. Come on, shoo!"

"This life is endless work!"

"And how! And to think that you were bored and moped about the bushes! This is how everything works. When I get tired from time to time, I only have to look at the bluetail female feeding her eleven gluttons or at the bushtit building her nest! It's a bit more troublesome than our job!"

They went barefoot to the stable. Hathor was dry and chewing phlegmatically. And Patch Pelt, too, had reasonably stayed indoors.

"Look how wise they are! They all returned to the cabin in time and now look at us with pity. Get out of here, Hiss-Hiss!" He chased the snake away and crouched down to milk the cow.

"Come on, Whatisit! Take a bunch of straw stuck under the thatch and wipe the Little One!"

Patch Pelt sniffed the greens and Whatisit's hands and graciously allowed him to touch her daughter. The baby was also favorably disposed to the operation.

When Panther finished, he poured a little milk into a small shard for the snake, then found a pot in the corner and said softly:

"Give a little to the Little One, too, but make sure Crane doesn't find out. Poor thing, mosquitoes bite it, and she's too young to enjoy fresh grass this spring. There, little baby, grow big, grow healthy!"

They watched it with pleasure. The snake stuck its head into the milk; the foal sucked at the pot with delight.

"Panther," said Whatisit. "Do you hear? What is it? What kind of bird is this?"

"This?" Panther listened. "This is a sign of a long rain coming. It's a viper!"

"Cannot be! Snakes are mute!"

"Come on, take a look. Only go soft. Quiet."

Walking carefully, slowly, towards the voice, they saw a snake on the path to the water. Half coiled, she only raised her head and issued a monotonous, very high-pitched *"trrrr!"*

Panther handed Whatisit his milking jar, stepped back to the shed without a rustle, and then, suddenly, leaped towards the reptile. He held a cane in his hand, and he struck with it again and again. The *trrr* ceased, a whitish belly flashed, and the dead reptile stretched like a limp piece of rope on the path. Panther crushed his head underfoot and then lifted the body with his stick and threw it far away into the bush.

"There you have him, the scoundrel! He rarely speaks, but he does have a voice. There was a multitude of this filth here when we first came. We killed them by the dozen. Hathor was bitten, and the mare and I. The others don't go about barefoot, so they escaped."

"Isn't the venom deadly?"

"Ha, ha! We have a doctor here to make sure we don't die. But I was quite sick for several days. Odrowąż taught me an herb treatment, which was helpful – I think. The farm animals seem to find it themselves; they know it by instinct."

They returned to the hut.

"The reptile trumpets! It will rain!" said Panther, nudging Whatisit and pointing to his companions with his eyes.

Crane was busy swathing the pink lily in some special cotton wool and blotting paper; Wolverine was blowing his eggs. Neither spoke.

"And on the table, nothing but bread and salt. Where is our supper?"

"It's Sunday; I'm not cooking," muttered Crane. Wolverine stopped blowing and asked:

"You killed the beast?"

"Yes! I killed it, and now I want potatoes richly dressed with sauce; I have had enough soups!"

Receiving no reply, he brought potatoes from the pantry and began to peel them with Whatisit.

"If it rains... what do we do? Boredom! Sit at home!" the boy said. "I was supposed to learn to swim tomorrow, draw a map, keep an eye on that thing in that oak! And now it turns out I must stay indoors!"

"A little rain is good sometimes! Work will pile up. You'll see what a workshop this place can be! Well, light the fire!"

Wolverine finished his work, left the hut, and, returning, said:

"Yes! It will be chilly and rainy for a few days. At last, I'll have the time to repair the nets and baskets."

"And I to catalog the herbarium!" added Crane.

"And I... to sew up all your rags," said Panther.

"And I?" asked Whatisit.

Wolverine pointed to the bookshelves:

"You will study the natural history of your new acquaintances!"

He lit his pipe, took the violin off the wall, and after a while, began to play.

"And this is a proper Sunday," Panther said. "It ends in a ball!"

Whatisit listened. Wolverine played strange, unfamiliar melodies. As if each melody were a fairy tale, a dream. After a while, Crane began to accompany him on a peculiar pipe made of several reeds. The sky, draped with clouds, grew darker and faded away. The coals on the fireplace glowed, a fire crackled in the stove; the distant chorus of frogs was quieter than usual, and, somehow, even the clarions of cranes were shorter than normal. But there was no sadness in it, neither outside nor inside. They could feel that the mighty sun was just behind the cloud and that it was only a moment of respite for reflection.

"Whose music is this, Uncle?" Whatisit asked when Wolverine stopped to retune.

"It's... ours. Forest people's. May's," the amateur musician said.

And Whatisit understood that it was the singing of the forest overheard by the human soul.

RAIN

The monotonous rumble of rain on the roof woke Whatisit. He had clearly overslept because there were all kinds of activity around him: the room was cluttered with bast rods, bast fiber, fish baskets, and Wolverine reigned among it, busy with his work.

"It's pouring," he said. "And it'll continue to rain for three days, at least. The others went to fetch Crane's flower."

Whatisit ran to the bath. Hathor and the mare stood in the open stable door and pondered whether to go out and get wet, yawning in turns. Hiss-Hiss, glistening with new skin, studied himself in the mirror of the spring; wet birds sat under their leaf umbrellas.

"What should I do?" the boy asked as he swallowed his breakfast.

"What would you like to do?"

"Why, learn basket-weaving from you!"

"Not much special art to this! Sharpen the knife well and cut me fibers, about this long. Selects them carefully, though: smooth, pliable, and long! There is plenty to choose from here."

And thus, Whatisit became acquainted with the fishing equipment, its original and cunning design, its names, and the theory of its use. Bast, hazel, birch, and hemp were the only material – the knife the only tool.

When he looked at Wolverine's hands, it seemed to him that the work was a breeze; the fiber bent so easily, split, took the desired forms, tied itself tightly and firmly, like a steel wire. But when he tried to weave and bind it himself, everything rose up in a rebellion, refused to listen to his hands, broke, and fell apart. At first, the boy lowered his hands in defeat and wanted to give up the work, but then he became ashamed and, gritting his teeth, began to struggle stubbornly with the bast.

"Damn you!" he growled. "I will make you submit!"

"Ha! That's not our way!" Wolverine shook his head. "You won't go far like that, violating our forest law. This sallow gave us its tendrils to use, but as I cut it, I thanked her for the gift, and now, as I pleat it, I think thankful thoughts. One must not get angry. Anger, like a boomerang, returns to him who hurled it. The inner disorder then passes into our hands, and then they tear, break, and despoil instead of creating. And around the angry and cursing person rises a kind of bad current. The thing to do, my boy, is to apologize to the fiber. The fiber is good fiber; only your hands are untrained. Watch and learn the easy movements, the easy knots; and when learning, think favorably about your material and learn about its character and qualities. Then, the job will be both easier and better!"

And he started to arrange the boy's fingers, calmly and patiently, to direct his movements.

"Please, Uncle, do you never get angry?"

"Hmm... it's better not to use words like 'never' and 'always.' All I can say is that I try to get angry the least I can. Now, be careful, don't pull that fiber too much. And this thicker spot... try warming it up over the fire before bending it. This will make it more flexible. And when you do that, hold the fingers of your left hand like that."

"Oy, dana, Oy, dana!" sang Panther, entering the room, all wet and smeared with earth. "We brought the 'princess slipper' on a litter, like imperial regalia. Downpour, wind, cold – and a pestilence of mosquitoes and other harmful vermin! I saw a whole herd of seagulls. It must blow hard on the Baltic to drive them this far[23]. Stubborn Crane went with a saw to collect those tree fungus, and I am supposed to cook lunch. Are there any fish?"

"One delicious-looking pike. The basket had a hole in it, so a trifle was lost."

"Oy, oy! I can see that Chief has cleaned him. We are lucky with our choice of Chief! But I guess Whatisit has blisters on his hands by now. Stop fiddling with bast, jump to the vegetable garden, get me a bunch of sorrels and some other greens, whatever is to hand! And to cover yourself, best take that pleated straw coat. We must preserve dry clothes!"

Whatisit ran and returned with wet sorrel and bad news.

"Something broke the fence and trampled the potatoes. Probably Hathor?"

"Please, do not blame Hathor baselessly! I'm sure it's the work of a moose or goat! I'll go see." And, using the excuse, he fled from cooking dinner.

"This one, heh! Any excuse is good to go running," Wolverine laughed and began to bustle in the kitchen.

Panther came back after about an hour, not so much wet as soaked like a sponge.

"Baaad! Wild boars have discovered our potatoes. We might as well say goodbye to them."

"They have good taste," said Wolverine philosophically.

"We could shoot them if they are pests," Whatisit blurted out.

"You may as well shoot us, too, because we, too, like potatoes."

"Yes, but these are ours!"

---

[23] 355 kilometers (200 miles)

"Hmm... There still are some people around who respect private property, yes? And these pigs are here on their own land! What right have we to plant potatoes here, let alone shoot them? We'll build a platform in the tree and watch them! And we'll get our potatoes from Odrowąż."

"About right!" Panther said, but Whatisit remained silent.

"I got so sweaty the other day, hoeing that plot!" he mumbled.

"So did we," Wolverine shrugged. "Work is pleasant and healthy in itself. And the pigs will repay us for the potatoes yet, you will see!"

Soon, Crane returned – another sponge – and it took the two until dinner to dry out.

But then the downpour and the chill intensified, and no one dared step over the threshold. Sleepy, Jake got out of his sheep's sleeve and, yawning, joined the company; a cold Stomper Junior buried himself in Panther's bed. And the forest folk got busy with their work.

Panther sat by the window and patched their clothes. Crane covered the whole table with his atlases and his herbarium. Wolverine kept throwing repaired baskets out in front of the hut. Despite his sore hands, Whatisit struggled on with the bast, but now, instead of cursing, he whistled *The Basket Weaver.*

"Maybe you could take a patching lesson from me, Private Whatisit! Look at what you did to this jacket! You must have hanged on a knot to tear the hole in the back like this!"

"I don't want such girly work!" the boy muttered dismissively.

"Girly work? As in: *a woman's job*? I am not ordering you to give birth and breastfeed, you louse! Every job is fit for every human being. Personally, I think I might even be better than Chief's housekeeper at this."

"Panther knows only one woman – my maid!"

"Well, she and I have now fought for fifteen years: long enough to develop a special fondness for each other!"

"Please, Panther, have you never been married?"

"Me? A wife? Do you have one?"

"Not yet, but you must be well past thirty!"

"Thirty and seven, Private. But it never occurred to me."

He began to laugh and turned to Crane:

"Doctor! Shall we each take a wife?"

"*Spirea prunifolia*," Crane purred, writing.

"But Uncle was married!" Whatisit said.

Wolverine didn't reply immediately because he was holding a birch twig in his teeth:

"Yes. I had a wife. And a mother! They both died but live in my memory, revered and beloved. That is why I am anxious when someone talks lightly about these things or jokes about them. And when I hear the expression, 'Woman's work,' it seems to me that such a person does not remember his mother, sister, or wife. Or that he cannot respect anyone."

Whatisit lowered his head and reddened, but Wolverine kindly pressed him on the head.

"Forest Law, boy! Love, respect!"

There was a moment's silence, and then restless Panther looked out the window and shouted: "Look! Did I not say? The hoopoe just flew out of our box!"

"Perfect excuse to skip work and get wet again!" Wolverine laughed.

"Nah. I've had enough. But why don't we sing, as we usually do when it rains? Only let Wolverine accompany us on the violin; otherwise, I can't stand it. Crane! You start!"

"Let's wait until evening with that. My work isn't yet finished, but I will be done in an hour, and Crane will have done with his work by then, too. Meanwhile, we can sing informally, just like yellowhammers!"

And he started to sing *The Basket Weaver*. Whatisit and Panther joined in eagerly but without much talent. Crane raised his hands to his ears with some irritation and finally began to hurriedly fold his plants and clear the table.

"Panther! I beg you – you take the first note fine, then skip three notes higher. Stop it, or you'll completely screw up your ear."

"Who cares, as long as it is fun?" the prankster replied with a laugh. "I did that on purpose, just to rile you. And now there will be a concert!"

Whatisit enjoyed himself thoroughly. Song followed song: folk songs and art songs, jumping *krakowiaks* and *obereks*[24], sad Ukrainian *dumkas*[25] flowed from their full lungs until the walls of the hut shook, their eyes laughed, and their faces turned bright. Jake jumped on the stove; terrified, Stomper Junior rolled off the bed and hid in the corner, and beyond the fence, staring with amazement at the window, appeared the heads of Hathor and Patch Pelt. But the men sang and laughed with delight in turns.

"I don't mind the rain if we spend it like this," Whatisit said.

And he didn't mind it, even though it lasted a week. But how much he learned during that week! On the third day, he managed to weave a very decent fish trap basket, nearly as fast as Wolverine and with evenly spaced openings. And how many mysteries of the forest he had heard, how many atlas entries he had digested, how many pages he had read from Naumann, Brehm, and Taczanowski, and how many new songs he had learned, and Panther's entertaining riddles and parables. And how many times he had got wet and cold, without any harm to his health, and how close he had grown to his companions, how at home he felt among them, they so much older and yet so young in the spirit!

Until one day, he was honored: Wolverine sent him in his place to check on a few nearby fish baskets!

Wolverine and Panther, in the meantime, set up a carpentry workshop in the main room. They prepared birch planks for building bird boxes – that Panther built most artfully every winter.

"Take two airbags under your arms, or you will drown!" said the incorrigible scoffer to the boy as he left.

But Whatisit was no longer a novice. He bailed water out of the canoe and copied Wolverine's movements: slow and calculated. He

---

[24] *Krakowiak, oberek*: traditional dance styles

[25] *Dumka*: a slow, meditative song style from Ukraine

even made up for the absence of a pipe by holding a calamus stalk in his teeth.

He became a little confused on the waterway, got stuck with the canoe in the mud a couple of times, and a few traps escaped him, but he suffered no accident and turned home with a large sack of fish.

Suddenly, in a tight passage among thick bulrushes, he heard a human voice right next to him.

How much he had learned to live like a forest creature – his reaction now showed. With one powerful stroke of the oar, he pushed himself away with all his might – and fled. He only managed to catch a glimpse of a human head rising above the bush.

When he got back and entered the main room carrying the fish, he announced dramatically:

"I saw a man!"

And he said it in such a tone as if he were saying, "I rode a hippopotamus."

"Now what! On a rainy day like today? It has to be someone terminally ill looking for Crane. The footbridges must be all underwater again."

Crane grunted heavily and awaited his fate.

"Or was it a forest spirit? Did you see: did he have one eye or a pair? Was there a horn on his forehead?"

But Whatisit honestly reported:

"I missed a couple of traps and ran aground twice. But I brought the fish. There are pikes and ides."

"Ho ho! How wise and talkative it is, this material for forest folk".

Panther shook the fish into a bucket and began to prepare them. Whatisit was changing his clothes at the fire when the entrance door squeaked, and a deep voice greeted them.

Everyone stood up. Wolverine's eyes flashed as they shone only for his beloved birds, Crane smiled happily, and all replied in one voice:

"Welcome, Father!"

A huge peasant entered the room. He had a narrow face with an aquiline nose, a pair of gray, attentive eyes, a trimmed gray mustache, and thick, short, stubby hair on his head. He was a rich example of Sarmatian[26] strength and dignity. He wore a straw coat and clogs on his feet. At his hip, he carried a bag made from badger pelt; on the other side, a basket. He had a muzzle-loaded gun on his back, and an ax tucked into his leather belt. He first saluted the icon of the Virgin and said the usual prayer, *Salve Regina,* then began to undress and hang his things in Panther's alcove in what seemed his accustomed places, then turned to speak to them and answer their questions.

"I would have been with you, my sons, a long time ago. I don't care about the footbridges; I know passages that are always open! But my daughter gave me a granddaughter and then fell a little sick. So, I had to be their maid and nanny. And then there was the christening! But now all this is done, and I can stay with you until hay-harvest[27]. Grass, I see, is good this year, but fish are poor. The water is too high and now so much rain. But after the new moon, the weather will turn fine. I see you have a boy for company. Yours? Or a stranger?"

"My sister's son!" Wolverine replied.

"Light-eyed and black-haired, like the rest of you.

"Firm and wiry, he'll live long if he has any sense. And a clever fellow, too! When I called him, he took one look at me and took off. Yes, boy, always do as you did today whenever you meet a stranger in the wilderness. Who can tell a stranger from an enemy?"

The old man clearly felt at home. He peeked into the pantry, inspected the hall, and looked into the bedroom. Then he washed his hands, hung his coat by the stove to dry, and sat down with his bag at the table.

"I brought a housewarming gift for you – last year's tobacco. It came out surprisingly good. And this fiber for your netting, I

---

[26] Poles used to claim descent from an ancient tribe know to Romans as Sarmatians

[27] In Northern Europe, one harvests hay twice: first growth in late May and second in June or July.

collected these stalk by stalk. It will not tear, and it will not rot. And this – do you have such a thing?"

"A penduline nest!" Panther shouted.

"And this is for the doctor! I got that on the sandy cliffs above the river. Life was hard back in those days when one had to cut trees and hunt game with stone axes!"

"That's a delicious specimen," rejoiced Crane.

"Jasiek[28] has collected a lot of this and is keeping it all stashed away for the doctor. There are these blades, and shells, and whole pots!"

"What treasures!"

"Depends for whom! It feels nice to please another man. Like I was once pleased by an ensign's rifle! You did not find it, by any chance?"

They shook their heads. It was the old man's mania: locating gun caches hidden at the time of the Uprising.

Panther received a pair of leather sandals, and the old man took the rest of his haul straight into the pantry.

"Magda stuffed it full of eggs and other goods. She says the lapwing eggs will bore you soon. And now, give me some work and tell me your news!"

And the stories began. The old man set about tying nets, and they did their work.

Before dinner, Whatisit sneaked out behind Panther to look after the animals and asked:

"Is this the famous Odrowąż? And who is he?"

"Sage of sages in all forest matters. He built this hut with us and taught us everything we know. For him, there are no secrets here."

"What a man! He seems to have stepped right out of a Matejko[29]!"

"His ancestors were retainers of Wolverine's great-grandfathers once, and all this land and water belonged to his family.

---

[28] Jasiek /ya-shek/ Johnny

[29] A noted figure painter

And so it continued until the catastrophe[30]. This Odrowąż was in the Uprising with Wolverine's uncle, saved him from death and exile in Siberia, and carried him over the border. Wolverine's family literally forced him to accept a farmstead as a reward. He has a farm, a manor house, a daughter who is as charming as there is in the land, a son-in-law – a bit gruff, but a very decent man – a Szczepanski, and Jasiek – who is their son, his grandson. And now a newborn granddaughter, still unknown to me. Every summer, they spend several weeks with us because they mow hay in the clearings, as much as strength allows them, and in this, we help them. The old man, as long as he has free time, stays with us. And in winter, he looks after our refuge."

When the animals came called by the bugle, Odrowąż looked them over carefully, picked off ticks that Panther had not noticed, praised the foal, noticed a leak in the roof of the shed, and immediately repaired it with rushes, and returned to the hut. He then looked around, scented, and then said to Wolverine:

"The weather will be fine tomorrow, and since the water is high, we can fish in the reed."

"Uncle, can I come, too?" Whatisit asked.

"Come-sham. You will stay ashore with me and hoe potatoes," Panther said. "Who lives by the pot, works by the pot."

Whatisit was silent, obedient to the forest hierarchy, but tried to figure out how to do both: get the hoeing done and take part in the fishing expedition. As soon as they cleared the dishes, he grabbed the hoe and, despite the rain, ran to the vegetable garden. He returned in triumph before evening and found only Crane in the hut.

"I did the whole patch! I should be free tomorrow!"

"And that's exactly what Panther wanted!"

"Where are the others?"

"They paddled off to check how high the water is. They should be back soon. Why don't you fetch some water from the spring?"

---

[30] The 1863 uprising

The two soon returned and busied themselves with a bizarre basket that Wolverine had brought down from the attic.

"It looks like a flycatcher, those things made out of glass," Whatisit observed.

"Your uncle is a bit of a fishing virtuoso; you just wait and see."

"Will you take me with you?"

"Hmm... We'll have to see if you are fit for the job. Fishing is like a card game – a bit of a blind thing. Sometimes, your companion brings you luck, and sometimes – bad. We'd have to see which one you are!"

"I can already set baskets! And you promised to teach me to swim. And I know all those ditches by the lake. And I know what every fish is called."

"Even the squeaking fish?" Odrowąż smiled. "And you can probably catch a gudgeon?"

"No, I don't know any squeaking fish. Or any gudgeons. But if you tell me about that shotgun from the Uprising, I'll stay up till midnight listening."

"Well, young man, fairy tales are told after St. Martin's. Or else basking in the sun on a hot Sunday afternoon. But one goes to sleep at sundown and wakes up with the cranes, yes?"

The old man drank a cup of milk for supper and immediately went to sleep in Panther's alcove. Panther went to sleep in the attic.

Whatisit decided that he could not oversleep daybreak, but it was not the crane clarions that woke him but the monotonous singing of the old man's voice. It was Odrowąż, reciting the hours[31] at the icon, and it was the clearest morning in the world.

"Well, the rain-witch is done," said Panther cheerfully, hopping down from the attic and stopping to listen.

"*Oh, you invincible honeycomb of Samson,*" he sniggled. "It'll be a while before the old man is done," he whispered. "Come on, let me show you how to swim."

---

[31] "Canonical hours" (also known as "The Divine Office") are prayers prescribed for each hour of the day

The world had been washed crystal clear by the rain, and the eyes hurt from all its beauty. They flew almost naked to the spring, and Panther immediately dragged the boy into a deep spot so that he began to drown helplessly, desperately thrashing about in the water. Then he held him up and, enjoying himself, showed him various tricks until the boy calmed down.

"It's not as scary as it seems," said Whatisit when he got ashore after his first lesson.

"There is nothing really terrible here because even if you drown, you only die once!" said Panther philosophically, wiping himself with a handful of rush and pulling on dry clothes.

When they returned for breakfast, Odrowąż had just finished chanting his prayers and was getting dressed.

"Shall we go soon?" Whatisit asked.

"Fish are not land animals; they do not feed at dawn. They like the sun, insects. I guess an hour from now will be fine."

They did not rush. At breakfast, they began telling each other various fishing stories; then, they smoked a few pipes and finally set off.

Wolverine sat at the front of the canoe, his odd basket at hand. Odrowąż sat in the back, and Whatisit crouched in the middle.

"No point visiting the traps – the water's higher than the nets. Let's go straight for the reed!" said Wolverine, pulling on the oar.

Whatisit was surprised to see how agile, light, and responsive the canoe was in his hands. It went easily through tight passes and winding paths. And all the time, while paddling casually, the two men talked about the game and the forest, about summer and winter life, and about the wilderness. Only there was no mention of men.

Finally, they emerged onto the boundless expanse of submerged lowlands, covered with reeds and calamus. Here and there, like flower bouquets, stood beds of bulrushes, and water-plantains floated on the water.

Attentive eyes of ospreys watched them from above. They fell silent. The two men pocketed their pipes and got ready to work.

Odrowąż grasped his oar. Wolverine took his oar in his left hand, and with the basket in his right, he stood at the front of the boat, where there were only maybe two feet of space and where the slightest movement threatened a fall.

"May I help you row, master?" Whatisit said.

"Psst! Sit quietly!" snapped the old man, watching Wolverine. The canoe moved slowly, its bottom almost brushing against the grass.

Wolverine explored the depths with his eyes, and from time to time, he used his oar to point out the direction. Whatisit's eyes widened, but he saw and understood nothing.

Suddenly, Wolverine threw the basket into the water and stamped it with his foot while keeping the boat in place with his oar. It was a blink of an eye, but in that second, Odrowąż pushed his oar into the bottom, and Wolverine withdrew his leg, lifted the basket, and shook a large pike out onto the bottom of the boat.

"We managed! Good timing!" Odrowąż smiled, waving his oar and pushing at the water again in a slow motion.

"How is that? How did you know there was a fish there?" Whatisit asked, surprised by the performance.

"I watch for movement in the grass, where the big fish prey. I don't always get it," Wolverine replied calmly.

"It's a great skill, Uncle, to keep it all in balance: yourself, the basket, and the boat. How do you manage it?" the boy wondered. "I would have had a bath, for sure!"

"And I would have dunked more than once. This kind of fishing requires a good steersman. Look, over there, a fish is prowling!"

He fell silent, refocused his eyes, and, ready to throw and jump, signaled with his left hand again.

Hunting fervor seized Whatisit. He rose, trembling with expectation. Another throw of the basket, another tug of the boat. Again, the fisherman's astounding skill at keeping his balance. And again, the flash of the white belly of the fish as it fell from the basket into the boat.

"The kid brings us luck!" said Odrowąż. "Now, boy, collect the fish in a bag and sit down because I can't see a thing!"

"Goodness! That I could do this!" the boy sighed.

There were failed throws, too. At such times, Wolverine cursed under his breath: "Missed it!" and Odrowąż spat into the water. Other times, the catch was miserable: a trifle, a little thing. Then Wolverine murmured: "And it made a stir as if it dragged a train!" and Odrowąż commanded: "Throw it back! Such diddly!"

They zigzagged over the green waters, doubling back, circling, consumed with hunting fever, without care for time or exhaustion. The sun was warm, and sweat was running down Wolverine's face. The boy saw red flakes floating before his eyes from staring so intently at the glowing surface.

Finally, something black and the size of a plate fell from the basket to the bottom of the boat.

"Ha! A dead skull, phew!" Odrowąż spat. "Now, we won't catch a thing."

"A turtle!" Whatisit shouted. "I'll take it for a pet!"

Wolverine looked at the sky, put down the basket, and, sitting down in the middle of the boat, took out his pipe.

"It's midday. The fish went down. We can rest. There is a bag of bread under the bench, Whatisit. Have at it, my boy!"

The men smoked and looked about. Waterfowl circled overhead, screaming. Lapwings cursed and berated the intruders.

"The kid is lucky!" said Odrowąż suddenly, expressing a thought he had nursed for some time. "Perhaps because he comes from a lucky family, even if his surname is different. Yes, boy, you can bear yourself proudly. And you should know what makes a family's good fortune: the ability to risk everything without fear and to give generously without calculation. When the time comes to give, yours have given everything without hesitation or regret. Fools and egoists can't do that! To master this, you have to lose everything many times. Many times give everything away! My grandfather, who was in the Insurrection[32] with yours, told me that not a foal was left in your

---

[32] Judging by the age of Odrowąż, it has to be the insurrection of 1830 (or 1848)

family stable then, and the family had sold even their jacket buttons for the cause. And when my grandfather worried about it, yours said: 'Why are you frowning as if I have spent it on city girls? I gave it for the Commonwealth[33]. Here I have the receipt!' and he stroked the scar on his face."

Odrowąż pondered; the pipe had gone out. Then he murmured to himself:

"Commonwealth. The Worthy Lady! When the time comes, you remember to give her your all, too. That's the ticket!"

He put away his pipe, took up the oar, and pushed the boat.

"Let's try near the Cursed Tree: there are good ides there, and if we're lucky, a wels might come onto the shoal."

Wolverine shook his head.

"The bottom there is peat – too dark to see, and the water's cold. Let's cross the lake to the Flooded Lye!"

The hunt began again.

"Uncle," Whatisit asked. "Can I try it once? I can see the shapes of the fish at the bottom. I think I understand how you catch them. Let me try it!"

"Let him try it! It's shallow here; the bottom is clear. Let him take a dunk – the water is warm!" Odrowąż supported him.

"I won't fall! I can do it!"

"Just in case, take off your shirt and your clogs!" said Wolverine.

"But I feel that I can do it!" the boy insisted. "It only seems so difficult at first. Now, I understand how it is done."

Wolverine yielded his place and gave him the oar and the basket.

Whatisit stepped up to the edge, staggered, and steadied himself with his oar.

"You must balance carefully on both legs!"

"I know, I know. There, look."

---

[33] The Commonwealth (Res Publica) was the official name of the Polish state before 1795

"And raise the oar because you are keeping the canoe pinned in place!" Odrowąż commanded.

"Moment, moment... It seems so easy. Now!"

And just then, he lost his balance and fell headfirst into the water.

"Now what?" said Odrowąż calmly.

"Didn't I say to take your shirt off?" added Wolverine just as calmly.

The boy jumped to his feet and gasped. He was a bit scared but, above all, embarrassed. He scrambled into the canoe, and Wolverine, as if nothing had happened, fished out the oar, the basket, and the hat and went back to his place.

"Everything seems easy to the eyes. Easy to imagine and easy to say," said Odrowąż. "But that's normal. You will take a bath once or twice, and eventually, you will learn it. Then you will take a bath a few more times when you throw the basket. But you will learn it all in time as long as you keep trying and have a passion for fishing. In time, the boat will obey you, and the water, and the fish. If I can do it, so can you."

"Father, look to the left! There's something big slinking underwater!" Wolverine whispered.

He leaned forward, tensed, and leaped. He threw the basket and jumped himself at the same time. Water splashed beneath him and boiled violently in the basket. He did not lift it but dipped his arm in through the opening at the top.

"There he is! A cannibal!" he exclaimed.

Odrowąż turned the canoe around. Whatisit, electrified, also jumped into the water and threw himself at the basket.

After some moments of struggle, Wolverine raised the prey, Odrowąż supported the basket with his oar, and Whatisit pulled it into the boat.

"A bearded wels! What a monster! Keep him under the basket, or he'll pop right out! Well, now, home! What a fairy-tale hunt!"

"Uncle! Why didn't you take off your shirt and your clogs before jumping?" Whatisit laughed when, both wet through, they clambered back into the boat.

"Because you didn't advise me to!" Wolverine smirked.

They paddled energetically to warm up, and Odrowąż knew such shortcuts and such secret passages that they soon arrived home.

Wolverine shouted, but no one answered him; only Jake flickered among the branches and complained that he was hungry. The mare spoke, too, and even the apathetic Hathor observed that it was well past midday.

Yet, the hut was empty. There was a note on the table from Crane that a peasant had come for him to help his sick wife and that he would only be back at night. But Panther had not reported anything about his whereabouts. Wolverine shook his head.

"He's either playing a trick on someone or fallen asleep in the wood. Come on, let's get to work! Light the fire, boy, and change your clothes! I will feed the householders and milk the cow. The fish need to be prepared immediately because it's hot. There, Jake, a few nuts for you, enough of your begging!"

Odrowąż did not care about dinner or rest. He dragged the wels onto the grass, clubbed it, and took off the mucus with ash. Whatisit jumped to help him.

"Panther said that he once found Jewish phylacteries in the stomach of a catfish. He said the wels had swallowed a barber who had drowned."

"And digested the slippers but not the phylacteries! Ho, ho, Panther has also seen the king of serpents – the one with the diamond on its head that makes him invisible? He uses this pebble a lot himself!"

"He also said that he gave an angry snake a linden twig to bite. And, well, the twig grew as thick as a peg. Could this be true?"

"Everything is true as long as someone believes it!"

"He promised to show it to me, but we haven't seen a viper since."

"Ha, my boy! The way things usually work is that when you come across a viper, no willow twig will be to hand!"

Wolverine brought them milk and bread; it was too late to cook lunch.

Then they sat about preparing the fish and were nicely winded when Panther finally appeared, carrying a delicious-looking green-headed drake.

"I was by the bees on Pine Hill!" he said to distract attention away from the topic of his absence. "Songbirds are moving in! And on my way back, I look, and what do I see? A goshawk takes off from a pine tree, and something glistens on the branch. He had brought the duck there and began to eat it. There, look, marks on the neck. But I see you three did well, too! Chief took a wels in the basket! Respect! Well, master fishermen, let me take over from you; you two smoke your pipes to chase away the damned mosquitoes!"

Odrowąż stood up, inspected the drake, and, puffing on his pipe, slowly said:

"With the wels was a bit of a miracle, too. There we were, happily paddling along. Then, suddenly, we look, and what do we see? *Bang!* – a goshawk dropped something into the boat. And it was this very wels."

"Ho, ho! A goshawk? Not a cormorant?"

"No. A goshawk. Probably the same one that caught your water duck."

And Odrowąż pointed to where the bird's neck had been torn by a hook.

Whatisit did not understand it, and he looked from one to the other until Panther burst out laughing and made it all clear.

"Oh, and he spotted it! Nothing escapes these elderly eyes. I told you, Private, a sage of sages, our teacher is."

"Well, then you will tell us how you got it? In a lake with a camouflage net on your head?"

"No! From the shore, at the Rainbow Bridge. Ducks feed there in flocks. I string a bunch of tadpoles on hooks and set them floating on the water, and I lie down and wait. And if I tie the strings to my toe, I can even take a nap. When a drake takes the bait, he will let me know by – as they say – pulling my leg!"

Wolverine prepared the fish in silence and did not say a word. Panther understood the silence, for, after a while, he began to justify himself.

"Actually, I thought that a pike might catch, but these ducks are so greedy that they shovel in mud, totally oblivious. And those drakes... they are the bad guys. I mean thoroughly rotten. They don't help with building nests, treat their ladies poorly, don't look after the little ones. Hooligans! Yes, Chief? They sleep around and would probably drink, too, if anyone distilled vodka on the lake."

"If you mean to be a missionary to the ducks, you won't improve their habits this way."

"Ha! One sinner less, in any case."

"The others won't acquire virtue but will only learn to avoid further missionary work!"

"It's all ready!" said Panther, straightening up from his work. "Now, let's have the good doctor cook us the wels' head in soup – and the fish into the oven! And to divert Chief from his displeasure over the drake, I will report a discovery I made today. Should I talk?"

"Prattle, prattler!" Odrowąż laughed.

"I found a duck's nest in a tree. By God's grace – on a pine tree!"

Wolverine shrugged. Whatisit laughed.

"It happens," confirmed Odrowąż. "I'll even tell you how the duck leads her litter out from such a nest because I have seen it myself once: she took each one in her beak, carried it down to the ground, and placed it on its back, with its legs up. And all lay calmly on their backs like that until she brought down the last one. Then she turned each of them over, set them on their feet, and they followed her single file to water."

Nobody denied him, and Whatisit began to ask that Panther should lead him to the nest right away.

"We'll go on Sunday. And now, Panther, clean up the house because Crane won't be back until dark. Besides, he served us well his month. It's your turn."

Panther loaded himself with fish and went to the hut, singing:

Oy dey dee dee, oy dey dee dee,
They put me in misery!
Oy dey dee dee, misery!
They set me to mending sieves!

Forest expeditions, wanderings in the wilderness, hunts, and adventures – all were over now. Now came a long month of cooking and cleaning.

He was sad at the thought for some time but soon came upon some happy thought, for he began to smirk and whistle and took up his work with great panache.

TOIL

The sun took full power over the earth now. Evening lights barely died down into an amber glow in the west when, fast on their heels, an opal glow appeared in the east, and the world woke to life again after the briefest of nights. Leaves and flowers were in full, lush bloom, the carpets on the forest floor exploded with color, and birds were feeding their young. The honey scent of flowery glades rose up towards the sky and intoxicated swarms of bees, stirring them to work. Orioles, the last spring arrivals, sounded everywhere like silver flutes. It was not full summer yet, but the hard work of growing flowers into fruits and raising the next generation was in full swing.

Wild strawberries glowed red in sunny spots under spruce; in the shadows, the first great bellflowers sprung up, and the meadows turned red with catchflies.

Panther digested all these signs as he sat chained to the hut, waiting for something that would free him from cooking and cleaning.

Peeling potatoes, cleaning, washing linen, chopping wood, he always looked towards the footbridges that led to distant human settlements.

Until one evening, as he was hanging fish to smoke, he heard a rustling in the brushwood, and a teenage boy appeared in the clearing.

"Jasiek! Where's your mother?" Panther shouted, fighting a great urge to make a double flip.

"She's coming with my father and sister. Because you know, we have a baby in the family now, Marynka! Where's grandpa?"

"In the woods. You're damn late this year!"

"We had to wait for my aunt to come back. She had taken a vow to go on pilgrimage to Calvary. We couldn't leave the house unattended! Do you know? This year, I'm going to mow!"

The boy stood tall as he said that, proud that he finally deserved the honor of the work. He carried a scythe and a rake on his shoulder, and his black eyes stared boldly at the world from under his straw hat. He carefully hung the scythe under the roof, got rid of his bag and his linen jacket, and, thirsty from the heat, went to the bucket with water.

Two others came into the clearing: a slender, tall woman with a child on her arm and her husband, a swarthy man, laden with scythes, rakes, a cradle, and bast bags.

"Praise be to Jesus!" the woman greeted Panther, smiling an angelic smile.

"For ages and ages!" replied Panther. "Well, hello, Mother! I've been awaiting your arrival! The meadows are all ruddy, ready to be cut, and you're not here!"

"But we have one worker more now!" she exclaimed cheerfully.

Panther took off his hat and bowed low with a broad gesture.

"Father, sir; Mother, ma'am! I ask humbly for your girl's hand in marriage!"

"Why, ever so gladly. There, take her right away!" she laughed, handing him the baby.

Panther took her in his arms.

"Hello, beautiful bride! I take these people as my witness that I hereby take you to wife! May I now kiss my bride? I see you copied your mother well. Your eyes are like periwinkles, and your hair is dark. Though, I see, we may have to wait for the braids and the teeth! Please, all come in. I will now weave a nest for our baby oriole."

Briefly, the new arrivals moved in as they did every summer. The woman with the baby took the alcove; Odrowąż's bedding was taken to the entrance hall. They laid plenty of hay in the attic for Whatisit and Szczepanski, and Szczepanska took over the kitchen.

Panther played with the child, teasing his mother and beaming with joy that he was at last free of his arduous duties after only ten days.

He had had the same luck every year. Barely his month of service began when Odrowąż came to mow the meadows, and Szczepanska took over the house.

Almost immediately, the three of them set out to inspect the meadows, and soon, they returned together, hooting in the forest.

Whatisit soon became acquainted with Jasiek and began to press him about the scythe.

"How is that!" he bothered Wolverine. "He's only thirteen and mowing, and I'm sixteen."

"Ho, ho, I'm thirty-seven and only today got married," Panther laughed. "I got your granddaughter, yes, yes. It was a very fast decision. A shotgun wedding, you might say. I had to hurry, lest Crane beat me to it!"

"And you left her in the care of your mother-in-law!"

"Yes, but I will do her share of mowing for her. Whatisit, you will get a scythe, do not lament – I have a spare one. And I will lend it to you because I owe you for making the excellent suggestion of marriage. A capital idea, my boy, I mean it!"

And to emphasize how serious he was, he ran into the woods, bleated like a goat, and shouted: "Well, boys? Jasiek, Whatisit? Who is chasing Panther?"

The boys gave him a chase.

"He'll lead them for an hour, hide somewhere, and they will look for him till evening," Odrowąż laughed.

Indeed, when Wolverine and Crane returned to the hut, they found Panther with the "wife" in his arms and Jake on his shoulder. He was just a little out of breath.

"And the boys?" asked Wolverine.

"Looking for Panther in the wilderness."

Wolverine and Crane welcomed Szczepanska, but Odrowąż did not let them talk too long.

"Sharpen your scythes while it's still daylight. We have to start tomorrow before daybreak."

Now each took an anvil, a hammer, and a scythe, and the careful, delicate hammering began.

"Hey, flowers, herbs! Sweetgrass, fescue, vernal grass – and who can know all your names? This is to your death! We sharpen these sabers for your death!" said Wolverine, as if with regret and so softly that only his friend Crane heard him.

"One dies so that another may live. But the root remains in the ground, like the immortal soul!" Crane replied. *"Ring, ring, ring!"* their hammers rang on steel as if they were giving a signal to attack, and Odrowąż, like a regimental commander, inspected each scythe like a saber blade – against the sun – and either found it worthy or ordered it redone. For Whatisit, he tapped out the blade himself.

Just then, the boys came running out of the forest, breathless and hot like horses, but amused and laughing, carrying Panther's hat and clogs in triumph.

"We hunted like bloodhounds, but Panther is faster than any hound!" cried Whatisit.

"I threw you a clog and a hat and watched as you ran with your noses to the ground. But I was sitting on Beggar Woman, low above the ground, and then I jumped down and returned to the hut. You recruits are hunters-punters!"

Odrowąż nodded to Whatisit and led him out into the clearing.

"Here is your scythe, young man. See how it is set. Here is the blade mounted on the haft and fastened with an iron ring and a wooden wedge, like the letter L. Though it may sometimes happen that one may mount it upright, and then the mowers are called scythemen and mow enemy heads. The instrument thereby becomes ennobled, so one must honor it and keep it in respect, the way soldiers keep their swords – because no one knows when and for what purpose they may be needed. Do you understand?[34]"

"I understand, Father!" Whatisit replied, involuntarily straightening up like a private before his commander.

"And that is proper. Once you learn to cut grass, I'll show you what is done when you mount it upright. Now, then, my boy, take it in your hands so, stand straight, legs apart, give your arms a proper swing, and with each swing, in the end, raise the tip up slightly with your hand, like so. Do not swing your arms like a windmill; only turn your whole upper body at the midriff, like so. Well, then, try it!"

Whatisit took up his position and began to swing.

"Not bad, young man. You are a quick learner!" the old man encouraged him. "Release your shoulder and do not slouch. Easy, easy, leave nothing standing, and raise the tip at the end. And when you feel it is going dull, tap it again. Like this! And to keep your motion steady, you can whistle to yourself: *Hey, sharp, hey, sharp, hey, sharp are our scythes.*"

"And when I set it straight up, then it will be '*Bartosz, Bartosz, do not lose heart*[35],'" sang Whatisit.

A smile formed in the furrows of the face of old Odrowąż.

"So, you know the song? Surely, your mother has taught you? Well, thank God! You'll turn out well."

"*God will bless us, save our fatherland,*" Jasiek continued the song.

"Master!" Odrowąż said to Wolverine. "Maybe these young men will see justice finally done and our fatherland returned to us."

---

[34] Odrowąż is referring to the peasant batallions who fought against Russia 1794–1795, using vertically mounted scythes for hand to hand combat: a Polish reader would understand this reference while a Russian censor may not

[35] Bartosz Glowacki commanded a unit of Scythe-men during the Kosciuszko uprising

"Maybe they, or maybe their children or their grandchildren. But there will be justice. That day must come," replied Wolverine seriously.

"Ring, ring, ring!" rang the steel of scythes. The boys cut swaths of grass before them furiously. They had to be called twice to supper. Afterward, they threw themselves sprawled on the fresh-cut hay.

"I'd like to go to America!" Jasiek said. "Father says our boys are organizing there, like an army, and will come and whip the Moscovites and the Germans."

"And in my school – they say that there is a secret military organization. That they practice at night. They have ranks and secret signs, and pseudonyms. But this is all a big secret, and they do not invite us, the younger boys, for fear that we may prattle. And for talking about this is only one punishment: death. The one in the lead is called Raven, and only two know which one he is."

"I'd like to be called 'Arrow.'"

"And I – 'Aurochs'!"

"Sleep, you puppies!" cried Panther from his bed. "You're barely out of your swaddling clothes and want to talk conspiracy? What warriors! Aurochs! Arrows! Afraid to go fetch water at night and barely out of the gate, he loses his way! Mouth ready to fight for fatherland, but in need – can't do a thing!"

"We will yet see when the time comes," Whatisit said boldly, and they began to whisper with Jasiek.

They didn't realize when they fell asleep and were mighty embarrassed when Panther began to pull them out of the hay by their feet, shouting that the mowers were waiting.

The morning was barely a pearly gray, and the sun had not yet risen as they followed Odrowąż in a line, leaving a trail in the dew. The old man was reciting his prayers in an undertone, and everyone was silent.

"No breakfast?" Whatisit asked Jasiek.

"Mowing goes smoother with dew. When the sun rises, Mother will bring us breakfast. Then we will sleep at noon."

Odrowąż led his group to a wide glade in the forest, crossed himself, and laid the first row. Behind him, Wolverine came, and they stretched out one by one, slicing straight lines and laying flat the grass.

Big deal! Whatisit thought, swinging impatiently right behind Crane, who scythed lightly, easily, as if without the least bit of effort. Thus came Odrowąż to the end of the clearing and, turning around, looked at their work.

"Why are you boys so hasty? You are too greedy for fame. Look, you leave stalks standing in places! Go slowly; easy does it, or you won't last until noon!"

"We won't last? No way! This is not hard at all!" Whatisit replied, sliding his hat off his forehead and stopping to sharpen his scythe.

"We will see how easy it is... tomorrow!" said Panther. "You wave your arms like a windmill, and your swath is clear for all to see afterward, it's so uneven. If you swing like this today, you won't be able to move your arms tomorrow. And when sharpening a scythe, do not look for thrush's nests, but watch what you're doing, or your blade won't last till noon!"

But Whatisit, in his arrogance, shrugged his shoulders and said:

"Please, Panther, you are always after me!"

They mowed a swath, and then another, and then another until Szczepanska appeared with breakfast. Then they rested in the shade for the brief moment of their meal and went right back to work. The sun began to warm up; they mowed. They were stripped down to their undershirts, sweat ran down their faces and hands, and their cheeks burned with heat. No one spoke; their lungs worked like bellows, their lips parched with thirst.

When they started cutting a new swath, there was scarcely time to wipe their faces with their sleeves as Odrowąż pushed forward and led the way.

And finally, he looked at the sun and stopped.

"Eleven o'clock!" he said. "Now we lie down, sleep, then eat a little and rest until the heat eases. It's a long time until the evening dew!"

At his call, his obedient army stopped working and leaned their scythes up against each other in tripods, like rifles.

It turned out that everyone had seen something while mowing. Wolverine now went back to a bush to collect a nest. Crane got busy digging up a root, Szczepanski cutting off an oddly-bent birch branch; Odrowąż sawing a fungus off a tree. And Panther went rooting for wild strawberries.

Only the boys threw themselves on the ground and fell asleep immediately.

They didn't hear the lunch bugle. It proved impossible to wake them up.

"Let them sleep," decided Wolverine. "We'll bring them food here. They are exhausted."

When the boys woke up, it was evening. They jumped up and looked around: they were all alone in the mowed clearing.

Next to them stood a clay pot with food and a jug of water.

"Sweet Jesus!" Jasiek shouted. "We slept the whole day!"

"And how do we face Panther now," said Whatisit morosely.

They fell to thinking.

"Damn, it's shameful!" Jasiek whispered, close to crying.

"It'd be better not to show up at all."

"And how?"

"Run away!"

"And?"

"Settle somewhere on our own, in the forest, on some inaccessible island in the bog."

"You can! I can't. My mother will kill me," said Jasiek seriously. "Unless I tell her first."

"Then go and tell her."

Jasiek ran off, and Whatisit began to compose his plan for this Robinson Crusoe existence: they would shelter in trees and eat berries and bird eggs. He was just warming up to the idea when Jasiek came running.

"Mother says Grandpa left an order for us to catch crayfish for supper. They left us here deliberately to do that."

"Maybe that's not true?"

"My mother said it, did you hear me? Mother wouldn't lie for a mountain of gold!" Jasiek was indignant and ready for a fight if Whatisit objected.

He brought nets and bags with him, and they made their way to the lake.

"Your bones hurt?" Whatisit asked.

"Nah! Not at all!" Jasiek muttered without much conviction. "Well, a bit."

The water refreshed them, and soon they were thrilled and delighted because they were catching a lot of crayfish, and they forgot their shame and weariness.

When they returned to the hut with their catch, the others were already back from mowing and fiercely tapping out their scythes. And it seemed as if no one had noticed their absence. During supper, Panther groaned about how his arms and legs hurt, and the others nodded agreement that theirs did too.

"We work like Poles, not like peasants[36]," said Odrowąż. "And, truth be told, even peasants will feel sore at the beginning. The only remedy is to bathe and rest and get over it. We will forget the pain in a few days! If only this heat does not bring rain."

They went to bed right away, and Whatisit dreamed that raindrops drummed on the roof and that they were allowed to stay in bed until noon.

But it was only a dream, and it seemed to him that he had rested only a moment when Panther began to shake him. A crystal clear dawn meant it was time to work.

Whatisit got up and, with a crash, fell right back on his pile of hay, overpowered by terrible pain in all his muscles, joints, and tendons. He felt tears welling up in his eyes. He felt nauseous.

---

[36] In the 19th century in the Polesie region (today's Byelarus) the landlord class was often Polish (Polish-speaking and Catholic) and the peasants (Byelorussian-speaking and Orthodox) used the words "Pole" and "finer folk" interchangeably, to mean the spoiled rich, while referring to themselves as "peasants" or "locals"

"I can't move!" he wailed. "Leave me alone! I think I am paralyzed!"

"Paralyzed? That's unlikely! You exhausted yourself – you're unused to manual work. Now get up! It's important to keep using your muscles, or else you will be down a week. Each of us is feeling a bit sore, but the feeling will go away as we work, I promise! Gather your strength and get up! Look at Jasiek, bent over double and crooked but moving."

"I'm not moving! I can't!" Whatisit cried.

"Come on, you cry-baby! We'll call you Strong-in-the-Mouth! How's that?" Panther sneered and went down the ladder.

Whatisit smarted as if slapped on the cheek and, making an extraordinary effort, got off his pile of hay.

He would rather die than stay behind. He would die but with pride. The pain contorted his face, but with a great effort, he managed to climb down the ladder. Everyone else was stiff too, and the sight of it comforted him.

"You feel broken, too?" he asked Jasiek.

"Don't ask. Everything hurts. I don't even want to mention it because if I do, my mouth gets sour just from thinking about it. The others won't show they are in pain, so we'll look weak if we do. Mother says to bathe in the river. She says cold water helps calm the pain. Let's go!"

Whatisit dragged himself to the stream and, indeed, the water helped enough that he was able to walk to the clearing without much agony. But as he stood in line with his scythe, he thought he would faint at the first stroke.

Fortunately, no one hurried him. They mowed small clearings now, little patches of meadow in the nooks and crannies of the forest: there was no need to keep up with the whole advancing row. Wolverine mowed behind him and took it slow. When, after a while, he stopped to sharpen his blade, he said:

"My dear boy! You will now understand the peasant's toil and honor his work because you yourself have endured it. You think you're learning to mow, but that's not so. You're learning how to perform physical labor and how to respect it. Tomorrow, you will find the work easier, but you will treasure the memory of this pain forever."

Whatisit saw that they were alone and said softly:

"But, uncle, why do we exhaust ourselves like this so that Odrowąż's cattle may have hay?"

Wolverine smiled.

"And why did you first look around before asking the question? Do you maybe feel that it is a shameful thought? If you feel this work is for nothing, stop."

"Well, no – but it really is."

"Hm... I see what you mean. So I should perhaps explain. This is how it is here, my boy, here in the forest. Here, we work for the sake of work. We work because we like the work and because we like the results it brings. It isn't all that important to me whose cattle benefit from my work as long as it gives sustenance to another creature. In winter frost, this hay will give warmth and strength to animals that had worked for man all summer. Cows and horses are man's best and never-failing friends. So when you rake in these sweetgrasses and fescues, these sweet-peas and timothies think of that: an animal will be grateful to you. And is it our animal? Or theirs? Let those wonder who do not understand that only our soul is our own, and everything else is merely rented. Merely temporary."

They fell silent, and only the grass fell with a soft rustle as he mowed, and Whatisit became ashamed of his words.

"Hop hop! Breakfast!" Szczepanska shouted. "What? How are you, young things? The joints still moving?"

"Yes, Mother, the pain is gone!" Jasiek replied.

"Hey, by tomorrow, we won't be able to keep up with these boys," said Crane.

"Tomorrow, we will send them to build haystacks."

"The weather willing. We must finish all the haystacks by Saturday. The hay will be golden like saffron! But we must hurry because by the full moon it will rain again. And God forbid that the Deaf Saint will hear us!"

"What deaf saint?" Whatisit asked.

"Why, the patron of rain. The Good Lord commanded him: "go where they sow." But he misheard and thought Lord God had said: "go where they mow." And since then, as soon as he hears the sharpening of scythes, he comes and pours!"

At midday, Crane called for Whatisit to help him dig some roots and led him to a clearing which they had already mowed. They sat down on the drying hay with a crunching sound, and Crane said:

"I can see you have a fever, my boy, and it could get worse. Take this powder and take your shirt off, and I will rub you with this extract. If you neglect your health, you'll be out for weeks."

"What a kind doctor you are!" Whatisit whispered, touched. "Thank you! I'm actually not feeling all that well!"

And he subjected himself to the massage patiently, then fell asleep in the shade, covered with fragrant hay, and he woke up refreshed as if born again.

At lunchtime, he found out from Jasiek that he, too, had been given the same cure.

"The Doctor's an angel!" Jasiek said. "Two years ago, he saved my life! I was down with typhoid. He watched over me day and night because my mother was too ill herself to get up!

"Come on, boys," Odrowąż commanded. "You start raking the hay now but try to keep up with us. Day after tomorrow, we'll build a haystack."

The change of tempo gave them relief, their arms now moved differently, and the motions weren't quite so monotonous.

But chiefly, the boys were glad to work under the command of their "mother."

Everyone called her "Mother Szczepanska." Or just "Mother."

For all these men, she was the symbol of nurturing care and, at the same time, charm and grace. So they gave her this name both to honor and comfort her.

In the morning, then, Whatisit took the cradle on his back, Jasiek took the rakes, "mother" took the "bride-to-be" in her arms, and they went to work.

They hung the cradle in the shade of a tree. Covered with cheesecloth to shelter her from insects, the child fell asleep, and soon the clearing resounded with song and laughter.

Whatisit learned quickly how the hay is first gathered into long rows, then raked up sideways and lifted on the rake high above the head and piled in huge heaps. They gathered the hay, and Mother arranged it. They raced against each other, excited, amused, and laughing, even though the heat burned their cheeks and sweat streamed down their backs. And when they finished a heap, the boys rested a little, taking turns to drink from a jug of water, while Mother went back to her child's cradle hanging on a branch, held her daughter, fed her and kissed her, and put her to sleep, rocking her cradle and humming to her.

The child was easy-going. She did not fuss, and as if she understood that they were too busy to play with her, she slept obediently.

Sometimes they heard the sound of the sharpening of scythes, and in the evening, Panther turned up, as he said, to woo his betrothed. He took the child in his arms and carried her around, showing her flowers and butterflies, and making up all kinds of nonsensical stories.

Mother would then leave them and go back to the hut.

She was a skilled housekeeper and somehow seemed to find sufficient time to get everything done in time. The hut was cleaned and decorated with flowers; floors were washed, linen washed, dinner cooked, and the cattle looked after. When the mowers returned from work, they could rest because even the firewood had been chopped. Their sheets were clean, and the woman was smiling, radiant with inner happiness; and she had a good word, a joke, and attention for everyone.

Whatisit's soul, tainted by the city, by the company of his schoolmates, and by fashionable books, now experienced shame and regret. How bold, disrespectful, and contrary he had been in his dealings with his own mother! And with the professor!

God, he suddenly froze in terror. Has Panther forgotten about the professor? Might he not joke about that business in front of

Szczepanska, and what would she think of him then? Or of the poems he wrote to Wanda Albersonówna, a girl he often passed in the staircase of their building, a disheveled, red-haired pension girl.

He had bragged to his friends about her glances and giggles. He often spoke of debauchery and mocked "timid virgins." Whatisit would not dare to speak to Jasiek that way, a boy with whom he had a different sort of friendship, more innocent, and with whom he now planned various daring trips and shared fantasies of great future adventures.

Their most immediate goal was to obtain a forest name and be accepted in the ranks of the forest folk.

"Your name isn't bad; they call you 'Jasiek,' but as for me, they never call me anything but 'Whatisit'!"

"You have to accomplish something memorable. Find some great prize. So that they might call you by some name related to that, like 'Fox.'"

"'Fox' would be great. But how do we capture one?"

"When we finish with the hay, let's go look for a fox nest. Chief will be happy because he abhors foxes. Or let's find an eagle's nest! But it's probably too late for it this summer. Oh, to be called 'Eagle!' Wouldn't that be great?"

These daydreams were put paid to by sleep, but perhaps they continued as dreams because Szczepanski or Pantera would nudge the boys and admonish them at night:

"Goodness gracious, what racket they make in their sleep, like frogs in mud!"

The boys froze silent, frightened.

"My goodness! What if they call us 'Frog' or 'Barker'!" Whatisit whispered.

When they amassed a dozen or so hay heaps, Panther came to their clearing, riding on Patch Pelt.

"Private Whatisit! You are now promoted from infantry to cavalry!"

"Aha, the haystacks go up tomorrow," Jasiek rejoiced.

"No! Not tomorrow! Today! We must gather all this hay by noon and then pile it up. By order of father Odrowąż, because he says it'll rain tomorrow!"

"Oh, that's great!" the boys blurted out.

"What's great? That the hay will get wet? Oy oy oy, you'll make poor farmers with only your hats for a barn! Well, get moving now, boys! You take the rope, Jasiek, and you, Whatisit, hop on the old nag! You don't need me to bring you a stool, do you? You start with the farthest heaps."

"And, Mother, I must now say hello to my future wife!"

He took the child in his arms and began to dance with her, singing:

Rain is falling, rain is falling,
Love me, wife, with all your faith!

"Oh no, son-in-law, son-in-law! Do not call the rain! And do go easy on your wife! Better help the boys," Szczepanska laughed.

"True! Whatisit probably does not know whether the horse pulls hay with its neck or tail!"

"There are some who only pull with their mouths!" Whatisit growled, but Panther only laughed.

"You are one saucy private! I will baptize you 'Shotgun Mouth'! You will see! Come on, boys, let's go!"

"Whatisit is in his rights to talk back when you make such cruel fun of him," said Szczpanska in his defense. "He's been doing the work of two, and his work is going well! He's a wonder!"

"Well, if 'Mother' comes to 'Wonder's' defense, I'll leave him alone. Now, Whatisit Wonder, we start with the furthest pile. Now stop! Hey ha!" Then he wrapped the rope around the pile of hay, tied it with a knot, attached it to the horse's harness, and slapped the mare on its hindquarters with the flat of his hand.

"Now go! Try to follow flat ground and take it to the other end of the clearing."

Patch Pelt clenched, pulled, and shifted, and the mound of hay slid on. Jasiek and Panther walked along, each to one side. When they had brought the first three heaps, Panther left the boys to it and set about collecting willow branches to build the platform for the haystack. By the lunchtime bugle, all the work was done, and the boys returned to the cottage riding on Patch Pelt.

"It'll rain for sure! Grandpa's never wrong. We will go on the lake, catch crayfish and pike, we will swim and dive!" they rejoiced like little kids.

Odrowąż kept looking at the sky and did not let them rest. They had hardly swallowed their food, and he was already ordering them about: "Hurry, hurry! Pitchforks, rakes! Everybody! Leave the cottage as it is. And fast, or we won't finish in time!"

They all ran back to the fields. The platform of the haystack was finished; the old man stood in the middle laying the hay and hurrying them to gather it fast.

Again, Whatisit found himself an inept recruit. While all the others were picking up huge piles of straw on their pitchforks, so huge that they bent under their weight and then tossed them expertly overhead onto the stack, his hay kept falling off and scattering, and he often found that his upraised pitchfork reached the top of the stack empty, and he had to gather it all again. He was close to tears, and he felt faint with all the wasted effort.

And his companions were so eager, they were in such a rush, they had so much work to do that no one minded him or bothered to mock him, but also no one stopped to show him how to do it properly. They worked in silence, sensing the storm gathering in the heavens and already darkening the horizon.

The haystack grew as the heaps were added to it one after another. Now it was so high that they set a ladder against it and drove a pole into the stack between its rungs. Szczepanski sat astride it, took their loads, and passed them up higher. They worked feverishly, without a moment's break, until Odrowąż's voice was heard from above: "We're good! I'm setting the roof. You straighten the sides and plait a rope. We are no longer afraid of rain."

And the rain had already come. The wind had risen, driving dark clouds over the forest, and the treetops roared like battle drums.

The men worked furiously.

"Now the rope! Just like this!" cried Jasiek, out of breath, as he fell with Whatisit against the haystack and began to pull loose strands of hay and feed them to Szczepanska, who twisted them into a rope.

The others, too, picked up the loose hay which had fallen by the wayside and passed them on, calling hoarsely: "There, take this! Here! Take this!"

Now the whirlwind began to grapple with them, tear at the hay, and tug at their loads.

"Pass the rope!" Odrowąż shouted.

He was given two ropes and crossed them at the top. They buried the ends in the haystack, and the old man slid down to the ground.

Then he crossed himself and made some signs in the air in the direction of the clouds.

"God was pleased by our industry. He has given us time and strength to accomplish the task. Praise and glory be to him."

"Forever and ever. Amen!" they replied.

And they all stood there for a while, leaning on their pitchforks, gasping for breath, and turning their faces to the wind. And just then, the heavens opened up, and lightning flashed in the clouds.

That evening, as Whatisit tried to pick up his spoon, he found he lacked the strength to close his hand around it. He was ashamed and wondered if anyone else was experiencing such exhaustion. But they were all chatting, and only Crane seemed to notice, nodded knowingly, and beckoned him secretly into the bed-chamber.

He told him to change and put on his nightshirt, then massaged his arms and hands. The boy was falling asleep, fatally weary, and only whispered: "Oh, ooh, ooh! Oh, if only I could have the strength to work with you again tomorrow! Oh, if only I could." And he fell asleep. Crane covered him and said softly to the entering Wolverine: "The spirit of the forest has won. Our soul now rises inside him."

"Thanks be to God! It will give him joy," replied Wolverine, stroking the dark hair of the sleeping youth gently.

It drizzled the whole next day, but Odrowąż ordered the men out to mow, so the boys did not have a break. But mowing wet grass was easier, and the heat did not overwhelm them, so they managed to keep up with the others.

Only two days later, when mountains of cut grass grew about them, but the rain didn't stop, did the mowers give it a rest and scattered, each to his own pursuit.

Wolverine and Odrowąż went fishing on the lake, Szczepanski, Crane, and Panther tore bast, and the boys ran into the forest to look for fox nests. And as they rummaged around, peering into the hollows and holes, they suddenly heard a strange noise in the air. A gray ball flew low over the clearing.

"It's a swarm[37]! A swarm!" Jasiek shouted and ran. Whatisit jumped after him, and a crazy chase began.

They jumped through bushes and ditches, throwing handfuls of earth, leaves, and twigs at the ball, screaming at the tops of their lungs, all scratched up and stung.

A hunting frenzy overcame them, the instinctive, primeval drive to husband bees. They'd probably run on through swamps, and ditches, and jungle without slowing down until their hearts burst. But the swarm stopped moving first. It settled on a viburnum bush to rest. It made a thick cluster, like a gigantic greyish fruit.

"Water, water! Sprinkle them with water, or they will fly again!" Jasiek commanded. Whatisit brought water in his hat, and they sprinkled it on the ball.

"Now what? What do we do with them?" Whatisit asked breathlessly.

---

[37] Swarming is how bee colonies multiply in the wild. Swarming usually happens after a new queen has appeared in the hive; the new queen then flies away from the hive with approximately half of the worker bees in the colony. The swarm will then find a new place to build a hive.

"Give me your shirt because mine is torn!" Jasiek gasped breathlessly, helping his companion undress. "Tie the collar and sleeves with a piece of withe, firmly, like this, only fast, before they come to their senses and start stinging. Now pass it here, under the branch. Be ready to close it as soon as I drop them in! Oh, get ready now! Don't let go! Hold it! Bear it! Ouch! Bear it. We're the forest folk; we don't care about a few stings."

Whatisit gritted his teeth, obeying orders. A gray cloud surrounded him: he felt burning stings on his body, heard their angry buzzing all around him, and smelled the sour smell of their venom. But he remained staunch in his resolve, neither squealed nor let go.

And, behold, the triumph! There they stood with their catch! They were sweaty, dirty, naked to their waist, and marked with sting marks all over.

But they held their prize, a bizarre sack made out of a shirt in which desperately roared the imprisoned bees.

"What will it be, hey? Because this will definitely earn us a name!" Jasiek said. "I will be glad to have the name Beekeeper! I love bees! But you also chased them and brought water and gave up your shirt, and, oh, boy, they stang you mercilessly! If you want it, you can carry it!"

Whatisit hesitated, thinking. This could be his first real prize; and would probably allow him to shed his current name, but he felt he didn't deserve it.

"No, you deserve it more. I would not have known what this was, or chased it, or known how to catch it. No. You take it!"

"Then I thank you for it! Now we are friends for life!" Jasiek exclaimed radiantly. "Put my shirt on. I'll carry the swarm. Oh, the Chief is going to like this! A midsummer swarm!"

The others were gathered in the cottage for lunch when Jasiek burst in, naked down to his waist, with his prize in hand, and breathlessly shouted:

"A prize! For Chief!"

Wolverine stepped out of the hut, and the boy recited the speech he had composed on the way.

"There flew the swarm! And I after it. The swarm on wings, I on foot! And I caught it. I snatched it in what I wore and brought it here. Now I ask for a forest name to recognize that I, too, am forest folk!"

Something got tangled up in the speech, but Wolverine understood it and, taking the prize from him, said without smiling, very seriously: "You are a sport! We will consider your wishes, and you will hear our decision tonight!"

"The boy's gone mad. Running naked in the woods! Are you not ashamed of yourself? Mother pushed Jasiek into the alcove.

"By evening, you must prepare the hive to receive your swarm!" Odrowąż called after him.

"Yes, grandpa! I have already decided which hollow to use," answered the boy, out of breath, twirling in his mother's hands, so as to get dressed soonest and head out to the hollow.

He hung the swarm on a branch in the shade, and soon they all set out to prepare the beehive. They took with them a long ladder, ropes, and tools, and Jasiek led them to his selected conifer.

"This boy will grow up alright," said Odrowąż when they stood by the old, lonely pine tree in the midst of a forest clearing. "He has a good eye! The hollow's pointing east, the branch above it is like a roof. As long as the interior is not too broad, this will serve well! Come on, boy; you do it yourself!"

Jasiek was already up the ladder, but, as it did not reach high enough, he tied a rope to a branch, and hanging from it at the mouth of the hollow, he worked with a chisel and an ax.

Unable to stand by merely watching, Panther now climbed the rope to the upper branch and sat astride it. And now they hammered together like two woodpeckers.

The others handed them tools, moss and clay from below, and finally, a piece of board and nails.

After a couple of hours of work, they slipped down the tree and lay down, faint with exhaustion. The hive was ready.

"This pine shall be called Piast[38]," said Wolverine. Odrowąż looked at the sun.

"Run, Jasiek, and bring the swarm! You can set them."

And now came the most challenging test of his beekeeping skill: without any cover for face and hands, without water to sprinkle on the bees, without smoke, Jasiek had to settle his angry swarm in their new home.

As he climbed the ladder, holding the roaring bees in his teeth, Odrowąż commanded:

"Now, do not hurry. Do not get nervous, eager, or angry. If they sit on you, do not chase them away. From the way they buzz, you can hear that the queen-mother is inside, so they will not break up. You have the spoon. Take a few at a time and let them into the hollow. But make sure you do not harm the queen."

"I'll help him!" said Wolverine, carried away by sudden enthusiasm, and pulled himself up the rope onto the upper branch.

"I think I'd rather watch from here," Panther muttered.

It was easier to work together. Wolverine held the shirt. Jasiek tied himself with the rope to the trunk. They opened the shirt, and a gray cloud surrounded them, but Jasiek brought the first handful to the hive's opening and quietly, joyfully whispered:

"They're going in!"

Both stared at the buzzing moving mass, and suddenly Wolverine tilted, leaned forward, and, hanging his head-down, plunged his hand into the swarm and whispered, "The Queen!"

"His fist was a grey ball of buzzing bees. He moved it to the beehive's mouth, and they both laughed softly.

"She's gone in!" they whispered.

"May she be happy here!" said Odrowąż from below and made a sign of the cross over the hollow.

Now the swarm rushed to the beehive, like a gray river, like a well-ordered army. They went in, humming a song, waving their

---

[38] Piast: the mythical founder of Poland's first royal family and therefore a symbol of hoary antiquity

wings like pennants, laden with honey and pollen and glistening with plaques of wax.

They had brought with them everything that was needed to establish their new kingdom, build it up, and multiply into the millions needed for a well-fed, disciplined, and immensely industrious nation.

Now, the beekeepers only had to wait for all the bees to enter the hive. Those that had flown up now settled down and marched peacefully. And those that had landed on people now walked over their faces and hands without stinging.

"What a gentle folk!" Jasiek said.

"And smart," added Wolverine. "When I held the queen mother in my hand, not one stung me. Look what a populous tribe! We'll have two liters of honey from them!"

"And I have a bouquet for them for their new settlement!" cried Crane from below and threw up a wreath of lemon balm and thyme.

Wolverine grabbed it and hung it over the beehive.[39]

"Come down already!" Panther called from below. "They can take it from there on their own, without you watching."

"But!" Jasiek objected. "Don't rush us! We are fine here. Such a miracle of life! And such a beautiful smell of resin, honey, and herbs. And the sight is so beautiful to watch them march like this."

"Different strokes, I guess, and you have to believe it. Chief's been hanging with his head down for a quarter of an hour, and you're tied up like a pig in your rope."

"Well, everyone knows that beekeeper's work is great fun!" said Jasiek.

"Well, enjoy it then. We will go sharpen our scythes."

That night, when they had eaten and lit their pipes, Wolverine said:

"Is there among us here one Jasiek Szczepanski?"

---

[39] Farmers in Eastern Europe place wreathes of herbs on the roof when they complete the construction of a house

The boy raised his eyes, but before he could open his mouth, Panther replied:

"There is no Jasiek Szczepanski here. Only the marsh Beekeeper, our friend and companion."

"And does this young Beekeeper love his bees? Does he not hurt them, rob them for profit or curse them when they sting?"

"He is not a slave driver but a loving caretaker," said Odrowąż.

"And I will be!" Jasiek whispered.

"And does this Beekeeper, who wants to be our friend, love God, the creator of this forest?"

"He loves God dearly, recites his prayers, and never lies!" his mother said.

"And does this Beekeeper love and protect from harm every creature of God that lives and grows in this forest?"

"As companions and friends! Loves them and respects them!" said Crane.

"And is there nothing in the forest which this Beekeeper might fear, day or night?"

"I am only afraid of shame!" Jasiek replied proudly.

"And does this Beekeeper know how to do all forest work so that he could live in the forest, even if he were stranded here alone?"

"Yes, he does," Szczepanski, normally always silent, said shortly.

"Then this Beekeeper is our friend and companion!" finished Wolverine, holding out his right hand to the boy.

Then Crane and Panther rose, and all shook hands, and then the boy got up and left because he did not want any of the elders to see the tears welling in his eyes. And his heart was pounding in his chest so much that he could not say a word. And from that day on, no one called him: 'Jasiek' because he would not answer to that name, and he only made an exception for his mother.

After this forest christening, the men started to sharpen their scythes, and Odrowąż said to Wolverine: "It may seem like child's play to us, but it is something that the boy will not forget his entire life.

This memory will lead him in life and protect him from corruption. A child has today become a Beekeeper."

Wolverine was silent for a moment, staring at the blade of his scythe, then he straightened up. His eyes ran over the forest and the sky with loving tenderness. He said thoughtfully:

"It seems to me a great treasure that we can all enjoy a childish soul here. How does a man enter the kingdom of heaven, but by becoming a child again?"

HOW WHATISIT EARNED HIS FOREST NAME

Ten proud haystacks now stood in the clearings, the fruit of their toil and pain. June was coming to an end, the month of the sun's majesty and triumph, of the splendor of colors, lushness, and scent. The forest was carpeted with flowers, humming with bird young, and already fruitful because blueberries had ripened and colored the earth.

Their toil made people swarthy and wiry and strong, and Whatisit had grown so much that he now wore Crane's clothes and had to duck his head when going through the cottage door. When the hay was all collected, Odrowąż sent Beekeeper home to see their corn, whether it was ready for harvest, and the rest devoted themselves to fishing, which they had neglected for some time. Wading in the dried lagoons, Panther and Whatisit made plans for the Kupala Pyre because it was the eve of St. John's[40]. They waded and pulled crayfish from their holes. The catch was tremendous, and the specimens huge.

"This has been my secret place for a while," laughed Panther. "It's unbelievably rich. And all this filth came here after wolves drowned a moose on the ice a year ago. They chased him onto the ice, and he crashed through; they were on top so that he couldn't climb out, and he drowned, and he was food for crayfish alone. I came upon his head and antlers as I rummaged around. Seventeen tines it had. Seventeen! A true patriarch. Chief and I fished out the skull and the horns, but as for the crayfish, well, I didn't brag about that. Sometimes, those two won't catch anything for three days running, I come here, and it's as easy as going to the pantry."

"What are we going to do next, now that the hay is ready?" Whatisit asked.

"We will help Odrowąż with the harvest, and then the Chief plans to build a causeway across The Drowning to the old Pine Hill so that he can investigate there. It should be possible to reach the crane nesting grounds from there and perhaps find a siskin nest at last. We will not run out of work, but today is a day of sadness for all."

"Why?"

"From tonight on, we lose the sun! Things will lean towards autumn, and earth, and winter. Such sadness!" he groaned, and as if to chase sad thoughts away, he added:

"We will light our Kupala Pyre on the Widow's Hill. It'll be visible for a dozen miles around, all the way to the dry land where people live. Well, we have a gallon of crayfish, enough for supper. Let's leave them for Mother in the hut and go build the pyre."

Szczepanska was in the midst of deep-cleaning the hut and took their catch with thanks. They did not wait for the return of their comrades and ran into the forest. When they got back at sunset, Panther said: "Chief! We're lighting Kupala tonight. We have built a pyre sky high."

---

[40] Midsummer, June 24/25

"Nice. We will all come! Only there is plenty of fish to prepare. You have to help if we are to finish by nightfall!"

Panther liked the sound of that less, but he went to work with the others all the same.

"We will not go hungry at Advent[41]," he said. "And if only we have a good mushroom harvest, we will live this winter like kings! Oh, look, Beekeeper is back!"

Beekeeper brought a sheaf of rye ears, a heavy bag of provisions, and various news of the world.

Odrowąż husked the grain in his hand, tasted it, and ground it with his teeth.

"We'll reap after Saint Peter's,"[42] he decided.

"Hurray! We have a whole week in the forest!" Beekeeper whispered happily to Whatisit.

"A blueberry week!" Said Szczepanska. "Crayfish are ready, come and get it!"

They sat around the table, around bowls full of color, and amid the crunch of broken claws, Panther said:

"You do realize, Whatisit, that you will have to go to Widow's Hill alone to light the pyre?"

"Why?"

"Because it's your first Kupala Pyre, and you haven't found your fern flower[43] yet."

"And you have?"

"Everybody here has!"

"Eh! I don't believe it!"

"Why don't you just admit that you are afraid of the dark and won't find your way."

"It'll be easy to find, and I'm not afraid."

"Oh, yes? Prove it."

---

[41] Advent: In the liturgical calendar, the thirty days leading up to Christmas when Catholics abstain from meat

[42] Saint Peter's Feast: June 29

[43] According to legend, the wish fulfilling fern flower blooms only at midnight on Midsummer Night

Whatisit looked at their faces. It seemed to him that Beekeeper was smiling secretly, that Wolverine was studying him, and that Odrowąż moved his eyebrows.

"What's so scary? I'll go!"

"In the forest? At night? It's scary!" said Szczepanska. Panther is just teasing you. Don't listen to him. We will all go together, singing. Anyone unaccustomed to walking at night can be afraid. And lose his way."

But that only egged the boy on. He jumped up, took his hat and matches, tucked the ax in his belt, and left.

"I'll light the way for you," he said, closing the door.

But once out of the light of the hut, darkness enveloped him, and he walked blindly for a long time along the familiar path. When his eyes grew accustomed to the dark, and he started making out shapes and felt he was not really certain where he was. But he walked boldly across the clearing, hoping to find the trail. Indeed, he found the worn track, but by following it, he plunged into the forest and lost sight of the starry night overhead. He was overwhelmed by the murmurs of the forest, mysterious and unnerving. He became unsettled by the uncertainty of the path, by the mysterious rustles in the dark, the nudging of branches, the bland glow of decaying wood, and finally, he stopped, feeling his heart hammering with fear and the dew of sweat cooling his temples.

Then he began to repeat in his mind the words of Beekeeper's baptism: "I am only afraid of shame," and he felt that his soul was strengthened.

And then he began to sing because he thought: *A song makes good company.*

And with that, his fear flew away like a broken spell. He looked about him soberly and recognized a large juniper next to him. Yes, he was on the right track.

"*Hey, brothers, falcons!*" he sang louder and louder and marched on, having mastered his fear. When he emerged out of the thicket, he realized that he had gone off track somewhat, but once in the glade, he oriented himself by the glowing sky, and now, sure of his direction, he triumphed:

"Panther is going to lose this one! I'll find my way! I only have to avoid that little dyke and find the footbridge over the peat." He was no longer afraid. He shuddered only once when an animal leaped from under his feet and crashed into the thicket with a tremendous racket. But that lasted only a moment, and he soon took off after the beast, thinking: "He'll lead me to the ford! Why should I look for it myself?"

And, indeed, he found the dry passage, lit a match, and studied the trail in the sand. "A boar!" he whispered. "As big as a house! A retired recluse!"[44]

And then he plunged into the ford and waded along, safe from drowning now.

Before him lay the Widow's Hill. It was the highest point of the entire wild country around, a hill of sand piled high by prehistoric works of nature.

For many centuries, mother nature, which hates a vacuum, had sowed stalks of grass there and taught the plants to thrive on the dune. Heathers settled in depressions, forming a compact rug; coarse grasses with gray fluff, mosses, and lichens clung to the bald patches of sand, and among them, like jewels, yellow strawflowers, dwarf thyme, and tiny red clove pinks shone in the summer.

"Look how our Widow got herself all pimped out," Panther had once said. "Amber, amethyst, and even rubies. She only pretends to be poor!"

At the top of the dune, an enormous pile of firewood blackened the sky. Whatisit stretched out on the ground next to it and awaited the arrival of his companions.

The night was quiet, clear, moonless, but full of stars and a kind of dreamy summer peace descended upon him.

Nightjars and owls flashed by silently, prowling for moths; from the thickets came the calls of feeding animals, crunchings, murmurs. Dogs barked in some very distant settlement.

---

[44] Very old boars leave the herd and live alone

Whatisit stared at the stars and mused. A kind of song flowed from his soul, and he seemed to have melted into this heaven, into the very being of nature.

He felt both very small and very powerful: an atom in the body of a giant. Then a melody came to him from afar. His companions were coming from the direction of the hut, and Wolverine was playing his fiddle.

Then Whatisit lit the pyre.

The flame ran up the dry needles and moss, as was its custom, hurriedly, greedily, up and up, clapping, whistling, gathering power to explode.

And now, human voices joined the fiddle: a woman's voice, very high – and then the men, and the call of the ancient song: "*Lada, Lada, Oh, Kupala.*"

And now the pyre was blazing. Fire shot straight up overhead, tinted the sky with purple and gold, and illuminated the whole hill.

"That's my boy, Whatisit !" Panther called. "It's midnight, Private! Your chance to find your fern flower!"

They surrounded the fire, finished their song, and then Wolverine said:

"Perhaps thousands of years ago, this hill alone stood above the mass of waters of some inland sea, and ancient men, living by the water, armed with flint, dressed in skins and bast, sang their ancient Indoeuropean songs this night."

"There are ancient fox holes here at the top of the hill," said Crane. "And in one of them, I once found a pair of flint arrowheads."

"What an abundance of bones and treasures lies buried in this earth," said Odrowąż.

"We lie here, as watchmen, on the ancient trail of robbers, wandering tribes, barbarian armies, like a dam protecting the land from flood. Throughout the ages, how many times have other fires burned on this hill, not to celebrate the summer like today, but as a warning: the Mongols are coming! The Cossacks are coming![45] As a

---

[45] A reader would understand the author means Russians, not Mongols

warning or as a call to arms. 'The strong to the colors! The weak to their hiding places!' You, father, have seen those signs; we have not, and that saddens us."

Wolverine stared at the fire, and then the boys whispered to each other and ran into the forest.

There was a rumble of axes, and they soon returned, bending under the weight of a greasy tar trunk. They shook it and threw it into the fire.

"Lada Kupala!" Beekeeper shouted. "Burn! Burn for our good fortune that we may yet hear the call to the colors!"

"Oh, do not be sad, Wolverine!" said Odrowąż. "The time will come, and you will hear that call. Where the spirit lives, death needs not be feared. This is not death; this is sleep!"[46]

And the boys looked at each other, straightened up, stood at attention, and sang: "*Poland has not been lost!*" and it sounded like a bugle.

Everyone stood up and uncovered their heads.

"Hey, you eastern frontiers of the Commonwealth! You who are silent, empty, suppressed, depopulated, murdered, displaced! You who are frozen under the gaze of the spy-executioner, held down by the bayonets of powers that be, imprisoned by *diktats* of mighty sovereigns and international congresses, removed from us, struck out of history.

"Such is your voice! Such bones and treasures lie in you and await their wake-up call."

When the song was over, Odrowąż began to tell a story, another bead in the endless rosary.[47]

"When they overran us at Horki,[48] four of us broke through and fled into the woods. Mr. Seweryn, your cousin, was wounded in the hand, but I only had my neck scratched a little. We had two friends

---

[46] i.e. "Poland has not yet been lost"

[47] Of anti-Russian uprisings

[48] Odrowąż remembers the 1863 uprising

from The Crown[49] with us: one from Podlasie[50], the other, an ensign from Warsaw. The former was close to forty, with a wife and kids. The ensign was merely a kid, hardly a little down on his chin, some hooligan from the Old Town, and his name was Stacho.

He was small, thin, blackish, saucy, quarrelsome and disputatious, and fierce and daring, like a badger. He got a bullet in the hip, and we carried him in our hands. He was bleeding a lot and fainting and only whispered to me: 'I'll give you my Sagalas rifle,[51] only hide me somewhere, so these dogs don't get the flag.'

"And he did not let go of that flag until fever completely overwhelmed him in a safe hiding place. And even then, he came to every now and then and cried out: 'My standard! My standard!'

"Well, then! We fell into such remote hiding places as only I knew, and we lay low. Mr. Seweryn, he knew how to treat wounds, treated everyone, then sent me out to scout. I sneaked to the manor and whispered with the women; I brought rags, bread, cordials, and ointments. And so we licked our wounds.

"When the master's fever eased, we got word that he had to flee abroad and that everything had been prepared, so we talked. Those two from the Crown – they had to stay. One was seriously wounded; the other had to keep an eye on him until I returned. After I took your cousin through the lines, then I would lead the two of them out.

"The ensign then says to me: 'My friend, remember this rifle is now yours because you did not let the dogs have the flag and because you carried me on your back. Something's telling me I will not rest in Powązki,[52] but here in your wood. And that's a fitting soldier's tomb: a green oak tree! As long as I lie with the standard! Our friend here will take care of this for me and deliver the rifle to you. God give you two a lucky scrape!'

---

[49] The Crown: central Poland

[50] Podlasie /pod-**la**-sheh/ a province of The Crown

[51] Sagalas was an 18th century gunsmith from the Kiev province

[52] /Po-**von**-ski/ A military cemetery in Warsaw

"And the other fellow says: 'Some damned fever's eating me, but I ought to get back to The Crown, because I have in trust a purse from the commander, the last of our unit's cash.

"And he ordered me, under oath, to go and deliver the sack to the National Council at a secret address. "Then you rush back to us, my friend."

"And if we die?" says Mr. Seweryn.

"And since we were soldiers and toughened up a bit, the Podlasiak[53] says: 'Whichever of the two of us lives will wait a month here, and after a month, he will assume you two are dead and move on alone.' Then we talked and agreed.

"It was high time for us two to move, as the other two would find it hard to live in the forest for a month without fire and warm food. And so we parted – it turned out: forever!

"At the border, a Russian horse-guard shot Mr. Seweryn, and I barely managed to carry him across, but first, we had to hide in empty sheds, mend and heal the wound, and it was seven weeks before I returned home. And by then, there were arrests, interrogations, torturings, hangings.

"I scraped through miraculously and came to this forest. The bunker was empty. I trampled all over, searched the woods, and asked every tree, every hand of dry land, every game, bird, reptile. I searched nests and shelters, and I examined every dyke and every fox hole. And I found nothing. Then I went to Podlasie and asked about our friend, but he had not come back.

"So I assume that they both lie here somewhere, waiting for the day of Christ's return."

"*The Angel of the Lord announced to the Virgin Mary,*" Szczepanska intoned the blessing. And they all returned: "*And she conceived of the Holy Spirit.*"

The pyre blazed, spattered, and bloomed with a glow in the sky as they remembered the dead.

---

[53] Podlasiak /pod-**la**-shak/ - a person from Podlasie

But Panther could not bear the solemnity any longer, and when they finished the prayer, he began to dare the boys to jump over the fire and various other tricks. Then, he took his "bride" to dance and sing around the fire. Then he persuaded people to sing again and to play the violin and the flute, and they sang song after song.

Finally, Szczepanska started telling fairy tales about the fern flower and treasures secreted in the forest. Stretched out by the fire, silent Wolverine listened. Others added a word from time to time: Panther, Odrowąż, Crane, even the normally quiet Szczepanski. But Wolverine was silent, staring at the sky.

"The chief has fallen asleep," said Panther. "And too bad, for he could spin us a forest yarn, too. One night, rumbling in the forest, he snagged a fern flower in his clog, you know."

"Ha! And I have it with me, always. And I will tell you this: that each of us has it!" Wolverine replied slowly.

Everyone looked at him, awaiting the story.

"It's like this," he continued. "The whole wisdom of existence lies in a fairy tale, and it is our challenge to put that fairy tale in practice. You see, in the fairy tale, the hero wins the princess, climbs a glass mountain, and wins the potion of eternal life. And we need that kind of goal in our life. The hero wins happiness because he sacrifices himself to free the weak, the oppressed, and the cursed. And we need to do that in real life. In a fairy tale, the strong support the weak, and the good and weak defeat the strong and evil. And all God's creatures: birds and beast, reptile and insect, return to friendship with man, to a mutual understanding. Which is how things should be.

"In a life lived like a fairy tale, health comes from pure springs and strength from a good harvest, and a shepherd is seated on the throne because he is a hero by soul and deed.

"Whoever understands the fairy tale and lives according to it, he has the fern flower. He has eyes that see and ears that hear. He lives by the wisdom of nature. And look at us: does anyone of us envy others, far away, and want what they have? No! And why? Because we have this fern flower secreted away in a place from which it can never fall: in our hearts."

Wolverine rose, stretched, and looked at the sky.

"Look. The day is breaking. And the cranes are starting to trumpet. It's time! Home!"

Nobody wanted to sleep. A lovely, fragrant, dewy dawn rose over the forest. Panther and the boys ran to swim, and Szczepanska said:

"Sunday is blueberry picking day. I won't feed anyone who does not bring me a jarful."

"I think we best obey Mother," said Wolverine.

"But I order dumplings for supper!" added Odrowąż.

When the boys returned from their bath, they found the hut empty and on the threshold – three slices of bread and three empty jars.

"Oh, I get it. The message is: 'Off you go for blueberries!" Panther translated, quickly getting hold of the smallest jar. "Here's our chance to sleep in the forest, eat blueberries and ask the thrushes to help us harvest."

"Let's go to the wild beehive because there are also wild strawberries there," said Beekeeper, and the two left.

But Whatisit, seeing Patch Pelt walking slowly out to pasture, jumped on her back and rode into the forest for a carefree stroll.

Behind the mare came little Agatka, the foal: dot-for-dot and patch-for-patch a perfect miniature of her mom, and, for fun, she nibbled at his clogs, inviting him to play. The day was hot, and Whatisit felt sleepy, so he pleaded with her:

"We'll play in the evening, Agatka, I promise, but for now, take me to the clearing, onto the moss, among the ferns and let me sleep a while!"

The mare was headed for open ground and took him to the Muraviev clearing, where her favorite scented bugleweed grew, and she began to graze diligently.

Whatisit slipped to the ground and studied it, looking for a comfortable bed.

Old, lonely oaks grew sparsely here, and great heaps of dead, chopped-up giants overgrown with weeds looked like green burial mounds. Whatisit climbed on one, nestled himself among the dry limbs, and, half-sitting and half-lying, watched the world and felt sleep descend upon him deliciously. The mare, while grazing, moved some distance away, but Agatka remained, nibbling on ferns under one of the giants.

There was such a silence that all one could hear was the thrumming of insects. The forest stood motionless, breathless, basking in the sunny noon.

And then suddenly, Whatisit heard the crack of a broken branch on the oak tree above Agatka.

He looked up and sprang to his feet like he'd heard a gunshot.

The whole drama lasted seconds. A jumping monster flashed in front of his eyes; thoughts shot through his mind like lightning: jungle – death – lynx! He flew like a bullet and leaped between the beast and the foal.

The beast fell on him, clawed his left arm, and knocked him to the ground.

Ah! The pain of the flesh torn to the bone, the terror stopping his breath, the primal instinct of defense! A red maw reeking of rotting flesh flashed in front of his face and eyes with slits of green pupils. The boy grabbed the beast by the throat, choking it with a desperate effort.

It took just seconds, and he couldn't have held on any longer: the shredded arm was losing its grip, blood from a ripped artery gushed in a stream, and his eyes became unfocused. One more second, and it would be over!

The desperate fight took place in silence, but then there was a thud, and with his fading eyes, Whatisit saw one last sight: distended nostrils, flashing pupils: the mare's head upraised in rage. Snorting wildly, she reached his side and jumped with both front hooves on the beast's back. The lynx's vertebrae gave in with a sickly crunch. The beast let out a desperate howl and –hung limply over the boy's chest. But the boy didn't see it and didn't feel it because he had passed out.

And now all hell broke loose. The mare, pinning the enemy with her hooves, raised her head and neighed wildly, and at this war cry of blood, Hathor rushed from the thicket and, reaching the place of death, lowed terrifyingly, kicking the ground with her hooves. And the trembling Agatka leaned her scrawny body against her mom and neighed, too, in a high-pitched whine.

This animal call was heard by Wolverine and Crane, who were busy nearby studying some lichen on a rotten aspen.

"Householders bay alarm! Something happened there! To the rescue!"

And they ran.

And they arrived in time.

There were signals, whistles, and calls.

The unconscious boy was brought to the hut and handed over to Crane for painful surgery.

Crane shook his head morosely, and they all stood over him in silence, petrified; only after the doctor tied the artery, stopped the bleeding, and bandaged the wound, Odrowąż said:

"Never fear! He will live! Let the doctor do his thing. I'll go home and fetch my drugs. I'm telling you, he will live. But he lost a lot of blood, so healing will take a long time. And you, Panther, Szczepanski, you skin the beast and bury the head in an anthill. This is a rare prize, and there must be a nest with young somewhere. Look, she's got milk!"

When Whatisit woke, he found himself lying in the bedchamber, on Wolverine's bed, and Szczepanska watching over him. At the table by the window, Crane was preparing a potion.

"Patch Pelt!" the boy whispered.

"What is it, child?" the woman asked.

"Patched Pelt saved me! Or I was done for! I'm thirsty. Doctor, have I lost my arm?"

"Here, drink this. Your arm will be fine! You'll play the violin one day, yet. You're wounded, but you will recover. How did it happen?"

"I saw the lynx jump down on Agatka from a branch... So I thought I'd push it away, hold it off with my hands, maybe strangle it! Well, actually, I didn't think anything. I was just worried about the foal. What a beast! If not for Patch Pelt!..."

He spoke in a whisper, his words broke off, and his mind began to wander in a gathering haze. In the evening, he became feverish and kept repeating: "See Panther? See? Panther will see that I am not a 'Shotgun Mouth'! Whatisit is not stupid! Aha, Panther! Aha!"

Everyone took turns watching over him. At dawn, Odrowąż returned with a bag full of bottles and jars, and he said to Crane:

"Will the good doctor allow me access to the patient?"

Crane smiled and looked at the forest all around them.

"I have been learning from you for years. How could I not?"

The old man then took the boy in his care. He washed his arm, rubbed it with an ointment, gave him a stew of herbs to drink, put a cooling compress on his hot head, and all his ministrations caused the fever to drop. After two days, the patient demanded a meal, and then he slept calmly and only woke to say:

"Food!"

Finally, one day he woke up feeling better and with a great sense of joy. Everything was silent and sunny. Summer warmth and the smell of resin wafted through the wide-open window of the alcove. Whatisit was alone, but there was the sound of someone moving in the other room.

"Mother!" he exclaimed.

But instead of Szczepanska, Odrowąż appeared with a bowl in his hand.

"Want to eat?"

"Eat and live and talk and sing! My weakness is all gone. I'm feeling so good! I thank you, sir!"

He began to devour with ravenous appetite a soup thick with fish and potatoes, enriched profusely with cream.

"Is Mother gone?"

"We're alone, just the two of us. Everyone's at the harvest, but every night someone comes to find out about you."

"My goodness! Will they leave any of that harvest for me? I'm going to get up. Only... my left hand isn't very good."

He sat up on the bed and felt fur under his feet. He looked down.

"The beast!" he said.

"You deserve to have it at your feet, and Panther even made you a hat."

And Odrowąż showed him two small lynx kitten pelts.

"He found them in a hollow in an oak tree. They scratched him something awful. And here you have the skull as a souvenir: the ants have cleaned it up beautifully."

"What a terrible beast! Surely there is nothing more dangerous in our forest!"

"No, there isn't, but luckily the beast is rare. In the past, it sometimes happened that it killed a bear. Now the bears are gone, but a lynx can kill a moose."

"Have you hunted lynx?"

"Not many. The last one was maybe ten years ago. It took a doe and ate until it was full and fell asleep in a tree. And there, I found it and shot it."

Whatisit sat listening.

"The forest is silent!" He whispered.

"It's high summer. July. The birds have finished their mating. Only insects still buzz in this heat."

"Have I been lying here long?"

"Your third week."

"Oh my God! I missed so much!"

"Only a little. You're strong! The wounds from lynx claws and bites often become infected and heal poorly, there is some dirt or venom in the maw, but you were lucky. It could have been months, not weeks."

He took his arm and rubbed it with an ointment.

"You'll have full use of your arm eventually, but not soon. That's nothing, though. You can collect mushrooms with one hand, and that will be our next task. We should see them with the new moon because the ground is ready."

Then quick steps sounded in the garden, and Beekeeper stood on the threshold, panting, and smiling.

"You're up! Thank God!"

He shook the patient's hand, kissed his grandfather's, and reported:

"Chief has sent me for honey because we'll hold the harvest feast tomorrow."

"Already? So fast!" said Odrowąż.

"Well, yes! Because as soon as people saw the good doctor in the field, they all ran to him for cures. And he says: 'The rye cannot wait; let someone help me with the scythe, then I'm going to treat you.' So five men came to mow and a bunch of women to bind sheaves. And then again, a crowd came to Chief to settle some dispute, and they did his bit for him in no time. So we collected all the rye and all barley and are taking oats now. The field is as crowded as a country fair, and work is going like wildfire. Chief told me to bring him his fiddle. I will go collect some honey now, but first I'd like some milk because the heat is terrible, and the doctor tells me not to drink water because I've got the runs. Oh, and Father is already taking sheaves to the barn."

And the boy ran off. Whatisit, too, got up to leave the hut but only made it as far as the threshold, and he sat there near crying that he could not go out, head into the woods, or work in the field.

"Don't worry!" Beekeeper consoled him when he returned with a jar full of honey and gave him a slice of honeycomb in a bowl, still warm and smelling of the beehive.

"Don't worry! They are readying something for you. Panther and Chief are making a big secret of it, but I overheard."

"What is it?"

"I'm not allowed to say! You will see!"

And laughing, the boy collected his honey and rushed away.

"Grandpa! What is it? You probably know?" Whatisit pressed Odrowąż.

"I do not know! But I think you have coming to you whatever is due to a brave man. Glory and honor!" the old man replied, stroking the boy's head.

Another quiet, hot summer day passed. Whatisit was out on the porch from early morning, enjoying the outdoor air. One could sense a turning point in nature, the end of the summer. Birds chirped among the branches of trees and shrubs, and fat chicks skipped from branch to branch, pestering their parents for food. Bumblebees, gnats, and butterflies danced in the hot air, and turtle doves cooed melancholically. Sometimes the relative calm was broken by the scream of a jay or buzzard, and the summer background chirping of crickets underpinned it all.

The sun grew strong.

The beads of rowans began to turn red, fat lilac bellflowers bloomed in the shade of birch trees, and on the trees themselves, here and there, single golden leaves already flashed.

The crickets, the flying insects, and the turtle doves finally put Whatisit to sleep, and he stretched out in the garden on a blanket and let the sun warm and heal him. And when he woke up, the day had leaned towards evening. Odrowąż emerged from the forest, and out of the folds of his coat, he poured a pile of yellow chanterelles and ruddy flirts[54] at his side.

"First mushrooms are here. It will be a great year for them."

"I thought you went to the harvest festival."

"And let the does[55] feed you, like some saint in the desert? Anyway, no point in going. By the time I got there, it would have been time to head back. They'll probably be here tonight."

The old man began to clean the mushrooms for supper and to tell various forest tales, and so their evening passed.

The boy wanted to stay up until the others arrived, but in the end, he went to bed right after supper because he was still very weak. And he preferred to sleep through the last hours of impatient anticipation of "what was in store for him."

The next day, the hut was full of ordinary bustle. From daybreak, there was the usual chattering of Panther as he saw to the animals, Wolverine's conversation with Odrowąż about the harvest, Beekeeper's whistling, quarrels between Jake and Crane, and Whatisit began to call to them and greet them.

---

[54] *Russula vesca*, a mushroom

[55] In various hagiographies, hermits are fed by wild animals (crows or does)

But most important of all, the dressing of the wound took place, and there was cause for great relief because the wound had closed, and then Panther saw to the sick patient's grooming.

"Like for the wedding, my young groom, like for the wedding!" he said, cutting his hair, washing it and brushing it, and helping him put on a fresh shirt.

"Wedding? What wedding?" Whatisit asked, helping with one hand as best he could.

But Panther only made faces and then disappeared into the forest, for he had missed his solitary roaming.

Soon all left, each to his passion: Odrowąż with Wolverine to fish, Beekeeper to tend the hive, and only Crane remained about the cottage, but he soon lost himself in the sorting, drawing, and filing of a multitude of stone tools, flint arrowheads and axes, clay pot shards and glass beads, that he collected as his doctor fees.

In the afternoon, Szczepanska came running. She hung the cradle with the "bride" in the alcove and went to work as she always did, filling the house with her bustle and singing.

"Look! Leave a house without a woman for a day, and trash piles up!" she laughed, pointing to Crane's collection.

"There can be no order without Mother!" he confirmed.

So Szczepanska started her thorough scrubbing, hung the house with flowers, and took dirty linen to the stream. Whatisit helped the best he could, impatiently waiting for the evening.

At last, when they were all seated at the supper table, Wolverine said:

"Is that fellow Whatisit here among us?"

The boy's heart skipped a beat.

"No Whatisit here!" Panther replied. "But there is our forest friend, Orlik,[56] who threw himself at a lynx with his bare hands."

"And why did he throw himself at the lynx? Was he defending his life?"

---

[56] Orlik: Lesser Spotted Eagle (*Clanga pomarina*)

"No! Not to defend his life but to defend the life of a weak creature. Of an animal that serves man quietly and obediently and only to be exploited and harmed by men as a reward for its pains. But Orlik, like this animal's brother and friend, jumped to her rescue and nearly lost his life. Therefore honor and glory to him for his merciful and courageous deed."

"Glory!" everyone said with one voice.

"And does Orlik honor God, the Master of this forest, who has made all these miracles? And does he feel like a brother to all His creatures?"

"I honor and respect them!" the boy whispered.

"And has Orlik mastered the fear of the forest at night? And is he not afraid of the depths of bogs and the currents of the water?"

"He is bold and brave!" said Crane.

"And does Orlik toil for the love of work?"

"A joyful worker he is," Szczepanska confirmed.

"Then Orlik is our brother and true friend after our heart!" said Wolverine solemnly, standing up and stretching out his right hand.

They all rose, but then there was movement, a scuffle, and neighing outside the hut.

Somehow, no one had noticed that Panther had slipped out of the room. Now the door of the hut opened wide, and Agatka entered, strangely decorated and clattering with her hooves.

She wore a wreath of golden everlasts around her neck, a lynx skin over her back, and a mane of lynx kitten furs by her ears. She stood in the middle of the room, a little frightened, and snorted.

At her call, the head of Patch Pelt appeared in the window, looking good-naturedly at the proceedings and huffing reassuringly.

Panther appeared behind Agatka and said:

"The householders have come to plead for their friend and to instruct me to give him his war trophies."

Whatisit was lost for words, but he embraced Agatka's neck and kissed her nostrils, wiping his tears surreptitiously on her mane.

And then the two went out onto the clearing and began to play together and were soon joined by Beekeeper.

Patch Pelt watched them patiently with Hathor at her side phlegmatically chewing cud. Jake, too, watched their frolicking from the fence but was a little afraid to join in.

And from that day on, no one called Orlik 'Whatisit' ever again because he had earned his forest name.

THE VIRGIN LAND

As Odrowąż had foretold, mushrooms spilled out the following week. Panther was the first to return from the forest with a full basket, thus giving them the sign to start the harvest.

The forest folk now became possessed by a fierce hunting lust. After all, it was a gift of nature, generous beyond all abundance, the gift of the wild, the fruit of the earth, primordial and primeval, their miraculous manna.

All activities were neglected, meal times were forgotten, and no one complained. As soon as the day broke, the hut emptied, and they dispersed one by one because everyone had his special secret places, which he kept to himself, wanting to show off the biggest catch.

Only Beekeeper accompanied Orlik to help him carry the basket, and Wolverine stayed near Szczepanska, helping her sometimes with the child.

The mushrooms were brought to the garden in the evening, sorted into piles by kind, and then counted and prepared for drying. They also made up their daily dinner because no one had time to go fishing, and no one cared to peel potatoes after a day spent wandering in the forest.

On the second day, Wolverine forbade further counting.

"Throw all your mushrooms together," he said. "To count and compare is to boast. Let us – forest folk – not do that."

"And that's the truth," Szczepanska said. "God has provided enough for all!"

Panther and the boys were silent, but they had to obey.

Every evening, they lit the stove to dry their harvest, but it was more than they could dry overnight, and the excess had to be sent beyond the Rainbow Bridge in a cart or taken to the footbridges and from there to the Odrowąż farm.

The folk were busy with work but radiant with joy, even though they wandered in the forest all day, dragging about heavy baskets, and had only bread to eat and wild blueberries to quench their thirst.

It was now so hot in the hut at night that they took to sleeping outside on a landing that Panther had built from a few wooden boards among the branches of an old tree. Szczepanska and the baby slept on the porch.

From these expeditions, from all that rummaging in all the nooks and crannies, they brought other trophies: rare mosses, snake skins, wood growths, redpoll nests, feathers. Orlik and Beekeeper found seven-year-old moose antlers and barely managed to drag them back, having between them only three hands.

The mushroom crop was stupendous that year. Mushrooms engulfed the whole country. Szczepanski came from the farm to report that whole villages were empty, and all fieldwork was neglected: everyone had gone into the woods. He also reported that a few peasants even crossed the footbridges to this side of the bog but soon fled in a panic because a forest devil appeared to them; or was it a werewolf?

Wolverine raised his eyes at Panther.

Panther and the boys knelt over a pile of mushrooms on the floor, cleaning and sorting them for drying, whispering something among themselves mysteriously. Now laughter flashed in their faces. They were intent on not noticing what was being said.

"One devil?" asked Wolverine, raising his voice. "I think I saw three."

Orlik could not resist the urge to look up and Panther rejoined:

"Chief's got a crystal ball."

"In three days, the mushrooms will be finished," said Odrowąż. "Look, how most are now full of bugs. It'll be a month before the autumn crop comes."

"I have a project for this month, then," said Wolverine as they sat down to supper. "It has been years since the water has been this low and the marsh so dry. We could build a levy over The Drowning. What do you think, father Odrowąż?"

"We could try. There are places over there that are totally inaccessible, in any weather, surrounded by bogs that do not freeze over in winter. So this summer might be our best chance in years to reach those places. We will need to lay a lot of osiers, though. There are a lot of us now, so the work should go quickly."

"We will start tomorrow then."

"First of all, let's check Pine Hill. There are mushrooms there which no one has ever picked since creation."

At dawn the next day, all six set off on a long journey. The forest was quiet, meditative, pensive, lost in thought, and heavy with seeds and fruit. Young birds were trying out songs, fat thrushes flew up from the blueberry beds, underfoot herbs and mosses crunched, dry from the heat, and the birch trees were covered with yellowing leaves. Rowans stood covered with purple corals and clouds of pink blooms colored viburnum and whortleberries.

The heathers were already in bud,[57] and the glades were covered with centaury and gentian – late-blooming flowers.

"Autumn is coming!" said Wolverine with a sigh.

"Time to start collecting rowan and herbs," observed Crane.

"Well, hazelnuts are not ripe yet. We still have another six weeks," Panther consoled himself, stepping out of line from time to time to pick a mushroom.

The boys inspected nests along the way, but all were empty, and only one mossy squirrel hut contained a late brood: four red "teenagers" who scampered into the branches at their sight.

"Jake! It's your kids!" Panther called.

But Jake, sitting on Crane's shoulder, was only interested in hazelnuts.

They finally stood at the edge of the peat bog, opposite the Pine Hill, and set to work. The bog had devoured the levy they had built in the spring, and they had to begin from scratch: cut osiers, bind them into bundles, and Odrowąż set the course choosing what seemed to his experienced eyes the safest trail.

At noon, crawling a little and sinking a little, they got to the Pine Hill and set up camp. Sweaty and thirsty, they ate bread and drank milk and, instead of resting, rushed to pick more mushrooms. No man has been here for years. Mushrooms grew in a compact mass, in whole colonies of different ages and different heights. They harvested them easily, without any need to look – just reach out and pull – and threw them onto a pile.

"But how can we get them home?" Orlik asked.

"We will dry them here. Start a fire!" commanded Odrowąż.

Following his instructions, they dug a wide and flat ditch and lit a fire inside it. The old man remained to watch over it, and they scattered to explore the backwoods.

Wolverine made a ladder out of a few fallen trees and climbed up to the wild bees' nest. Panther and the boys disappeared in the thicket and soon triumphantly brought two empty penduline nests.

---

[57] In Northern Europe, heathers bloom in September

Crane made his way to the farther side and found a whole colony of fieldfares, a few score nests on birch trees, and a swarm of birds feeding in the mistletoe.

Wolverine, having found the bees full, rich, and especially warlike, also set off on an expedition. Orlik followed after him.

"Uncle, can I come along?"

Wolverine nodded. They dove into the thicket, and the boy said in a whisper:

"The forest is different here from that on the other side, near our cottage. It feels like we're in a church. It sounds different here, too."

"It is the holy of holies, my boy. Men have rarely made it over here, and not for many years. And have you noticed the passages in the bush? These are moose and deer paths. Let's go quietly. We may see something beautiful."

The forest seemed to grow thicker and wilder. Old spruce trees cast deep shadows with their great overhanging branches. The undergrowth was pierced by the silver lances of young birches and aspen, and heaps of stinging blackberries covered the ground. Little clearings made by fallen trees were shrouded over with crawling hops and bindweed. Reeds covered the lower areas, pressing together into dense green walls, frozen waves, ramparts, fortifications.

And among all this, here and there ran narrow, well-worn animal tracks, along which the forest folk now moved slowly, trying to tread without making a rustle, without brushing against the plants. The silence was so profound that they could hear the hammering of a woodpecker beyond The Drowning, the buzzing of bees working in the buckthorn, and the beating of their hearts.

They didn't speak. Sometimes Wolverine stood still to point out a rare nest, a flower, a squirrel on a spruce tree, an owl hugged to a tree trunk and almost invisible, or a nightjar folded in to sleep, like a knot in the branch. They walked on, reading the book of the forest.

Suddenly they shuddered and stood still in the shade of spruce trees. Somewhere to the right, in the thicket, they heard a bellow. It was a deep dull grunt, and it was followed by the crash of broken branches.

Wolverine took Orlik by the arm and pulled him in the shadow of overhanging branches. Now invisible, they froze motionless, waiting, straining their eyes and ears.

Then the thicket came to life. Some great power shook and shattered the young trees and bush, as if a hurricane was bending trees. They heard a dull, gloomy snorting and thumping like of wooden knockers. In answer to the boy's inquiring gaze, Wolverine whispered almost soundlessly:

"Moose. A giant!"

Suddenly the thicket in front of them opened as if blown away by the wind, and into the glade, not ten steps ahead, a monstrous and fantastic shape emerged.

It was something beyond Orlik's comprehension.

Was it a beast, or was it a walking forest?

Its long legs remained buried in the dense undergrowth, and its monstrous head was half-camouflaged by a mass of green branches and leaves and vines wrapped about its tremendous antlers. It had collected them as it ripped through the forest: hops, blackberries, stinging nettles, thistles, cones, twigs. And now, alarmed by something, the moose stood upright, in all its enormous glory. It snorted and scented. Serious, black, gigantic eyes looked around. Wet, distended nostrils seemed to be tasting the air. It seemed to pick up an unknown, mysterious scent against which its instinct warned it: that of fire smoke.

The moose was not frightened. It trusted in its tremendous strength and the swiftness of its legs. Here it was on its own territory. It snorted twice with disgust, and, with a grunt, it began to tear through the thicket again and slowly moved off, its hooves clopping on the forest floor.

The men followed the beast, taking advantage of the noise it made.

"It's rooting season!" Wolverine whispered.

"It put a wreath on its head! What a mighty giant! Ugly as night, but in a magical way – wonderful."

"A forest god! The beast will lead us to its kingdom."

The moose did not follow a trail. It pressed on, crashing through the bush, through young trees, sallow and reed, as easily as if it were crossing a smooth meadow. Eventually, it came to the brink of a wide stretch of bogs that surrounded Pine Hill, like a sea surrounding an island.

The moose stopped, sniffed, and lowed loudly.

It stared at the island opposite, blackening in the distance.

For a moment, the beast stood listening to some sound from the other side, then it turned to the right and slid down into a narrow stream meandering through the bog, among the clumps and low thickets of the morass.

The moose waded and sank but kept its green-wreathed head above the mud and finally disappeared into the gray of the reeds on the other side. For a moment yet, they heard the splashing of the water and the less and less audible snorting, and then the beast was gone like a prehistoric dream.

Following its trail, Wolverine slipped into the water and tried the ground.

"Even Odrowąż does not know this passage. Look, we can wade here, and in places, it is deep enough to swim. It is a safe, ancient passage for the big game. We can cross here tomorrow. Panther will find his crane nesting grounds, and next spring, we will probably find capercaillie there because we hear them shouting every year somewhere in that direction."

They turned back, now talking normally, excited, and happy. They didn't have to find their way: they had the strong scent of drying mushrooms to guide them.

For Odrowąż had by now set up his primitive drying rack. He covered the ditch with glowing coals with a grill of sallow rods and laid out the mushrooms on top.

"By tomorrow, they will wither, then we'll add a little to the coals, and it will be all done by noon. They will be as light as air to carry."

The comrades were all gathered together. Crane was cleaning some roots, Beekeeper was weaving a basket, and Panther had set up his own fire and was roasting milk caps.[58]

"Why so silent, Panther?" Asked Wolverine, stretching on the ground.

"Can't you see what I am doing?"

"I can. You're roasting milk caps. I just don't understand why you're not salting them."

"I am! I am salting them with my tears! My salty tears! Red rowans, golden birch leaves flying everywhere, and now milk caps! It's autumn, Chief! Autumn!"

"Eh, yes. And so everything grows silent and somber. But unless there is the rest and gloom of autumn and the hard test of winter, there would be no happiness of resurrection in the spring. You must have the trust and wisdom of birds, plants, and animals. We pass away, but we continue."

Here he turned to Odrowąż and asked:

"Do you know the animal ford to Medvidleh?"

"No," said Odrowąż. "We were lying in Medvidleh then, after the uprising, but we got there by way of the lake."

"Just now, a moose showed us the way. We'll try it tomorrow. Let's spend the night here. Mother is at home. She will look after the householders."

I have not been to Medvidleh for twenty years. The river there became swamped up, and it's a bog on all sides now, and there is not much reason to go. There are no meadows there and no mushrooms that I have seen. Eternal backwoods, primeval forest. I once tried to go there to shoot capercaillie, but I fell in the mud up to my waist and turned around."

"Let's try the moose ford tomorrow, then. Now, boys! Cut some branches for our shelter but look out for vipers because I've seen many here. Then let's eat and rest."

---

[58] Saffron milk cap, a choice wild mushroom

"Perhaps the ensign is buried there?" Orlik whispered to Beekeeper. "And maybe this moose, and these capercaillies, who have lived there for ages, know his grave?"

"And maybe giant bees live there too, bees from ancient beehives and whole trees are full of honey?"

"And maybe lynxes breed there and live to hoary old age?"

"And maybe there are still bears?"

"And surely, there must be a bounty of nuts!" said Panther, placing roasted milk caps on leaves for supper.

The exhaustion from a day of heat and toil soon overwhelmed them. They buried themselves in the moss of the lean-to. Odrowąż lit a wet, smokey spruce fire at the entrance, and thus protected from mosquitoes and vipers, they went to sleep, dreaming of great discoveries and miracles.

The refreshing chill of the morning awakened them.

White dew lay on the ground. Odrowąż, muttering his hours, picked the dried mushrooms from the grate. Crane searched in vain for water to bathe in at the edge of the marsh. Wolverine peeled forest ticks from Beekeeper's back, and Panther roasted milk caps for breakfast. Everyone was rushing through their tasks, urged on by curiosity.

"Lead on, Orlik!" commanded Wolverine.

"Just make sure you find your way!" Panther laughed.

But Orlik knew the way: he had learned to read the forest like a book. He moved to the front of the pack and led them without hesitation, recognizing the signposts he had memorized the day before.

"We walked past that alder, that one there, with a broken limb. Then past that rowan, then the aspen with a hollow, from which a woodpigeon flew out. It must have little ones there! And then over this pile with feathers from a hawk kill, and then this spruce – it had a squirrel in it, and then this turn, here. It had a bundle of deer hair on it. He remembered and led on without hesitation until at last, he stopped and said:

"Here, out of these thickets, the moose came out and stood in front of us. And we were..."

"And did you notice the magpie nest behind you?" Panther asked.

"No! I stared at the beast like an apparition. And then it went this way to the ford."

Soon they stood over the black waterway. Wolverine stepped forward and began to undress.

"Everyone strip and put your clothes in a bundle on your head because it may happen that some of us go under."

"Oh, but the leeches will eat us alive," protested Panther.

"Nah, we'll live. Then we'll clean ourselves off once on the other side and get dressed again. But spending the whole day in wet, muddy clothes would be a major pain in the neck."

So they undressed, and Wolverine slipped into the black, thick, hideous muck.

The bottom was slushy, but they moved forward, grimacing and snorting in disgust at the rotten, foul-smelling exhalations of the swamp. The water was waist-high, then chest-high, and finally, Wolverine began to swim. A harrier sprang from a clump of reeds, screaming with surprise and fear. The ford meandered and twisted. It sometimes seemed that it would never end. Orlik became so exhausted with the effort that, for a moment, he thought of stretching out on one of the clumps of vegetation to rest.

And then Wolverine shouted:

"We're through! I feel the bottom underfoot, and Medvidleh is right in front."

A narrow channel of water led between two solid walls of reeds, stinging bushes, and shapeless corpses of fallen trees. Wolverine crawled out onto the first of the logs to catch his breath.

One by one, the others emerged out of the mire and sat on the mossy black log, panting, silent. They were all black with muck right up to their faces and completely exhausted.

Odrowąż looked at the sun and said:

"We were wading for an hour and a half. Must be two kilometers. That's one serious mud crawl."

"Time to peel off the leeches!" Panther said. "And there's nowhere to rinse off! This filthy swamp smells! At times, I wanted to put my nose in my pocket, but the pockets were in a bundle on my head."

"We have not had such a dry summer in eight years. This dry heat has opened up this ford. Without it, there would have been no passage here," said Odrowąż. "Not shallow enough for us."

They dressed hastily and jumped off the trunk onto the dry land. But there, they quickly sank up to their shoulders in a tangled mass of weeds and bushes and stood helplessly.

"Jake is lucky to be up in the trees. There's no way to move along the ground here!"

"You prefer going by water?"

"No! Not again! Please! Maybe we can cut our way through with axes."

"Could we please find a special prize to make this worthwhile?" grunted Beekeeper and started to slash and chop.

They set to work in the hope that they might eventually reach an area of less dense growth a little higher up. But the backwoods were as tight: when they got out of the coastal beds and bulrush, they found in front of them a tangled wall of hazel, bird cherry, buckthorn, rowan, and viburnum, all tangled with hops.

When the sun began to bake them, they lay down on the fallen trunks, completely exhausted.

They only had bread and dried fish for supplies. Fortunately, the thicket was full of raspberries and blackberries, and they could quench their thirst that way. And the hazel was covered with a myriad of tiny, delicious, soft, yellow, half-ripe nuts.

Odrowąż and Wolverine, instead of lying down and resting, pressed on.

"In those days, further back somewhere, there was a clearing among the spruce trees. But that was forty years ago!" said the old man, overwhelmed suddenly with memories.

They crawled under overturned logs. Sometimes they straightened up, scrambled on top, and tried to orient themselves to make sure they weren't meandering. And then another trench of bogs barred their path.

Impatient, Wolverine slid straight down into it.

"That moose was going somewhere. It had some goal! Maybe to the lakes? The marsh is shallow here."

Their hands and faces were covered in blood from prickly plants and the stings of gnats and mosquitoes, and their shirts were muddy and torn. It was easier to wade in mud than to struggle with the thicket.

Snakes, sunning themselves on logs, watched them with interest. Jays and nutcrackers flew up from the bush, screeching.

Suddenly they heard a splash and a bleating.

They barely managed to duck down when a herd of deer galloped by, headed by an antlered male.

"Nice horns on him!" Odrowąż said, the hunter's regret in his voice. But Wolverine looked after them with a smile of joy.

They climbed out of the mud onto the animals' path. Wolverine whistled to signal his companions.

"There's a boar's nest somewhere nearby: you can smell the bed," Odrowąż noticed and immediately pointed out a low, ruddy shadow slinking by.

"A vixen! At this time of day? She's got some loot! Oh, there! There goes another!" They pressed forward and suddenly emerged onto a trampled glade.

"So that's what it was!" the old man said, pointing.

In the middle of the clearing, on the withering, heavily trampled weeds lay a dead young moose. Its vertebrae were broken, its gut was disemboweled, and its whole body was trampled with hooves.

Wolverine leaned over the carcass.

"I bet the giant moose has murdered him, the one we saw yesterday. But the youngster was not a pushover, and the fight was stiff. See how they trampled the ground!"

"And see how many tracks there are! I count there were... let's see... four, five, six... seven females here. Something to fight for, I reckon. Quite a healthy youngster, too! The foxes have already started on him, and the wolves will finish him at night. If we had a gun, we could sit in that tree and take a lot of pelts!"

Wolverine began to whistle to his mates with a signal that they all knew meant "come here."

They responded, time and again, coming closer and closer, and at last, everyone gathered and filled the forest with their chattering.

"Look, you boys, what love has done!" said Panther to the boys, giggling.

And Crane examined the body and said:

"It's a pity we didn't see the fight. The young moose fought bravely. One of its antlers is knocked off and both front legs are broken. It fell, and then the elder moose ripped him open and trampled him.it."

"And then went off with the girls. That way! They walked in a row, like a wedding procession!"

Ever practical, Panther and Odrowąż lit a fire, and the old man started skinning the young bull.

The boys stared curiously. Crane was examining the horns, and only Wolverine stretched out on the ground and turned his gaze away from the scene.

Suddenly, after a long silence, he said:

"You forest folk want to make a feast, devour the corpse, and then take its skin and horns?"

"Naturally!" Panther replied.

"Then think about how you'll take it over the moose ford!"

They stopped working. Wolverine had a point.

Finally, Panther, sticking a piece of meat on a wooden spit, said:

"We're bound to think of a way once we have eaten."

"Eating does not improve wit," muttered Wolverine as he lit his pipe and set off on the moose trail.

Orlik caught up with him after a while.

"You've robbed me of my appetite," he said.

"I haven't eaten meat for a long time, and I feel more and more disgusted by it. As we came upon the carcass, the gravedigger flies were already swarming it. The guts had been mangled by foxes, and I am sure wolves are sharpening their fangs in the forest. No, I will not share in that feast.

"Anyway, I'm not hungry. I have bread, and there is no shortage of berries. Instead, I will see where the wedding procession went; they have cleared a nice trail for us."

But the trail led them again to the immeasurable plane of swamps. The moose had crossed yet another bog to yet another distant line of forest. But as the men emerged from the thicket, suddenly to their right and very close, a flock of cranes burst into the air with a deafening cry.

"Cranes' nesting ground!" exclaimed Wolverine.

Now a whole cloud of gigantic birds rose in the air and circled overhead, and out of it, suddenly, one dove down and fell at their feet.

Instinctively, Orlik rushed towards it to grab it in his arms.

"Watch out!" Wolverine shouted.

But it was too late! The bird pecked the boy with its beak square in the face and so hard that he gasped in pain and let go. The crane spread its wings to take off but fell again. Its left wing was broken. The bird tried to escape on foot, but, with lightning speed, Wolverine threw his shirt over its head, to overwhelm it, then tied it up, and took it under his arm.

"A broken wing is a death sentence for this fellow. Let's have him join us as a household member. Now, this is a trophy worth taking and keeping. We can go back now and set up camp for the night. With God's grace, we can be home by tomorrow night.

"And cross that awful ford again!" the boy grunted.

"I saw you barely made it. Going back will be easier. We will build a raft of reeds, load the skin and the antlers and you and the crane on it, and pull you back to Pine Hill.

"Heh! The others are still trying to figure out what to do."

"Oh, I am sure Odrowąż has already chopped up alder for the raft!" Wolverine smiled.

They found their comrades sated with roast meat and fast asleep. The hide of the moose hung on three poles pitched by the fire. The skull and horns lay on a huge anthill, black with a swarm of bone cleaners. The victim's other remains had been dragged into the thickets, and the camp had taken on a decent and orderly appearance. From the direction of the ford, there came the sound of an ax: Odrowąż was working on the raft.

He inspected the crippled bird.

"You'll have to keep it in a dark shed, bring it water, fish, snails, and worms, and visit it several times a day to give it the chance to get used to you. It'll take a few weeks, but the bird will learn to eat from your hand, and then you can start letting it out on its own. They make good companions. I had one for a few years in my yard. They make good night guards, too."

"Are you building a raft?" Orlik asked.

"Yes. There's no other way. The doctor would hate leaving the skull and horns behind, and Panther would not give up the skin. But with a raft, we can manage. We have to go back to the cottage tomorrow because there is no bread and the drinking water here is very bad here. And tonight we will have a wolf concert. The boars were here but smelled the smoke and went away. That a-way. A sow with seven piglets and two teenagers. Foxes are prowling about, too. Now, you guys gather withe to bind these hazel rods and some moss to stop the gaps."

By evening, they had finished the raft. It was narrow and very primitive, but it stayed up on the surface as Wolverine pulled it along for a distance to test it.

"It will hold," decided Odrowąż.

They returned to the camp and woke their companions.

In the depth of the forest, darkness fell.

Their captive replied pathetically to the twilight clarion call of its fellow cranes, then tried to tear at its bonds for a long time, eventually gave up, and finally curled up to sleep. But it refused to eat what they gave it.

"You stupid beast!" Panther said to him. "Personally, I'd be happy to accept a piece of bread right now, even from a Moscovite."

"And I would sting him," cried Beekeeper with a swollen mouth.

"I see you found a wild beehive," observed Wolverine.

"Yes, a strange one, in a fallen log. Very rich, but..."

"And they turned your face into a full moon. A perfect likeness!"

"They followed him all the way here, and the doctor got stung too. We barely managed to smoke them away."

"Come on, fellows, go gather enough firewood for the whole night before it gets dark," ordered Odrowąż. "We will have to take turns keeping watch. Wolves can smell a dead carcass kilometers away, and they will be here tonight. They will want the moose, but they are not particular. You forest folk slept off your feast this afternoon, so you will keep watch. The three of us have been working. We will sleep."

When it became completely dark, the three of them turned in, but Crane and Panther stayed up, watching over the fire. Panther, since he always fell asleep as soon as he stopped working or playing tricks, started to weave clogs in order to stay awake. Crane listened to the night.

It wasn't exactly the beautiful calm of a night in the wilderness. In their lean-to, Odrowąż snored like a horse, and Beekeeper groaned in pain; and all around them, in the forest, there was a lot of traffic and animal calls. There were stompings, rustlings of dry reeds, creepings, the clatter of owls' crooked beaks and the warning fluttering of their wings, and finally, a gloomy, short howl, a signal or a threat, rang out somewhere far away.

It was answered by the bleating of goats and a mighty grunt of a moose.

And again, they heard the howl, followed by a hoarse, short, staccato barking and the splashing of water.

"The scoundrels are coming over the bog as easily as if it were a highway," Panther muttered. "If it weren't for the fire, they'd eat the moose first, then us for dessert. There, can you hear? Quite a pack! They're coming from all directions! They are already here! Do you hear them? We should have poisoned the carcass!"

"You think? But I think that if they exist in nature, then they are there for a reason. They must be somehow useful."

"I don't believe it!" Panther shrugged. "If this were so, then you shouldn't kill even a flea. Let us ask the opinion of the defenseless and weak, doomed to death at the dawn of life!"

"Hmm... perhaps danger trains defense? And the killers kill off the weak and sick, improving the breed? Anyway, we look at this with our human eyes and judge them by our standards, which may not be fair."

He poked the fire and then threw a burning log into the thicket because he thought "something" had moved in the shadow by the hanging skin.

There was a kind of chattering now, more and more frequent and closer. There was a kind of rage and fear in it, and sometimes it merged into a gloomy, hair-raising choir.

"Just one shot with a rifle, and it would all go quiet! It'll be a long night!" Panther yawned. "I'm all itchy from sweat, filth, insects, and these cursed leeches. I am happy to leave this virgin land as it is! Maybe in the spring, it might be worth returning here for the nests. I think I saw an eagle's nest on an oak tree over that way. Cranes, mistle thrush, fieldfares, crossbills, eagle owls, capercaillies! But to stay here... no way! Way too hard! I bet our good doctor misses his bath in the stream, yes?"

And he sighed with longing for their refuge, then began to nod and – fell asleep.

Wolverine and Odrowąż took the midnight watch, then woke everyone up at daybreak. They discovered that despite the fire, the moose's entrails had been dragged wide across the thicket. They began to prepare for the return trip.

It was a slow, long, and arduous journey.

"We could all play the role of forest devils now," Wolverine decided as they reached Pine Hill and rested before the final crossing to their mainland.

And when they finally stood in front of the hut in the evening, Szczepanska wrung her hands: "Almighty God! How will I ever wash these clothes? And who bled you like this? Sweet Jesus!"

"It's nothing. It's just leeches," Beekeeper reassured her. "But we got a prize! And a crane! And a ton of hazel!"

"Eat!" Panther gasped.

"Bathe!" Crane cried.

"Wipe your skin with salt and ash to clean off the vermin," said Odrowąż.

Wolverine placed the captive bird in an improvised hut in the corner of the stable.

"After that trip, our stretch of the forest here seems to me like the main street in town by comparison," Orlik said as he followed Crane to the water.

"And what does our new guest think about it?" wondered Crane.

But precisely at that moment, the evening clarions resounded, and the pathetic voice of the crippled prisoner answered them from the stable.

A CALL FROM THE OTHER SIDE

On Panther's suggestion and with Crane's permission, the broken-winged crane was named "Doctor." Odrowąż estimated that the bird was three years old and guessed that it could be tamed.

But for the first few weeks, the bird put up such a fierce resistance that Wolverine had to feed it by force. The crane bristled and huddled in a helpless rebellion, hissing like a viper whenever someone approached.

And then, one day, as if it had burnt through all its despair, overcome with resignation and hunger, the crane accepted its first meal from the hands of Wolverine.

"Now you are one of us!" the man smiled.

And yes, the bird's instinctive fear and hatred of its eternal hunters had been overcome. The crane stopped hissing and pecking, and finally, one day, upon hearing the whistling that heralded the arrival of man, it went forward to meet him and spoke its own brief greeting.

"You know, brother, we can be friends," Wolverine said to the crane. "I would not dare to deprive you of your greatest treasure – freedom – if you were healthy, whole, and strong, if you could fly across the seas in close formation with your comrades and return to us again. Alas, brother, with that wing, you were doomed to starvation and a frosty death! I felt sorry for your young life, and that is why I took you. But this is not for life. Never fear. I will take you back to your nesting grounds in the spring so that you and your brothers may spend a happy summer together again."

"The bird listened, fed from his hand, looked at him calmly, and then, one day, Wolverine left the door to the stable open and, whistling, went back to the cottage.

The prisoner went out into the clearing, into the sun, and began to look around. It unfolded and folded its wings and began to feed in the grass and then to preen its feathers.

Then, lured by the familiar whistling, the crane walked slowly towards the cabin.

"Now it's one of us!" they rejoiced.

The next seasonal occupation of the forest folk was the hazelnuts.

Wolverine and Odrowąż went out each day to fish, but the rest were beavering after hazelnuts and brought home whole sacks every evening.

There was an abundance of fruit everywhere, and there was plenty to do. In the evening, mountains of their harvest were piled up in the garden and on the porch: nuts and mushrooms, berries and fish.

"And now, let's prepare them!" Panther called.

Before they went to rest, they had to prepare the fish, shell the nuts, salt the mushrooms, and their oven barely kept up with the task of drying all these treasures.

It had been a dry, fruitful, happy summer, punctuated only with a few powerful storms. The great heat then exploded with thunderbolts, sweated with brief torrential rains, and then the radiant weather returned.

Wolverine and Odrowąż had fantastic catches because the drought had narrowed fish paths, forcing fish into traps, and completely trapped some in deeper pits that had become isolated. One time they brought a boatful of delicious ides and perches, and once, in a ditch cut off from the river, they caught a monster pike, a "cannibal" as they said, whom they had to kill with an ax. Cutting it open, Crane found a shapeless mass the size of a fist. When he cut it open, he found the remains of a metal medallion inside.

Odrowąż studied it and gave it to Wolverine.

"You have better eyes than me. Look, is this the Virgin of Kodeń[59]? Our Podlasiak had one like this."

But neither eyes nor the magnifying glass were of any use.

"Many people have fed the fish in these bogs," said Panther.

"And many of them would deserve monuments."

"Once you are on the other side, even our monuments here are not worth more than this, I am sure! And the accounts they keep over there last a lot longer and are far more reliable," said Wolverine, putting the find away.

After one terrible night's storm, the fishermen set off on the lake around noon, searching for catfish. But the day was not fruitful, with hardly any catch, and they were just setting up the double net for perhaps the hundredth time, and with not much hope when, suddenly, Wolverine looked up, listening.

The bugle played far away. An agreed signal: two short, successive tones.

"This meant: 'Wolverine!'"

Wolverine raised his bone whistle to his mouth and answered them.

"The boys need something," he said, sitting down to row.

"A broken leg or arm, surely," Odrowąż muttered.

---

[59] A miraculous icon of Virgin Mary

"No! For that, they call Crane. They are not calling us to them. Rather, someone is coming our way. It's some news. They found something!"

The trumpet repeated the call again, then fell silent: the seeker had heard the reply, and soon, Orlik emerged from the reeds, sweating, dusty, muddy, and began to shout something from far away.

Odrowąż turned the boat towards him.

"Hey, hey, Chief!" the boy shouted, catching his breath. "We found the grave! Ensign, shotgun, and the Eagle[60]! Our ensign! We found him! Come! We called the others already. Beekeeper stands guard!"

Impressed, without a word, they got ashore and followed the boy. And he, overwhelmed by their concentration and silence, also fell silent.

They remained silent until they arrived at the spot, in the black forest, by a sleepy lagoon. The night storm had overturned a huge, half-rotten, primordial oak. Its crown fell into the water, and its trunk split open, revealing the rotten interior. Next to it stood Beekeeper, erect, frozen at attention, and next to him, Crane and Panther, with their heads bare, in silence.

Wolverine and Odrowąż came forward.

In the interior of the oak, they saw a skeleton. A small, slender skeleton of a teenager, intact, just as it had been buried within the trunk of the tree. To his right side lay an old rifle, chewed through with rust, and on the left side, by the heart, a cloth of amaranth-red with a twinkle of silver thread.

Deep eye sockets stared at the sun, and the slightly open, healthy teeth seemed to smile. And so he lay with his gun at his side and his regimental color by his heart.

The Ensign.

Wolverine straightened up and, uncovering his head, sang:

You, God, who have for so many centuries

---

[60] The Polish armorial white eagle in a red field, on a military standard

Beekeeper's arms twitched as if he wanted to present arms, and the others joined in:

Clothed our Poland with glory and might.

Odrowąż knelt down and prayed, and tears ran down his face like beads of a sultry rosary.

And when he finished, they covered the hero's remains with spruce branches. Everyone gathered for a council, and even Panther had a solemn expression.

"I think I know what happened," said Odrowąż. "When they ran out of food, and the October cold squeezed them, they had to come nearer people, and they came this way. And here the wounded boy gave up his ghost, and the Podlasiak found a rotten oak and buried him in it, and then he went on further and, not knowing the way, probably drowned in the marsh."

"What shall we do now?" asked Panther.

"Bury him as he deserves," answered Wolverine.

"On Widow's Hill, where they used to light war signals," Orlik exclaimed.

"He will watch over the whole country," added Beekeeper.

"Right!" confirmed Wolverine.

Odrowąż pondered and suddenly stood up, then nodded at his grandson and at Panther.

"We will go to the farm and bring planed boards here in secret, at night, so that the Muscovites don't catch wind of this."

"And we will hold a wake for him."

"And in the morning, we will build a coffin and take him up to Widow's Hill."

Three kept vigil over him. Orlik remembered that night for his whole life. It was moonlit and full of strange majesty. Wolverine talked. He told them what he had heard about those times, from his family, from the neighboring folk. About that time of battles, sacrifices, ruin, and the years of repression that followed.

And then they were silent, meditating on the pain, their hatred of the executioner, their bitterness, helplessness, and despair of captivity.

Until, unexpectedly, Crane said:

"Listen, you two! We would be right to despair and indulge in hopelessness if we had to sit here and hold this vigil by the remains of some scoundrel. But this boy teaches us something else. He accepted his inheritance, fulfilled his duty, and kept his faith. We have no more to do than that ourselves. Keep the faith, fulfill our duty, abide, survive. That's it! The rest is up to God."

"Thank you, brother, for those words," said Wolverine. "We aren't being fair to him. He deserves a heroic song, not dejection and sadness. You have your flute, Crane. Play us a song."

And these stayed in Orlik's heart for the rest of his life: this night, this grave in the forest, and these words:

We got up to work with larks,
And slept late with evening light!
In our tombs, we are God's troops!

The men returned from the Odrowąż farm with wooden planks long before daybreak. Szczepanski brought the tools, and a small coffin was ready by morning.

They placed the bones on a bed of herbs and flowers and covered them with the flag's remains. Each one took a silver thread as a souvenir, and they read prayers from Odrwaz's old prayer book.

Then Wolverine handed him the rifle, and the old man received it like a holy relic and passed it on to Beekeeper.

"There, you keep it. And remember."

"Yes, grandfather!" The boy said simply.

In the touchwood decay, they found a few more buckles, buttons, the remains of leather bags, and a medallion of the Virgin of Czestochowa and laid them all in the coffin. Then they took it on their shoulders and, taking turns, carried the casket to the top of the hill.

The boys ran ahead, and when the procession reached the Widow's Hill, a freshly dug grave awaited them. Szczepanska was there with the baby, and the boys stood guard. And when the coffin was lowered into the grave, Orlik fired two shots and presented arms.

Then they threw flowers on the coffin, and Odrowąż said prayers, and when he finished, Wolverine gave a speech, they recited a prayer and sang a hymn. And then, they buried him.

On the way home, they discussed how to honor the grave. Some suggested building a cross, others planting a tree, but Odrowąż shook his head and advised against it.

"Too many Moscovite informers around. Moscovites will come and despoil the grave and probably destroy it, too. And no point planting trees, either. Better we do something that only a few can recognize. I will make a tombstone. But a secret one. Flat. Not seen from far away. And no one will know, only we."

A week later, a stone appeared on the grave, and on it, Odrowąż had carved some mysterious symbols. He explained them now, pointing them out one by one.

"This is a cross. And this is the eagle. Here is its crown. And here, the year: '63'. His name was Stacho, but I don't remember the family name, so I only carved an 'S.' And one reads this inscription like this: 'A follower of Christ, an ensign in the Uprising, Stacho.' And here I added a 'W' for 'Warsaw.'"

The wind blew the white sand and sprinkled the ground with needles and leaves. Soon, the ensign's grave melted into the earth, and merged with her colors, and only his memory remained in the hearts of the forest folk.

DEPARTURES

One day, Wolverine returned from a lonely hike and, sitting down at the table, said:

"All the songbirds are gone. And heathers are blazing in glory."

Nobody replied because they understood what that meant. Only after a moment did Panther grunt:

"Good for the birds! Who can survive the migration will sate himself with sun and warmth. But I... I will go back to Wolverine's housekeeper."

They couldn't help laughing.

"And I... back to school," said Orlik.

"And I... back to the farm," added Beekeeper.

"And I to my laboratory," muttered Crane.

"And I – to my library and books," Wolverine said. "But each back to his work, so no reason to complain."

"Oh, yes? So why is Chief not singing with delight?" growled Panther rebelliously.

"Because no forest creature sings this time of year," said Wolverine and added: "Well, Panther, it is time for you to prepare the wagon for the return trip."

"I'd rather catch dogs than take that road. We still have time, right?"

"Let's wait until our cranes fly off. Any day now, because those from farther north are already passing overhead."

"Yes. A little more time to say goodbye," Orlik sighed.

"And why are you so gloomy! You're going back to your Mrs. Professor!" Panther laughed.

"Please, Panther, you forget that I am no longer Private Whatisit but Orlik!" the boy replied proudly.

"Oh, never mind him. He always turns nasty this time of year and is just looking for a fight," said Wolverine.

Their cottage emptied. Szczepanska returned home to help with the harvesting of flax. Odrowąż and Beekeeper to thresh. Wolverine now went alone to fish and brought back his baskets and traps and stored them in the attic. The rest scattered across the forest; they collected rowans, acorns, nuts, and pine cones; and built birdhouses in trees for the wintering birds.

Orlik worked with Crane because Panther, unless he was delivering their supplies across the Rainbow Bridge, spent days wandering through the woods, "saying goodbye to his old friends," as he said. The sun conjured up her last carpets of flowers and threw them over glades, hills, and wastelands. A feathery cloud of heathers lined the ground. Against it, huge toadstools, russulas, and leccinums raised their hats – the last mushrooms of the season.

Mornings rose lazy, wrapped in cold mists. Dried mosses, herbs, and ferns crunched underfoot, and the silence was such that in the evening, from a great distance, from the direction of the settlements, one could hear the prolonged, sad, monotonous playing of shepherd's flutes.

The forest stood pensive and said goodbye to the summer with a rainbow of colors of fading leaves.

"They dress for death as if it were a wedding! Not like us, foolish men, afraid of it," said Wolverine looking at the golden and purple trees.

Every evening Panther listened to the cranes and followed each formation of birds in the sky with his eyes until, one night, he whispered to Orlik as they were going to sleep:

"It was quiet on the nesting grounds tonight, and Doctor shouted all day. He must have recognized them when they passed overhead. They're gone."

"Maybe Chief hasn't noticed," Orlik whispered back.

"Oh, don't count on it! He hears everything! I fear about tomorrow."

But that 'tomorrow' was a Sunday and, after prayers, Wolverine ordered an expedition.

"Take bread in your bags because we won't be back till late tonight. We have to visit the winter feeding grounds, inspect everything, and look everywhere."

"Last rounds!" said Panther.

Wolverine said nothing, and they went with their light, skilled gait, with which they covered miles without tiring. They looked in on the bees, on the lake, various nooks and crannies, birdhouses, badger and fox holes. They walked around the haystacks, retraced their summer trails, and fords in the swamps. At noon they rested in heather, lulled by the humming of bees busily taking their last harvest.

Flocks of black grouse flew up from the ground at their feet, and flocks of wintering birds accompanied them through the trees.

"Look," Panther pointed them out to Orlik. "Look, these don't fly away. They winter here. See how they gather into a large flock, such a mixed crowd: great tits and blue tits and coal tits and longtails. They will adopt a couple of finches and a couple of woodpeckers, too, and plunder together, and keep together the whole winter for warmth."

Sometimes the silence of the forest was broken by the hoarse scream of a jay or a nutcracker, and otherwise, they walked in silence, and only leaves rustled and dry twigs crackled under their feet.

On the way back, Wolverine led them past the insurgent's grave, and they sang him a hymn, and then, in silence, they returned to the cottage.

The sun was dying. There were no crane clarions. Cool mists rose from the swamps, and trees laid long shadows across clearings. They met their householders coming back from foraging, and Doctor came out to them upon hearing their voices, joyfully welcoming them.

They also found Beekeeper, who had brought them honey and fresh, new bread.

"It is bright, and it still smells like a summer field. Later, the flour turns musty in the storage room, and the bread tastes different. Like winter. So my mother sent me now, while it still was warm, to wish you all good health.

"And we have collected thirteen gallons of honey, and we sowed the first rye yesterday. And I can hardly move my arms: grandfather and I threshed for three days straight!"

"We could hear it from here! Wham-bam!Wham-bam!"

Here Beekeeper nudged Orlik and whispered:

"I brought a military horn; it's lying in the bushes. We'll blow it after supper. I will show you how!"

They sat down to eat. They ate the light-colored bread with the golden honey and had the impression that they were eating the summer sun stored in this primordial food. And then Panther put a jug of foaming milk on the table, and they had to light a fire in the stove because of the chill.

The boys slipped out of the room in silence, and soon they heard the pathetic lowing of the horn. There was silence in the hut, and finally, after a while, Wolverine took his fiddle off the wall and began to improvise something.

"It's the rhapsody of our summer," said Crane.

Beekeeper and Orlik returned somewhat short of breath, and everyone listened. It was dark in the room, and only the ruby light glowed in front of the icon. And then the moon rose over the clearing and, looking in through the window, cast a long silver path across the floor.

With a long chromatic chord, Wolverine finished his playing and stood up. He stood at the window for a while, looking at the moon, as if he hesitated, and then slowly and calmly, he said:

"Beekeeper. You will go to see your grandfather tomorrow and tell him that we have left."

Nobody said a word.

"Time for us to go! Our cranes have flown. God had given us a good summer. How many new flowers did you find, Crane?"

"One hundred and thirty-seven," replied Crane precisely.

"My harvest is smaller. Only eleven new bird species added to my collection and three empty penduline nests."

"Next year, we will explore Medvidleh and find eagles and capercaillies and watch pendulines build their nests," said Panther.

"I am glad to hear that you are thinking about spring already."

"How else can I get through the winter months? Besides, I will not be alone this winter. I have Beekeeper now. And we two will come by here from time to time and get everything ready for the spring."

"Oh, yes! I've already spoken to my mother about it! I will visit you every couple of days. We have a young colt now. It will serve[61]. And Chief said I could look at his books in the library."

"As much and as long as you want."

"And I will join you every winter break," said Orlik.

"Well, well, then: *Away, away, all sorrow!"* Panther sang sharp in profound sarcasm.

"Let's go outside and enjoy the moonlight!" said Crane. They left the room and sat on the threshold.

"Just like last April! Do you remember?" said Panther.

The clearing was glowing with the silver of the moon, and trees stood in dense rising fog. It seemed otherworldly.

---

[61] i.e. "I'll be able to ride it to your place"

Only silence and concentration and great solemnity reigned over the night. Everything alive focused and gathered and preserved its strength to survive until the next resurrection, to survive the coming, apparent death.

It was so quiet that one could hear the leaves falling on the ground, falling down to protect the power of rebirth contained in the root, and the rustle of the worm that burrowed a hiding place under the bark from which it would come to life in the spring.

The men were silent, too, thinking about their own survival. Only Wolverine's eyes, staring at the silver distance, were beaming, and sometimes his lips twitched with an inner word.

Crane nudged him on the shoulder.

"Go ahead! Speak!" he whispered.

Quietly and slowly, Wolverine began, as if his thoughts detached from the bottom of his soul and floated upwards, looking to find expression:

"Hail to you, master of the wonders of beauty and wisdom! You are here with us in every shape, sound, and fragrance, and with you, we have spent this summer. We thank you for everyone and for everything. We thank you for opening our eyes and ears to understand your beauty and to live it like bread."

"Amen, amen, amen!" they all said solemnly, staring at the sky, listening to the silence.

And so the last summer day of the forest folk came to an end.

TRANSLATOR'S SPECIAL REQUEST

Translating and publishing this book has been a labor of love for me.
I grew up reading it, and I have always wanted to be able
to share it with my American friends. And so here it is.
It will not make me rich, but if you liked the book, would you please
recommend it to a friend? And give it a review? As you now know,
the book deserves to be known
and our reading friends will thank you.

ABOUT THE TRANSLATOR

Tom Pinch is the penname of a translator and a publisher
based in Luxembourg.

ABOUT THE PUBLISHER

Mondrala Press is a located in Luxembourg and dedicated to
publishing English translations of Polish classics:
the greatest books you have never heard of.

Made in the USA
Las Vegas, NV
28 November 2022

60495602R00125